"In case you haven't noticed, honey, I'm the one on top...

"You answer *my* questions."

"I did and you didn't believe me," she snapped. "Sorry, but I don't have my American Express card with me. For God's sake, do I look like a terrorist? You nearly broke my arm, then you knocked me out. You've bounced me on the ground like a rubber ball, and you've got the utter gall to act like *I'm* dangerous? My goodness, you'd better search me, too, so you'll be able to sleep tonight. Who knows? I might have a bazooka strapped to my leg, since I'm such a dangerous character!" Her voice had risen furiously, and he cut her off by resting all his weight on her rib cage. When she gasped, he eased up again.

"No, you're unarmed. I've already had your clothes off, remember?"

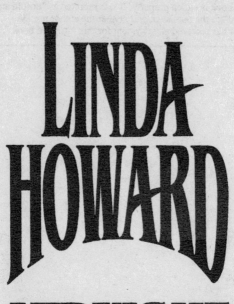

LINDA HOWARD

MIDNIGHT RAINBOW

MIRA BOOKS

ISBN 1-55166-153-5

MIDNIGHT RAINBOW

Copyright © 1986 by Linda Howard.

MIRA and the star colophon are trademarks of MIRA Books.

Printed in U.S.A.

MIDNIGHT RAINBOW

Chapter One

He was getting too old for this kind of crap, Grant Sullivan thought irritably. What the hell was he doing crouched here, when he'd promised himself he'd never set foot in a jungle again? He was supposed to rescue a bubble-brained society deb, but from what he'd seen in the two days he'd had this jungle fortress under surveillance, he thought she might not *want* to be rescued. She looked as if she was having the time of her life: laughing, flirting, lying by the pool in the heat of the day. She slept late; she drank champagne on the flagstone patio. Her father was almost out of his mind with worry about her, thinking that she was suffering unspeakable torture at the hands of her captors. Instead, she was lolling around as if she were vacationing on the Riviera. She certainly wasn't being tortured. If anyone was being tortured, Grant thought with growing ire, it was he himself. Mosquitoes were biting him, flies were stinging him, sweat was running off him in rivers, and his legs were aching from sitting still for so long. He'd been eating field rations again, and he'd forgotten how much he hated field rations. The humidity made all of his old wounds ache, and he had plenty of old wounds to ache. No doubt about it: he was definitely too old.

He was thirty-eight, and he'd spent over half his life involved in some war, somewhere. He was tired, tired enough that he'd opted out the year before, wanting

nothing more than to wake up in the same bed every
morning. He hadn't wanted company or advice or anything, except to be left the hell alone. When he had burned
out, he'd burned to the core.

He hadn't quite retreated to the mountains to live in a
cave, where he wouldn't have to see or speak to another
human being, but he had definitely considered it. Instead,
he'd bought a run-down farm in Tennessee, just in the
shadow of the mountains, and let the green mists heal him.
He'd dropped out, but apparently he hadn't dropped far
enough: they had still known how to find him. He supposed wearily that his reputation made it necessary for
certain people to know his whereabouts at all times.
Whenever a job called for jungle experience and expertise, they called for Grant Sullivan.

A movement on the patio caught his attention, and he
cautiously moved a broad leaf a fraction of an inch to clear
his line of vision. There she was, dressed to the nines in a
frothy sundress and heels, with an enormous pair of sun-
glasses shading her eyes. She carried a book and a tall glass
of something that looked deliciously cool; she arranged
herself artfully on one of the poolside deck chairs, and
prepared to wile away the muggy afternoon. She waved to
the guards who patrolled the plantation grounds and
flashed them her dimpled smile.

Damn her pretty, useless little hide! Why couldn't she
have stayed under Daddy's wing, instead of sashaying
around the world to prove how "independent" she was?
All she'd proved was that she had a remarkable talent for
landing herself in hot water.

Poor dumb little twit, he thought. She probably didn't
even realize that she was one of the central characters in a
nasty little espionage caper that had at least three government and several other factions, all hostile, scrambling to

find a missing microfilm. The only thing that had saved her life so far was that no one was sure how much she knew, or whether she knew anything at all. Had she been involved in George Persall's espionage activities, he wondered, or had she only been his mistress, his high class "secretary"? Did she know where the microfilm was, or did Luis Marcel, who had disappeared, have it? The only thing anyone knew for certain was that George Persall had had the microfilm in his possession. But he'd died of a heart attack—in *her* bedroom—and the microfilm hadn't been found. Had Persall already passed it to Luis Marcel? Marcel had dropped out of sight two days before Persall died—if he had the microfilm, he certainly wasn't talking about it. The Americans wanted it, the Russians wanted it, the Sandinistas wanted it, and every rebel group in Central and South America wanted it. Hell, Sullivan thought, as far as he knew, even the Eskimos wanted it.

So where was the microfilm? What had George Persall done with it? If he had indeed passed it to Luis Marcel, who was his normal contact, then where was Luis? Had Luis decided to sell the microfilm to the highest bidder? That seemed unlikely. Grant knew Luis personally; they had been in some tight spots together and he trusted Luis at his back, which said a lot.

Government agents had been chasing this particular microfilm for about a month now. A high-level executive of a research firm in California had made a deal to sell the government-classified laser technology his firm had developed, technology that could place laser weaponry in space in the near future. The firm's own security people had become suspicious of the man and alerted the proper government authorities; together they had apprehended the executive in the middle of the sale. But the two buyers had escaped, taking the microfilm with them. Then one of

the buyers double-crossed his partner and took himself and
the microfilm to South America to strike his own deal.
Agents all over Central and South America had been
alerted, and an American agent in Costa Rica had made
contact with the man, setting up a "sting" to buy the microfilm. Things became completely confused at that point.
The deal had gone sour, and the agent had been wounded,
but he had gotten away with the microfilm. The film
should have been destroyed at that point, but it hadn't
been. Somehow the agent had gotten it to George Persall,
who could come and go freely in Costa Rica because of his
business connections. Who would have suspected George
Persall of being involved in espionage? He'd always
seemed just a tame businessman, albeit with a passion for
gorgeous "secretaries"—a weakness any Latin man would
understand. Persall had been known to only a few agents,
Luis Marcel among them, and that had made him extraordinarily effective. But in this case, George had been
left in the dark; the agent had been feverish from his
wound and hadn't told George to destroy the film.

Luis Marcel had been supposed to contact George, but
instead Luis had disappeared. Then George, who had always seemed to be disgustingly healthy, had died of a heart
attack . . . and no one knew where the microfilm was. The
Americans wanted to be certain that the technology didn't
fall into anyone else's hands; the Russians wanted the
technology just as badly, and every revolutionary in the
hemisphere wanted the microfilm in order to sell it to the
highest bidder. An arsenal of weapons could be pur-
chased, revolutions could be staged, with the amount of
money that small piece of film would bring on the open
market.

Manuel Turego, head of national security in Costa Rica,
was a very smart man; he was a bastard, Grant thought,

but a smart one. He'd promptly snatched up Ms. Priscilla Jane Hamilton Greer and carried her off to this heavily guarded inland "plantation." He'd probably told her that she was under protective custody, and she was probably stupid enough that she was very grateful to him for "protecting" her. Turego had played it cool; so far he hadn't harmed her. Evidently he knew that her father was a very wealthy, very influential man, and that it wasn't wise to enrage wealthy, influential men unless it was absolutely necessary. Turego was playing a waiting game; he was waiting for Luis Marcel to surface, waiting for the microfilm to surface, as it eventually had to. In the meantime, he had Priscilla; he could afford to wait. Whether she knew anything or not, she was valuable to him as a negotiating tool, if nothing else.

From the moment Priscilla had disappeared, her father had been frantic. He'd been calling in political favors with a heavy hand, but he'd found that none of the favors owed to him could get Priscilla away from Turego. Until Luis was found, the American government wasn't going to lift a hand to free the young woman. The confusion about whether or not she actually knew anything, the tantalizing possibility that she *could* know the location of the microfilm, seemed to have blunted the intensity of the search for Luis. Her captivity could give him the edge he needed by attracting attention away from him.

Finally, desperate with worry and enraged by the lack of response he'd been getting from the government, James Hamilton had decided to take matters into his own hands. He'd spent a small fortune ferreting out his daughter's location, and then had been stymied by the inaccessibility of the well-guarded plantation. If he sent in enough men to take over the plantation, he realized, there was a strong possibility that his daughter would be killed in the fight. Then someone had mentioned Grant Sullivan's name.

A man as wealthy as James Hamilton could find someone who didn't want to be found, even a wary, burnt-out ex-government agent who had buried himself in the Tennessee mountains. Within twenty-four hours, Grant had been sitting across from Hamilton, in the library of a huge estate house that shouted of old money. Hamilton had made an offer that would pay off the mortgage on Grant's farm completely. All the man wanted was to have his daughter back, safe and sound. His face had been lined and taut with worry, and there had been a desperation about him that, even more than the money, made Grant reluctantly accept the job.

The difficulty of rescuing her had seemed enormous, perhaps even insurmountable; if he were able to penetrate the security of the plantation—something he didn't really doubt—getting her out would be something else entirely. Not only that, but Grant had his own personal experiences to remind him that, even if he found her, the odds were greatly against her being alive or recognizably human. He hadn't let himself think about what could have happened to her since the day she'd been kidnapped.

But getting to her had been made ridiculously easy; as soon as he left Hamilton's house, a new wrinkle had developed. Not a mile down the highway from Hamilton's estate, he'd glanced in the rearview mirror and found a plain blue sedan on his tail. He'd lifted one eyebrow sardonically and pulled over to the shoulder of the road.

He lit a cigarette and inhaled leisurely as he waited for the two men to approach his car. "Hiya, Curtis."

Ted Curtis leaned down and peered in the open window, grinning. "Guess who wants to see you?"

"Hell," Grant swore irritably. "All right, lead the way. I don't have to drive all the way to Virginia, do I?"

"Naw, just to the next town. He's waiting in a motel."

The fact that Sabin had felt it necessary to leave headquarters at all told Grant a lot. He knew Kell Sabin from the old days; the man didn't have a nerve in his body, and ice water ran in his veins. He wasn't a comfortable man to be around, but Grant knew that the same had been said about himself. They were both men to whom no rules applied, men who had intimate knowledge of hell, who had lived and hunted in that gray jungle where no laws existed. The difference between them was that Sabin was comfortable in that cold grayness; it was his life—but Grant wanted no more of it. Things had gone too far; he had felt himself becoming less than human. He had begun to lose his sense of who he was and why he was there. Nothing seemed to matter any longer. The only time he'd felt alive was during the chase, when adrenaline pumped through his veins and fired all his senses into acute awareness. The bullet that had almost killed him had instead saved him, because it had stopped him long enough to let him begin thinking again. That was when he'd decided to get out.

Twenty-five minutes later, with his hand curled around a mug of strong, hot coffee, his booted feet propped comfortably on the genuine, wood-grained plastic coffee table that was standard issue for motels, Grant had murmured, "Well, I'm here. Talk."

Kell Sabin was an even six feet tall, an inch shorter than Grant, and the hard musculature of his frame revealed that he made it a point to stay in shape, even though he was no longer in the field. He was dark—black-haired, black-eyed, with an olive complexion—and the cold fire of his energy generated a force field around him. He was impossible to

read, and was as canny as a stalking panther, but Grant
trusted him. He couldn't say that he liked Sabin; Sabin
wasn't a man to be friendly. Yet for twenty years their lives
had been intertwined until they were virtually a part of
each other. In his mind, Grant saw a red-orange flash of
gunfire, and abruptly he felt the thick, moist heat of the
jungle, smelled the rotting vegetation, saw the flash of
weapons being discharged...and felt, at his back, so close
that each had braced his shoulders against the other, the
same man who sat across from him now. Things like that
stayed in a man's memory.

A dangerous man, Kell Sabin. Hostile governments
would gladly have paid a fortune to get to him, but Sabin
was nothing more than a shadow slipping away from the
sunshine, as he directed his troops from the gray mists.

Without a flicker of expression in his black eyes, Sabin
studied the man who sat across from him in a lazy
sprawl—a deceptively lazy sprawl, he knew. Grant was, if
anything, even leaner and harder than he had been in the
field. Hibernating for a year hadn't made him go soft.
There was still something wild about Grant Sullivan,
something dangerous and untamed. It was in the wary,
restless glitter of his amber eyes, eyes that glowed as fierce
and golden as an eagle's under the dark, level brows. His
dark blond hair was shaggy, curling down over his collar
in back, emphasizing that he wasn't quite civilized. He was
darkly tanned; the small scar on his chin wasn't very noticeable, but the thin line that slashed across his left
cheekbone was silver against his bronzed skin. They
weren't disfiguring scars, but reminders of battles.

If Sabin had had to pick anyone to go after Hamilton's
daughter, he'd have picked this man. In the jungle Sullivan was as stealthy as a cat; he could become part of the
jungle, blending into it, using it. He'd been useful in the

concrete jungles, too, but it was in the green hells of the world that no one could equal him.

"Are you going after her?" Sabin finally asked in a quiet tone.

"Yeah."

"Then let me fill you in." Totally disregarding the fact that Grant no longer had security clearance, Sabin told him about the missing microfilm. He told him about George Persall, Luis Marcel, the whole deadly cat-and-mouse game, and dumb little Priscilla sitting in the middle of it. She was being used as a smokescreen for Luis, but Kell was more than a little worried about Luis. It wasn't like the man to disappear, and Costa Rica wasn't the most tranquil place on earth. Anything could have happened to him. Yet, wherever he was, he wasn't in the hands of any government or political faction, because everyone was still searching for him, and everyone except Manuel Turego and the American government was searching for Priscilla. Not even the Costa Rican government knew that Turego had the woman; he was operating on his own.

"Persall was a dark horse," Kell admitted irritably. "He wasn't a professional. I don't even have a file on him."

If Sabin didn't have a file on him, Persall had been more than a dark horse; he'd been totally invisible. "How did this thing blow open?" Grant drawled, closing his eyes until they were little more than slits. He looked as if he were going to fall asleep, but Sabin knew differently.

"Our man was being followed. They were closing in on him. He was out of his mind with fever. He couldn't find Luis, but he remembered how to contact Persall. No one knew Persall's name, until then, or how to find him if they needed him. Our man just barely got the film to Persall before all hell broke loose. Persall got away."

"What about our man?"

"He's alive. We got him out, but not before Turego got his hands on him."

Grant grunted. "So Turego knows our guy didn't tell Persall to destroy the film."

Kell looked completely disgusted. "*Everyone* knows. There's no security down there. Too many people will sell any scrap of information they can find. Turego has a leak in his organization, so by morning it was common knowledge. Also by morning, Persall had died of a heart attack, in Priscilla's room. Before we could move in, Turego took the girl."

Dark brown lashes veiled the golden glitter of Grant's eyes almost completely. He looked as if he would begin snoring at any minute. "Well? Does she know anything about the microfilm or not?"

"We don't know. My guess is that she doesn't. Persall had several hours to hide the microfilm before he went to her room."

"Why the hell couldn't she have stayed with Daddy, where she belongs?" Grant murmured.

"Hamilton has been raising hell for us to get her out of there, but they aren't really close. She's a party girl. Divorced, more interested in having a good time than in doing anything constructive. In fact, Hamilton cut her out of his will several years ago, and she's been wandering all around the globe since. She'd been with Persall for a couple of years. They weren't shy about their relationship. Persall liked to have a flashy woman on his arm, and he could afford her. He always seemed like an easygoing good time guy, well-suited to her type. I sure as hell never figured him for a courier, especially one sharp enough to fool me."

"Why don't you go in and get the girl out?" Grant asked suddenly, and he opened his eyes, staring at Kell, his gaze cold and yellow.

"Two reasons. One, I don't think she knows anything about the film. I have to concentrate on finding the film, and I think that means finding Luis Marcel. Two, you're the best man for the job. I thought so when I... ah... arranged for you to be brought to Hamilton's attention."

So Kell was working to get the girl out, after all, but going about it in his own circuitous way. Well, staying behind the scenes was the only way he could be effective. "You won't have any trouble getting into Costa Rica," Kell said. "I've already arranged it. But if you can't get the girl out..."

Grant got to his feet, a tawny, graceful savage, silent and lethal. "I know," he said quietly. Neither of them had to say it, but both knew that a bullet in her head would be a great deal kinder than what would happen to her if Turego decided that she did know the location of the microfilm. She was being held only as a safety measure now, but if that microfilm didn't surface, she would eventually be the only remaining link to it. Then her life wouldn't be worth a plugged nickel.

So now he was in Costa Rica, deep in the rain forest and too damned near the Nicaraguan border for comfort. Roaming bands of rebels, soldiers, revolutionaries and just plain terrorists made life miserable for people who just wanted to live their simple lives in peace, but none of it touched Priscilla. She might have been a tropical princess, sipping daintily at her iced drink, ignoring the jungle that ate continuously at the boundaries of the plantation and had to be cut back regularly.

Well, he'd seen enough. Tonight was the night. He knew her schedule now, knew the routine of the guards, and had already found all the trip lines. He didn't like traveling through the jungle at night, but there wasn't any choice. He had to have several hours to get her away from here before anyone realized she was missing; luckily, she always slept late, until at least ten every morning. No one would really think anything of it if she didn't appear by eleven. By then, they'd be long gone. Pablo would pick them up by helicopter at the designated clearing tomorrow morning, not long after dawn.

Grant backed slowly away from the edge of the jungle, worming himself into the thick greenery until it formed a solid curtain separating him from the house. Only then did he rise to his feet, walking silently and with assurance, because he'd taken care of the trip lines and sensors as he'd found them. He'd been in the jungle for three days, moving cautiously around the perimeter of the plantation, carefully getting the layout of the house. He knew where the girl slept, and he knew how he was going to get in. It couldn't have been better; Turego wasn't in the house. He'd left the day before, and since he wasn't back by now, Grant knew that he wasn't coming. It was already twilight, and it wasn't safe to travel the river in the darkness.

Grant knew exactly how treacherous the river was; that was why he would take the girl through the jungle. Even given its dangers, the river would be the logical route for them to take. If by some chance her departure were discovered before Pablo picked them up, the search would be concentrated along the river, at least for a while. Long enough, he hoped, for them to reach the helicopter.

He'd have to wait several more hours before he could go into the house and get the girl out. That would give everyone time to get tired, bored and sleepy. He made his way to the small clearing where he'd stashed his supplies, and carefully checked it for snakes, especially the velvety brown fer-de-lance, which liked to lie in clearings and wait for its next meal. After satisfying himself that the clearing was safe, he sat down on a fallen tree to smoke a cigarette. He took a drink of water, but he wasn't hungry. He knew that he wouldn't be until sometime tomorrow. Once the action was going down he couldn't eat; he was too keyed up, all his senses enhanced so that even the smallest sound of the jungle crashed against his eardrums like thunder. Adrenaline was already pumping through his veins, making him so high that he could understand why the Vikings had gone berserk during battle. Waiting was almost unbearable, but that was what he had to do. He checked his watch again, the illuminated dial a strange bit of civilization in a jungle that swallowed men alive, and frowned when he saw that only a little over half an hour had passed.

To give himself something to do, to calm his tightly wound nerves, he began packing methodically, arranging everything so he would know exactly where it was. He checked his weapons and his ammunition, hoping he wouldn't have to use them. What he needed more than anything, if he was to get the girl out alive, was a totally silent operation. If he had to use his carbine or the automatic pistol, he'd give away their position. He preferred a knife, which was silent and deadly.

He felt sweat trickle down his spine. God, if only the girl would have sense enough to keep her mouth shut and not start squawking when he hauled her out of there. If he had to, he'd knock her out, but that would make her dead weight to carry through vegetation that reached out to wrap around his legs like living fingers.

He realized that he was fondling his knife, his long, lean fingers sliding over the deadly blade with a lover's touch, and he shoved it into its sheath. Damn her, he thought bitterly. Because of her, he was back in the thick of things, and he could feel it taking hold of him again. The rush of danger was as addictive as any drug, and it was in his veins again, burning him, eating at him like an acid—killing him and intensifying the feeling of life all at once. Damn her, damn her to hell. All this for a spoiled, silly society brat who liked to amuse herself in various beds. Still, her round heels might have kept her alive, because Turego fancied himself quite a lover.

The night sounds of the jungle began to build around him: the screams of the howler monkeys, the rustles and chirps and coughs of the night denizens as they went about their business. Somewhere down close to the river he heard a jaguar cough, but he never minded the normal jungle sounds. He was at home here. The peculiar combination of his genes and the skills he'd learned as a boy in the swamps of south Georgia made him as much a part of the jungle as the jaguar that prowled the river's edge. Though the thick canopy blocked out all light, he didn't light a lamp or switch on a flashlight; he wanted his eyes to be perfectly adjusted to the dark when he began moving. He relied on his ears and his instincts, knowing that there was no danger close to him. The danger would come from men, not from the shy jungle animals. As long as those reassuring noises surrounded him, he knew that no men were near.

At midnight he rose and began easing along the route he'd marked in his mind, and the animals and insects were so unalarmed by his presence that the din continued without pause. The only caution he felt was that a fer-de-lance or a bushmaster might be hunting along the path he'd chosen, but that was a chance he'd have to take. He carried a long stick that he swept silently across the ground before him. When he reached the edge of the plantation he put the stick aside and crouched down to survey the grounds, making certain everything was as expected, before he moved in.

From where he crouched, he could see that the guards were at their normal posts, probably asleep, except for the one who patrolled the perimeter, and he'd soon settle down for a nap, too. They were sloppy, he thought contemptuously. They obviously didn't expect any visitors in as remote a place as this upriver plantation. During the three days he'd spent observing them, he'd noted that they stood around talking a great deal of the time, smoking cigarettes, not keeping a close watch on anything. But they were still there, and those rifles were loaded with real bullets. One of the reasons Grant had reached the age of thirty-eight was that he had a healthy respect for weapons and what they could do to human flesh. He didn't believe in recklessness, because it cost lives. He waited. At least now he could see, for the night was clear, and the stars hung low and brilliant in the sky. He didn't mind the starlight; there were plenty of shadows that would cover his movements.

The guard at the left corner of the house hadn't moved an inch since Grant had been watching him; he was asleep. The guard walking the grounds had settled down against one of the pillars at the front of the house. The faint red glow near the guard's hand told Grant that he was smoking and if he followed his usual pattern, he'd pull his cap over his eyes after he'd finished the cigarette, and sleep through the night.

As silently as a wraith, Grant left the concealing jungle and moved onto the grounds, slipping from tree to bush, invisible in the black shadows. Soundlessly, he mounted the veranda that ran alongside the house, flattening himself against the wall and checking the scene again. It was silent and peaceful. The guards relied far too heavily on those trip lines, not realizing they could be dismantled.

Priscilla's room was toward the back. It had double sliding glass doors, which might be locked, but that didn't worry him; he had a way with locks. He eased up to the doors, put out his hand and pulled silently. The door moved easily, and his brows rose. Not locked. Thoughtful of her.

Gently, gently, a fraction of an inch at a time, he slid the door open until there was enough room for him to slip through. As soon as he was in the room he paused, waiting for his eyes to adjust again. After the starlight, the room seemed as dark as the jungle. He didn't move a muscle, but waited, poised and listening.

Soon he could see again. The room was big and airy, with cool wooden floors covered with straw mats. The bed was against the wall to his right, ghostly with the folds of mosquito netting draped around it. Through the netting he could see the rumpled covers, the small mound on the far side of the bed. A chair, a small round table and a tall floor lamp were on this side of the bed. The shadows were deeper to his left, but he could see a door that probably opened to the bathroom. An enormous wardrobe stood against the wall. Slowly, as silently as a tiger stalking its prey, he moved around the wall, blending into the darkness near the wardrobe. Now he could see a chair on the far side of the bed, next to where she slept. A long white garment, perhaps her robe or nightgown, lay across the chair. The thought that she might be sleeping naked made his mouth quirk in a sudden grin that held no real amusement. If she did sleep naked, she'd fight like a wildcat when he woke her. Just what he needed. For both their sakes, he hoped she was clothed.

He moved closer to the bed, his eyes on the small figure. She was so still.... The hair prickled on the back of his neck in warning, and without thinking he flung himself to the side, taking the blow on his shoulder instead of his neck. He rolled, and came to his feet expecting to face his assailant, but the room was still and dark again. Nothing moved, not even the woman on the bed. Grant faded back into the shadows, trying to hear the soft whisper of breathing, the rustle of clothing, anything. The silence in the room was deafening. Where was his attacker? Like Grant, he'd moved into the shadows, which were deep enough to shield several men.

Who was his assailant? What was he doing here in the woman's bedroom? Had he been sent to kill her or was he, too, trying to steal her from Turego?

His opponent was probably in the black corner beside the wardrobe. Grant eased the knife out of its sheath, then pushed it in again; his hands would be as silent as the knife.

There...just for a moment, the slightest of movements, but enough to pinpoint the man's position. Grant crouched then moved forward in a blurred rush, catching the man low and flipping him. The stranger rolled as he landed and came to his feet with a lithe twist, a slim dark figure outlined against the white mosquito netting. He kicked out, and Grant dodged the blow, but he felt the breeze of the kick pass his chin. Moving in, he caught the man's arm with a numbing chop. He saw the arm fall uselessly to the man's side. Coldly, without emotion, not even breathing hard, Grant threw the slim figure to the floor and knelt with one knee on the good arm and his other knee pressed to the man's chest. Just as he raised his hand to strike the blow that would end their silent struggle, Grant became aware of something odd, something soft swelling beneath his knee. Then he understood. The too-still form on the bed was so still because it was a mound of covers, not a human being. The girl hadn't been in bed; she'd seen him come through the sliding doors and had hidden herself in the shadows. But why hadn't she screamed? Why had she attacked, knowing that she had no chance of overpowering him? He moved his knee off her breasts and quickly slid his hand to the soft mounds to make certain his weight hadn't cut off her breath. He felt the reassuring rise of her chest, heard the soft, startled gasp as she felt his touch, and he eased a little away from her.

"It's all right," he started to whisper, but she suddenly twisted on the floor, wrenching away from him. Her knee slashed upward; he was unguarded, totally vulnerable, and her knee crashed into his groin with a force that sent agony through his whole body. Red lights danced before his eyes, and he sagged to one side, gagging at the bitter bile that rose in his throat, his hands automatically cupping his agonized flesh as he ground his teeth to contain the groan that fought for release.

She scrambled away from him, and he heard a low sob, perhaps of terror. Through pain-blurred eyes he saw her pick up something dark and bulky; then she slipped through the open glass door and was gone.

Pure fury propelled him to his feet. Damn it, she was escaping on her own. She was going to ruin the whole setup! Ignoring the pain in his loins, he started after her. He had a score to settle.

Chapter Two

Jane had just reached for her bundle of supplies when some instinct left over from her cave-dwelling ancestors told her that someone was near. There hadn't been any sound to alert her, but suddenly she was aware of another presence. The fine hairs on the back of her neck and her forearms stood up, and she had frozen, turning terrified eyes toward the double glass doors. The doors had slid open noiselessly, and she had seen the darker shadow of a man briefly outlined against the night. He was a big man, but one who moved with total silence. It was the eerie soundlessness of his movements that had frightened her more than anything, sending chills of pure terror chasing over her skin. For days now she had lived by her nerves, holding the terror at bay while she walked a tightrope, trying to lull Turego's suspicions, yet always poised for an escape attempt. But nothing had frightened her as much as that dark shadow slipping into her room.

Any faint hope that she would be rescued had died when Turego had installed her here. She had assessed the situation realistically. The only person who would try to get her out would be her father, but it would be beyond his power. She could depend on only herself and her wits. To that end, she had flirted and flattered and downright lied, doing everything she could to convince Turego that she was both brainless and harmless. In that, she thought, she'd succeeded, but time was fast running out. When an aide had brought an urgent message to Turego the day before, Jane had eavesdropped; Luis Marcel's location had been discovered, and Turego wanted Luis, badly.

But by now Turego surely would have discovered that Luis had no knowledge of the missing microfilm, and that would leave her as the sole suspect. She had to escape, tonight, before Turego returned.

She hadn't been idle since she'd been here; she'd carefully memorized the routine of the guards, especially at night, when the terror brought on by the darkness made it impossible for her to sleep. She'd spent the nights standing at the double doors, watching the guards, clocking them, studying their habits. By keeping her mind busy, she'd been able to control the fear. When dawn would begin to lighten the sky, she had slept. She had been preparing since the first day she'd been here for the possibility that she might have to bolt into the jungle. She'd been sneaking food and supplies, hoarding them, and steeling herself for what lay ahead. Even now, only the raw fear of what awaited her at Turego's hands gave her the courage to brave the black jungle, where the night demons were waiting for her.

But none of that had been as sinister, as lethal, as the dark shape moving through her bedroom. She shrank back into the thick shadows, not even breathing in her acute terror. Oh, God, she prayed, what do I do now? Why was he there? To murder her in her bed? Was it one of the guards, tonight of all nights, come to rape her?

As he passed in front of her, moving in a slight crouch toward her bed, an odd rage suddenly filled Jane. After all she had endured, she was damned if she'd allow him to spoil her escape attempt! She'd talked herself into it, despite her horrible fear of the dark, and now he was ruining it!

Her jaw set, she clenched her fists as she'd been taught to do in her self-defense classes. She struck at the back of his neck, but suddenly he was gone, a shadow twisting away from the blow, and her fist struck his shoulder instead. Instantly terrified again, she shrank back into the shelter of the wardrobe, straining her eyes to see him, but he'd disappeared. Had he been a wraith, a figment of her imagination? No, her fist had struck a very solid shoulder, and the faint rippling of the white curtains over the glass doors testified that the doors were indeed open. He was in the room, somewhere, but *where*? How could a man that big disappear so completely?

Then, abruptly, his weight struck her in the side, bowling her over, and she barely bit off the instinctive scream that surged up from her throat. She didn't have a chance. She tried automatically to kick him in the throat, but he moved like lightning, blocking her attack. Then a hard blow to her arm numbed it all the way to her elbow, and a split second later she was thrown to the floor, a knee pressing into her chest and making it impossible to breathe.

The man raised his arm and Jane tensed, willing now to scream, but unable to make a sound. Then, suddenly, the man paused, and for some reason lifted his weight from her chest. Air rushed into her lungs, along with a dizzying sense of relief, then she felt his hand moving boldly over her breasts and realized why he'd shifted position. Both terrified and angry that this should be happening to her, she moved instinctively the split second she realized his vulnerability, and slashed upward with her knee. He sagged to the side, holding himself, and she felt an absurd sense of pity. Then she realized that he hadn't even groaned aloud. The man wasn't human! Choking back a

sob of terror, she struggled to her feet and grabbed her
supplies, then darted through the open door. At that point
she wasn't escaping from Turego so much as from that
dark, silent demon in her room.

Heedlessly, she flung herself across the plantation
grounds; her heart was pounding so violently that the
sound of her blood pumping through her veins made a
roar in her ears. Her lungs hurt, and she realized that she
was holding her breath. She tried to remind herself to be
quiet, but the urge to flee was too strong for caution; she
stumbled over a rough section of ground and sprawled on
her hands and knees. As she began scrambling to her feet,
she was suddenly overwhelmed by something big and
warm, smashing her back to the ground. Cold, pure terror froze her blood in her veins, but before even an instinctive scream could find voice, his hand was on the back
of her neck and everything went black.

Jane regained consciousness by degrees, confused by her
upside down position, the jouncing she was suffering, the
discomfort of her arms. Strange noises assailed her ears,
noises that she tried and failed to identify. Even when she
opened her eyes she saw only blackness. It was one of the
worst nightmares she'd ever had. She began kicking and
struggling to wake up, to end the dream, and abruptly a
sharp slap stung her bottom. "Settle down," an ill-
tempered voice said from somewhere above and behind
her. The voice was that of a stranger, but there was something in that laconic drawl that made her obey instantly.

Slowly things began to shift into a recognizable pattern, and her senses righted themselves. She was being
carried over a man's shoulder through the jungle. Her
wrists had been taped behind her, and her ankles were also
secured. Another wide band of tape covered her mouth,
preventing her from doing anything more than grunting or

humming. She didn't feel like humming, so she used her limited voice to grunt out exactly what she thought of him, in language that would have left her elegant mother white with shock. A hard hand again made contact with the seat of her pants. "Would you shut the hell up?" he growled. "You sound like a pig grunting at the trough."

American! she thought, stunned. He was an American! He'd come to rescue her, even though he was being unnecessarily rough about it...or was he a rescuer? Chilled, she thought of all the different factions who would like to get their hands on her. Some of those factions were fully capable of hiring an American mercenary to get her, or of training one of their own to imitate an American accent and win her trust.

She didn't dare trust anyone, she realized. Not anyone. She was alone in this.

The man stopped and lifted her from his shoulder, standing her on her feet. Jane blinked her eyes, then widened them in an effort to see, but the darkness under the thick canopy was total, she couldn't see anything. The night pressed in on her, suffocating her with its thick darkness. Where was he? Had he simply dropped her here in the jungle and left her to be breakfast for a jaguar? She could sense movement around her, but no sounds that she could identify as him; the howls and chittering and squawks and rustles of the jungle filled her ears. A whimper rose in her throat, and she tried to move, to seek a tree or something to protect her back, but she'd forgotten her bound feet and she stumbled to the ground, scratching her face on a bush.

A low obscenity came to her ears, then she was roughly grasped and hauled to her feet. "Damn it, stay put!"

So he was still there. How could he see? What was he doing? No matter who he was or what he was doing, at that moment Jane was grateful for his presence. She could not conquer her fear of darkness but the fact that she wasn't alone held the terror at bay. She gasped as he abruptly lifted her and tossed her over his shoulder again, as effortlessly as if she were a rag doll. She felt the bulk of a backpack, which hadn't been there before, but he showed no sign of strain. He moved through the stygian darkness with a peculiar sure-footedness, a lithe, powerful grace that never faltered.

Her own pack of pilfered supplies was still slung around her shoulders, the straps holding it even though it had slid down and was bumping against the back of her head. A can of something was banging against her skull; she'd probably have concussion if this macho fool didn't ease up. What did he think this was, some sort of jungle marathon? Her ribs were being bruised against his hard shoulder, and she felt various aches all over her body, probably as a result of his roughness in throwing her to the floor. Her arm ached to the bone from his blow. Even if this was a real rescue, she thought, she'd be lucky if she lived through it.

She bounced on his shoulder for what seemed like days, the pain in her cramped limbs increasing with every step he took. Nausea began to rise in her, and she took deep breaths in an effort to stave off throwing up. If she began to vomit, with her mouth taped the way it was, she could suffocate. Desperately she began to struggle, knowing only that she needed to get into an upright position.

"Easy there, Pris." Somehow he seemed to know how she was feeling. He stopped and lifted her off his shoulder, easing her onto her back on the ground. When her weight came down on her bound arms she couldn't suppress a whimper of pain. "All right," the man said. "I'm going to cut you loose now, but if you start acting up, I'll truss you up like a Christmas turkey again and leave you that way. Understand?"

She nodded wildly, wondering if he could see her in the dark. Evidently he could, because he turned her on her side and she felt a knife slicing through the tape that bound her wrists. Tears stung her eyes from the pain as he pulled her arms around and began massaging them roughly to ease her cramped muscles.

"Your daddy sent me to get you out of here," the man drawled calmly as he began easing the tape off of her mouth. Instead of ripping the adhesive away and taking skin with it, he was careful, and Jane was torn between gratitude and indignation, since he'd taped her mouth in the first place.

Jane moved her mouth back and forth, restoring it to working condition. "My daddy?" she asked hoarsely.

"Yeah. Okay, now, Pris, I'm going to free your legs, but if you look like you're even thinking about kicking me again, I won't be as easy with you as I was the last time." Despite his drawl, there was something menacing in his tone, and Jane didn't doubt his word.

"I wouldn't have kicked you the first time if you hadn't started pawing at me like a high school sophomore!" she hissed.

"I was checking to see if you were breathing."

"Sure you were, and taking your time about it, too."

"Gagging you was a damned good idea," he said reflectively, and Jane shut up. She had yet to see him as anything more than a shadow. She couldn't even put a name to him, but she knew enough about him to know that he would bind and gag her again without a moment's compunction.

He cut the tape from around her ankles, and again she was subjected to his rough but effective massage. In only a moment she was being pulled to her feet; she staggered momentarily before regaining her sense of balance.

"We don't have much farther to go; stay right behind me, and don't say a word."

"Wait!" Jane whispered frantically. "How can I follow you when I can't see you?"

He took her hand and carried it to his waist. "Hang on to my belt."

She did better than that. Acutely aware of the vast jungle around her, and with only his presence shielding her from the night terrors, she hooked her fingers inside the waistband of his pants in a death grip. She knotted the material so tightly that he muttered a protest, but she wasn't about to let go of him.

Maybe it didn't seem very far to him, but to Jane, being towed in his wake, stumbling over roots and vines that she couldn't see, it seemed like miles before he halted. "We'll wait here," he whispered. "I don't want to go any closer until I hear the helicopter come in."

"When will that be?" Jane whispered back, figuring that if he could talk, so could she.

"A little after dawn."

"When is dawn?"

"Half an hour."

Still clutching the waistband of his pants, she stood behind him and waited for dawn. The seconds and minutes crawled by, but they gave her the chance to realize for the first time that she'd truly escaped from Turego. She was safe and free . . . well almost. She was out of his clutches, she was the only one who knew what a close call she'd had. Turego would almost certainly return to the plantation this morning to find that his prisoner had escaped. For a moment she was surprised at her own lack of elation, then she realized that she wasn't out of danger yet. This man said that her father had sent him, but he hadn't given her a name or any proof. All she had was his word, and Jane was more than a little wary. Until she was actually on American soil, until she knew beyond any doubt that she was safe, she was going to follow poor George Persall's iron-clad rule: when in doubt, lie.

The man shifted uncomfortably, drawing her attention. "Look, honey, do you think you could loosen up on my pants? Or are you trying to finish the job you started on me with your knee?"

Jane felt the blood rush to her cheeks, and she hastily released her hold. "I'm sorry, I didn't realize," she whispered. She stood stiffly for a moment, her arms at her sides; then panic began to rise in her. She couldn't see him in the darkness, she couldn't hear him breathing, and now that she was no longer touching him, she couldn't be certain that he hadn't left her. Was he still there? What if she was alone? The air became thick and oppressive, and she struggled to breathe, to fight down the fear that she knew was unreasonable but that no amount of reason could conquer. Even knowing its source didn't help. She simply couldn't stand the darkness. She couldn't sleep without a light; she never went into a room without first reaching in and turning on the light switch, and she always left her lights on if she knew she would be late returning home. She, who always took extraordinary precautions against being left in the dark, was standing in the middle of a jungle in darkness so complete that it was like being blind.

Her fragile control broke and she reached out wildly, clawing for him, for reassurance that he was still there. Her outstretched fingers touched fabric, and she threw herself against him, gasping in mingled panic and relief. The next second steely fingers grasped her shirt and she was hurled through the air to land flat on her back in the smelly, rotting vegetation. Before she could move, before she could suck air back into her lungs, her hair was pulled back and she felt the suffocating pressure of his knee on her chest again. His breath was a low rasp above her, his voice little more than a snarl "Don't ever—*ever*—come at me from behind again."

Jane writhed, pushing at his knee. After a moment he lifted it, and eased the grip on her hair. Even being thrown over his shoulder had been better than being left alone in the darkness, and she grabbed for him again, catching him around the knees. Automatically he tried to step away from her entangling arms but she lunged for him. He uttered a startled curse, tried to regain his balance, then crashed to the ground.

He lay so still that Jane's heart plummeted. What would she do if he were hurt? She couldn't possibly carry him, but neither could she leave him lying there, injured and unable to protect himself. Feeling her way up his body, she scrambled to crouch by his shoulders. "Mister, are you all right?" she whispered, running her hands up his shoulders to his face, then searching his head for any cuts or lumps. There was an elasticized band around his head, and she followed it, her nervous fingers finding an odd type of glasses over his eyes. "Are you hurt?" she demanded again, her voice tight with fear. "Damn it, answer me!"

"Lady," the man said in a low, furious voice, "you're crazier than hell. If I was your daddy, I'd *pay* Turego to keep you!"

She didn't know him, but his words caused an odd little pain in her chest. She sat silently, shocked that he could hurt her feelings. She didn't know him, and he didn't know her—how could his opinion matter? But it did, somehow, and she felt strangely vulnerable.

He eased himself to a sitting position, and when she didn't say anything, he sighed. "Why did you jump me like that?" he asked in resignation.

"I'm afraid of the dark," she said with quiet dignity. "I couldn't hear you breathing, and I can't see a thing. I panicked. I'm sorry."

After a moment he said, "All right," and got to his feet. Bending down, he grasped her wrists and pulled her up to stand beside him. Jane inched a little closer to him.

"You can see because of those glasses you're wearing, can't you?" she asked.

"Yeah. There's not a lot of light, but enough that I can make out where I'm going. Infrared lenses."

A howler monkey suddenly screamed somewhere above their heads, and Jane jumped, bumping into him. "Got another pair?" she asked shakily.

She could feel him hesitate, then his arm went around her shoulders. "Nope, just these. Don't worry, Pris, I'm not going to lose you. In another five minutes or so, it'll start getting light."

"I'm all right now," she said, and she was, as long as she could touch him and know that she wasn't alone. That was the real terror: being alone in the darkness. For years she had fought a battle against the nightmare that had begun when she was nine years old, but at last she had come to accept it, and in the acceptance she'd won peace. She knew it was there, knew when to expect it and what to do to ward it off, and that knowledge gave her the ability to enjoy life again. She hadn't let the nightmare cripple her. Maybe her methods of combating it were a little unorthodox, but she had found the balance within herself and she was happy with it.

Feeling remarkably safe with that steely arm looped over her shoulders, Jane waited beside him, and in a very short

time she found that she could indeed see a little better.
Deep in the rain forest there was no brilliant sunrise to an-
nounce the day—the sunrise could not be seen from beneath the canopy of vegetation. Even during the hottest
noon, the light that reached the jungle floor was dim, filtered through layers of greenery. She waited as the faint
gray light slowly became stronger, until she could pick out
more of the details of the lush foliage that surrounded her.
She felt almost swamped by the plant life. She'd never been
in the jungle before; her only knowledge of it came from
movies and what little she'd been able to see during the trip
upriver to the plantation. During her days at the plantation she'd begun to think of the jungle as a living entity,
huge and green, surrounding her, waiting. She had known
from the first that to escape she would have to plunge into
that seemingly impenetrable green barrier, and she had
spent hours staring at it.

Now she was deep within it, and it wasn't quite what
she'd expected. It wasn't a thick tangle, where paths had
to be cut with a machete. The jungle floor was littered with
rotting vegetation, and laced with networks of vines and
roots, but for all that it was surprisingly clear. Plant life
that lingered near the jungle floor was doomed. To com-
pete for the precious light it had to rise and spread out its
broad leaves, to gather as much light as it could. She stared
at a fern that wasn't quite a fern; it was a tree with a buttressed root system, rising to a height of at least eight feet,
only at the top it feathered into a fern.

"You can see now," he muttered suddenly, lifting his
arm from her shoulders and stripping off the night vision
goggles. He placed them carefully in a zippered section of
his field pack.

Jane stared at him in open curiosity, wishing that the
light were better so she could really see him. What she

could see gave wing to hundreds of tiny butterflies in her stomach. It would take one brave *hombre* to meet this man in a dark alley, she thought with a frightened shiver. She couldn't tell the color of his eyes, but they glittered at her from beneath fierce, level dark brows. His face was blackened, which made those eyes all the brighter. His light colored hair was far too long, and he'd tied a strip of cloth around his head to keep the hair out of his eyes. He was clad in tiger-striped camouflage fatigues, and he wore the trappings of war. A wicked knife was stuck casually in his belt, and a pistol rode his left hip while he carried a carbine slung over his right shoulder. Her startled eyes darted back up to his face, a strong-boned face that revealed no emotion, though he had been aware of her survey.

"Loaded for bear, aren't you?" she quipped, eyeing the knife again. For some reason it looked more deadly than either of the guns.

"I don't walk into anything unprepared," he said flatly.

Well, he certainly looked prepared for anything. She eyed him again, more warily this time; he was about six feet tall, and looked like...looked like... Her mind groped for and found the phrase. It had been bandied about and almost turned into a joke, but with this man, it was deadly serious. He looked like a lean, mean, fighting machine, every hard, muscled inch of him. His shoulders looked to be a yard wide, and he'd carried her dead weight through the jungle without even a hint of strain. He'd knocked her down twice, and she realized the only reason she wasn't badly hurt was that, both times, he'd tempered his strength.

Abruptly his attention left her, and his head lifted with a quick, alert motion, like that of an eagle. His eyes narrowed as he listened. "The helicopter is coming," he told her. "Let's go."

Jane listened, but she couldn't hear anything. "Are you sure?" she asked doubtfully.

"I said let's go," he repeated impatiently, and walked away from her. It took Jane only a few seconds to realize that he was heading out, and in the jungle he would be completely hidden from view before he'd gone ten yards. She hurried to catch up to him.

"Hey, slow down!" she whispered frantically, catching at his belt.

"Move it," he said with a total lack of sympathy. "The helicopter won't wait forever; Pablo's on the quick side anyway."

"Who's Pablo?"

"The pilot."

Just then a faint vibration reached her ears. In only a moment it had intensified to the recognizable beat of a helicopter. How could he have heard it before? She knew that she had good hearing, but his senses must be almost painfully acute.

He moved swiftly, surely, as if he knew exactly where he was going. Jane concentrated on keeping up with him and avoiding the roots that tried to catch her toes, she paid little attention to their surroundings. When he climbed, she climbed; it was simple. She was mildly surprised when he stopped abruptly and she lifted her head to look around. The jungle of Costa Rica was mountainous, and they had climbed to the edge of a small cliff, looking down on a narrow, hidden valley with a natural clearing. The helicopter sat in that clearing, the blades lazily whirling.

"Better than a taxicab," Jane murmured in relief, and started past him.

His hand closed over her shoulder and jerked her back. "Be quiet," he ordered, his narrowed gaze moving restlessly, surveying the area.

"Is something wrong?"

"Shut up!"

Jane glared at him, incensed by his unnecessary rudeness, but his hand was still clamped on her shoulder in a grip that bordered on being painful. It was a warning that if she tried to leave the protective cover of the jungle before he was satisfied that everything was safe, he would stop her with real pain. She stood quietly, staring at the clearing herself, but she couldn't see anything wrong. Everything was quiet. The pilot was leaning against the outside of the helicopter, occupied with cleaning his nails; he certainly wasn't concerned with anything.

Long minutes dragged past. The pilot began to fidget, craning his neck and staring into the jungle, though anyone standing just a few feet behind the trees would be completely hidden from view. He looked at his watch, then scanned the jungle again, his gaze moving nervously from left to right.

Jane felt the tension in the man standing beside her, tension that was echoed in the hand that held her shoulder. What was wrong? What was he looking for, and why was he waiting? He was as motionless as a jaguar lying in wait for its prey to pass beneath its tree limb.

"This sucks," he muttered abruptly, easing deeper into the jungle and dragging her with him.

Jane sputtered at the inelegant expression. "It does? Why? What's wrong?"

"Stay here." He pushed her to the ground, deep in the green-black shadow of the buttressed roots of an enormous tree.

Startled, she took a moment to realize that she'd been abandoned. He had simply melted into the jungle, so silently and swiftly that she wasn't certain which way he'd gone. She twisted around but could see nothing that indicated his direction; no swaying vines or limbs.

She wrapped her arms around her drawn-up legs and propped her chin on her knees, staring thoughtfully at the ground. A green stick with legs was dragging a large spider off to be devoured. What if he didn't come back . . . whoever he was. Why hadn't she asked him his name? If something happened to him, she'd like to know his name, so she could tell someone—assuming that she could manage to get out of the jungle herself. Well, she wasn't any worse off now than she had been before. She was away from Turego, and that was what counted.

Wait here, he'd said. For how long? Until lunch? Sundown? Her next birthday? Men gave such inexact instructions! Of course, this particular man seemed a little limited in the conversation department. Shut up, Stay here and Stay put seemed to be the highlights of his repertoire.

This was quite a tree he'd parked her by. The bottom of the trunk flared into buttressed roots, forming enormous wings that wrapped around her almost like arms. If she sat back against the tree, the wings would shield her completely from the view of someone approaching at any angle except head on.

The straps of her backpack were irritating her shoulders, so she slid it off and stretched, feeling remarkably lighter. She hauled the pack around and opened it, then began digging for her hairbrush. Finding this backpack had been a stroke of luck, she thought, though Turego's soldiers really should be a little more careful with their belongings. Without it, she'd have had to wrap things up in a blanket, which would have been awkward.

Finally locating the hairbrush, she diligently worked through the mass of tangles that had accumulated in her long hair during the night. A small monkey with an indignant expression hung from a branch overhead. It scolded her throughout the operation, evidently angry that she had intruded on its territory. She waved at it.

Congratulating herself for her foresight, she pinned her hair up and pulled a black baseball cap out of the pack. She jammed the cap on and tugged the bill down low over her eyes, then shoved it back up. There wasn't any sun down here. Staring upward, she could see bright pinpoints of sun high in the trees, but only a muted green light filtered down to the floor. She'd have been better off with some of those fancy goggles that What's-his-name had.

How long had she been sitting there? Was he in trouble?

Her legs were going to sleep, so she stood and stomped around to get her blood flowing again. The longer she waited, the more uneasy she became, and she had the feeling that a time would come when she'd better be able to move fast. Jane was an instinctive creature, as sensitive to atmosphere as any finely tuned barometer. That trait had enabled her to hold Turego at bay for what seemed like an endless succession of days and nights, reading him, sidestepping him, keeping him constantly disarmed, and even charmed. Now the same instinct warned her of danger. There was some slight change in the very air that stroked her bare arms. Warily, she leaned down to pick up her backpack, slipping her arms through the straps and anchoring it this time by fastening the third strap around her middle.

The sudden thunderous burst of automatic weapon fire made her whirl, her heart jumping into her throat. Listening to the staccato blasts, she knew that several weapons were being fired, but at whom? Had her friend been detected or was this something else entirely? Was this the trouble he'd sensed that had made him shy away from the clearing? She wanted to think that he was safe, observing everything from an invisible vantage point in the jungle, but with a chill she realized that she couldn't take that for granted.

Her hands felt cold, and with a distant surprise she realized that she was trembling. What should she do? Wait, or run? What if he needed help? She realized that there was very little she could do, since she was unarmed, but she couldn't just run away if he needed help. He wasn't the most amiable man she'd ever met, and she still didn't exactly trust him, but he was the closest thing to a friend she had here.

Ignoring the unwillingness of her feet and the icy lump of fear in her stomach, Jane left the shelter of the giant tree and began cautiously inching through the forest, back toward the clearing. There were only sporadic bursts of gunfire now, still coming from the same general direction.

Suddenly she froze as the faint sound of voices filtered through the forest. In a cold panic she dove for the shelter of another large tree. What would she do if they were coming in this direction? The rough bark scratched her hands as she cautiously moved her head just enough to peer around the trunk.

A steely hand clamped over her mouth. As a scream rose in her throat, a deep, furious voice growled in her ear, "Damn it, I told you to stay put!"

Chapter Three

J ane glared at him over the hand that still covered her mouth, her fright turning into relieved anger. She didn't like this man. She didn't like him at all, and as soon as they were out of this mess, she was going to tell him about it!

He removed his hand and shoved her to the ground on her hands and knees. "Crawl!" he ordered in a harsh whisper, and pointed to their left.

Jane crawled, ignoring the scratches she incurred as she squirmed through the undergrowth, ignoring even the disgusting squishiness when she accidentally smashed something with her hand. Odd, but now that he was with her again, her panic had faded; it hadn't gone completely, but it wasn't the heart-pounding, nauseating variety, either. Whatever his faults, he knew his way around.

He was on her tail, literally, his hard shoulder against the back of her thighs, pushing her onward whenever he thought she wasn't moving fast enough. Once he halted her by the simple method of grabbing her ankle and jerking her flat, his urgent grip warning her to be quiet. She held her breath, listening to the faint rustle that betrayed the presence of someone, or something, nearby. She didn't dare turn her head, but she could detect movement with her peripheral vision. In a moment the man was close enough that she could see him plainly. He was obviously of Latin ancestry, and he was dressed in camouflage fatigues with a cap covering his head. He held an automatic rifle at the ready before him.

In only a moment she could no longer see or hear him, but they stayed motionless in the thick tangle of ferns for long, agonizing minutes. Then her ankle was released and a hand on her hip urged her forward.

They were moving away from the soldier at a right angle. Perhaps they were going to try to get behind their pursuers, then take off in the helicopter while the soldiers were still deep in the jungle. She wanted to know where they were going, what they would do, who the soldiers were and what they wanted—but the questions had to remain bottled up inside her. Now was definitely not the time for talking, not with this man—what *was* his name?—practically shoving her through the undergrowth.

Abruptly the forest cleared somewhat, allowing small patches of sunlight to filter through. Grasping her arm, he hauled her to her feet. "Run, but be as quiet as you can," he hissed in her ear.

Great. Run, but do it quietly. She threw him a dirty look, then ran, taking off like a startled deer. The most disgusting thing was that he was right behind her, and she couldn't hear him making a sound, while her own feet seemed to pound the earth like a drum. But her body seemed cheered by the small amount of sunlight, because she felt her energy level surge despite her sleepless night. The pack on her shoulders seemed lighter, and her steps became quick and effortless as adrenaline began pumping through her veins.

The brush became thicker, and they had to slow their pace. After about fifteen minutes he stopped her with a hand on her shoulder and pulled her behind the trunk of a tree. "Rest a minute," he whispered. "The humidity will wipe you out if you aren't used to it."

Until that moment Jane hadn't noticed that she was wringing wet with sweat. She'd been too intent on saving her skin to worry about its dampness. Now, she became aware of the intense humidity of the rain forest pressing down on her, making every breath she drew lie heavily in her lungs. She wiped the moisture from her face, the salt of her perspiration stinging the small scratches on her cheeks.

He took a canteen from his pack. "Take a drink; you look like you need it."

She had a very good idea what she looked like, and she smiled wryly. She accepted the canteen and drank a little of the water, then capped it and returned it to him. "Thanks."

He looked at her quizzically. "You can have more if you want."

"I'm okay." She looked at him, seeing now that his eyes were a peculiar golden brown color, like amber. His pupils seemed piercingly black against that tawny background. He was streaked with sweat, too, but he wasn't even breathing hard. Whoever he was, whatever he was, he was damned good at this. "What's your name?" she asked him, desperately needing to call him something, as if that would give him more substance, make him more familiar.

He looked a little wary, and she sensed that he disliked giving even that much of himself away. A name was only a small thing, but it was a chink in his armor, a link to another person that he didn't want. "Sullivan," he finally said reluctantly.

"First or last?"

"Last."

"What's your first name?"

"Grant."

Grant Sullivan. She liked the name. It wasn't fancy; he wasn't fancy. He was a far cry from the sleekly sophisticated men she usually met, but the difference was exciting. He was hard and dangerous, mean when he had to be, but he wasn't vicious. The contrast between him and Turego, who was a truly vicious man, couldn't have been more clear-cut.

"Let's go," he said. "We need to put a lot more space between the hounds and the foxes."

Obediently she followed his direction, but found that her burst of adrenaline was already dissipating. She felt more exhausted now than she had before the short rest. She stumbled once, catching her booted foot in a liana vine, but he rescued her with a quick grab. She gave him a tired smile of thanks, but when she tried to step away from him he held her. He stood rigid and it frightened her. She jerked around to look at him, but his face was a cold, blank mask, and he was staring behind her. She whirled again, and looked down the barrel of a rifle.

The sweat congealed on her body. For one moment of frozen terror she expected to be shot; then the moment passed and she was still alive. She was able then to look past the barrel to the hard, dark face of the soldier who held the rifle. His black eyes were narrowed, fastened on Sullivan. He said something, but Jane was too upset to translate the Spanish.

Slowly, deliberately, Sullivan released Jane and raised his arms, clasping his hands on top of his head. "Step away from me," he said quietly.

The soldier barked an order at him. Jane's eyes widened. If she moved an inch this maniac would probably shoot her down. But Sullivan had told her to move, so she moved, her face so white that the small freckles across her nose stood out as bright dots of color. The rifle barrel jerked in her direction, and the soldier said something else. He was nervous, Jane suddenly realized. The tension was obvious in his voice, in his jerky movements. God, if his finger twitched on the trigger...! Then, just as abruptly, he aimed the rifle at Sullivan again.

Sullivan was going to do something. She could sense it. The fool! He'd get himself killed if he tried to jump this guy! She stared at the soldier's shaking hands on the rifle, and suddenly something jumped into her consciousness. He didn't have the rifle on automatic. It took her another moment to realize the implications; then she reacted without thought. Her body, trained to dance, trained in the graceful moves of self-defense, went into fluid motion. He began moving a split second later, swinging the weapon around, but by then she was close enough that her left foot sliced upward under the barrel of the gun, and the shot that he fired went into the canopy over their heads. He never got a chance at another shot.

Grant was on him then, grabbing the gun with one hand and slashing at the man's unprotected neck with the side of the other. The soldier's eyes glazed over, and he sank limply to the ground, his breathing raspy but steady.

Grant grabbed Jane's arm. "Run! That shot will bring every one of them swarming down on us!"

The urgency of his tone made it possible for her to obey, though she was rapidly depleting her reserves of energy. Her legs were leaden, and her boots weighed fifty pounds each. Burning agony slashed her thighs, but she forced herself to ignore it; sore muscles weren't nearly as permanent as being dead. Urged on by his hand at her back, she stumbled over roots and through bushes, adding to her collection of scratches. It was purely a natural defense mechanism, but her mind shut down and her body operated automatically, her feet moving, her lungs sucking desperately at the heavy, moist air. She was so tired now that she no longer felt the pain in her body.

The ground abruptly sloped out from under her feet. Her senses dulled by both terror and fatigue, she was unable to regain her balance. Grant grabbed for her, but the momentum of her body carried them both over the edge of the hill. His arms wrapped around her, and they rolled down the steep slope. The earth and trees spun crazily, but she saw a rocky, shallow stream at the bottom of the slope and a small, hoarse cry tore from her throat. Some of those rocks were big enough to kill them and the smaller ones could cut them to pieces.

Grant swore, and tightened his grip on her until she thought her ribs would splinter under the pressure. She felt his muscles tighten, felt the desperate twist he made, and somehow he managed to get his feet and legs in front of him. Then they were sliding down in a fairly upright position, rather than rolling. He dug his heels in and their descent slowed, then stopped. "Pris?" he asked roughly, cupping her chin in his hand and turning her face so he could see it. "Are you hurt?"

"No, no," she quickly assured him, ignoring the new aches in her body. Her right arm wasn't broken, but it was badly bruised; she winced as she tried to move it. One of the straps on the backpack had broken, and the pack was hanging lopsidedly off her left shoulder. Her cap was missing.

He adjusted the rifle on his shoulder, and Jane wondered how he had managed to hold on to it. Didn't he ever drop anything, or get lost, or tired, or hungry? She hadn't even seen him take a drink of water!

"My cap came off," she said, turning to stare up the slope. The top was almost thirty yards above them and the slope steep enough that it was a miracle they hadn't crashed into the rocks at the streambed.

"I see it." He swarmed up the slope, lithe and sure-footed. He snatched the cap from a broken branch and in only a moment was back beside her. Jamming the cap on her head, he said, "Can you make it up the other side?"

There was no way, she thought. Her body refused to function any longer. She looked at him and lifted her chin. "Of course."

He didn't smile, but there was a faint softening of his expression, as if he knew how desperately tired she was. "We have to keep moving," he said, taking her arm and urging her across the stream. She didn't care that her boots were getting wet; she just sloshed through the water, moving downstream while he scanned the bank for an easy place to climb up. On this side of the stream, the bank wasn't sloped; it was almost vertical and covered with what looked like an impenetrable tangle of vines and bushes. The stream created a break in the foliage that allowed more sunlight to pour down, letting the plants grow much more thickly.

"Okay, let's go up this way," he finally said, pointing. Jane lifted her head and stared at the bank, but she didn't see any break in the wild tangle.

"Let's talk about this," she hedged.

He gave an exasperated sigh. "Look, Pris, I know you're tired, but—"

Something snapped inside Jane, and she whirled on him, catching him by the shirt front and drawing back her fist. "If you call me 'Pris' just one more time, I'm going to feed you a knuckle sandwich!" she roared, unreasonably angry at his continued use of that hated name. No one, but no one, had ever been allowed to call her Priscilla, Pris, or even Cilla, more than once. This damned commando had been rubbing her face in it from the beginning. She'd kept quiet about it, figuring she owed him for kicking him in the groin, but she was tired and hungry and scared and enough was enough!

He moved so quickly that she didn't even have time to blink. His hand snaked out and caught her drawn back fist, while the fingers of his other hand laced around her wrist, removing her grip from his shirt. "Damn it, can't you keep quiet? *I* didn't name you Priscilla, your parents did, so if you don't like it take it up with them. But until then, climb!"

Jane climbed, even though she was certain at every moment that she was going to collapse on her face. Grabbing vines for hand holds, using roots and rocks and bushes and small trees, she squirmed and wiggled her way through the foliage. It was so thick that it could have been swarming with jaguars and she wouldn't have been able to see one until she stuck her hand in its mouth. She remembered that jaguars liked water, spending most of their time resting comfortably near a river or stream, and she swore vengeance on Grant Sullivan for making her do this.

Finally she scrambled over the top, and after pushing forward several yards found that the foliage had once again thinned, and walking was much easier. She adjusted the pack on her back, wincing as she found new bruises. "Are we heading for the helicopter?"

"No," he said curtly. "The helicopter is being watched."

"Who are those men?"

He shrugged. "Who knows? Sandinistas, maybe; we're only a few klicks from the Nicaraguan border. They could be any guerrilla faction. That damned Pablo sold us out."

Jane didn't waste time worrying about Pablo's duplicity; she was too tired to really care. "Where are we going?"

"South."

She ground her teeth. Getting information out of this man was like pulling teeth. "South *where*?"

"Limon, eventually. Right now, we're going due east."

Jane knew enough about Costa Rica to know what lay due east, and she didn't like what she'd just been told. Due east lay the Caribbean coast, where the rain forest became swamp land. If they were only a few kilometers from the Nicaraguan border, then Limon was roughly a hundred miles away. In her weariness, she felt it might as well have been five hundred miles. How long would it take them to walk a hundred miles? Four or five days? She didn't know if she could stand four or five days with Mr. Sunshine. She'd known him less than twelve hours, and she was already close to death.

"Why can't we just go south and forget about east?"

He jerked his head in the direction from which they'd come. "Because of them. They weren't Turego's men, but Turego will soon know that you came in this direction, and he'll be after us. He can't afford to have the government find out about his little clandestine operations. So...we go where he can't easily follow."

It made sense. She didn't like it, but it made sense. She'd never been in the Caribbean coastal region of Costa Rica, so she didn't know what to expect, but it had to be better than being Turego's prisoner. Poisonous snakes, alligators, quicksand, whatever...it was better than Turego. She'd worry about the swamp when they were actually in it. With that settled in her mind, she returned to her most pressing problem.

"When do we get to rest? And eat? And, frankly, Attila, you may have a bladder the size of New Jersey, but I've got to *go*!"

Again she caught that unwilling twitch of his lips, as if he'd almost grinned. "We can't stop yet, but you can eat while we walk. As for the other, go behind that tree there." He pointed, and she turned to see another of those huge, funny trees with the enormous buttressed roots. In the absence of indoor plumbing it would have to do. She plunged for its shelter.

When they started out again he gave her something hard and dark to chew on; it tasted faintly like meat, but after examining it suspiciously she decided not to question him too closely about it. It eased the empty pains in her stomach, and after washing a few bites down with cautious sips of water, she began to feel better and the rubbery feeling left her legs. He chewed a stick of it, too, which reassured her in regard to his humanity.

Still, after walking steadily for a few hours, Jane began to lose the strength that had come with her second wind. Her legs were moving clumsily, and she felt as if she were wading in knee-deep water. The temperature had risen steadily; it was well over ninety now, even in the thick shelter of the canopy. The humidity was draining her as she continued to sweat, losing water that she wasn't replacing. Just when she was about to tell him that she couldn't take another step, he turned and surveyed her with an impersonal professionalism.

"Stay here while I find some sort of shelter for us. It's going to start raining in a little while, so we might as well sit it out. You look pretty well beat, anyway."

Jane pulled her cap off and wiped her streaming face with her forearm, too tired to comment as he melted from sight. How did he know it was going to start raining? It rained almost every day, of course, so it didn't take a fortune-teller to predict rain, but she hadn't heard the thunder that usually preceded it.

He was back in only a short while, taking her arm and leading her to a small rise, where a scattering of boulders testified to Costa Rica's volcanic origin. After taking his knife from his belt, he cut small limbs and lashed them together with vines, then propped one end of his contraption up by wedging sturdier limbs under the corners. Producing a rolled up tarp from his backpack like a magician, he tied the tarp over the crude lean-to, making it waterproof. "Well, crawl in and get comfortable," he growled when Jane simply stood there, staring in astonishment at the shelter he'd constructed in just a few minutes.

Obediently she crawled in, groaning with relief as she shrugged out of her backpack and relaxed her aching muscles. Her ears caught the first distant rumble of thunder; whatever he did for a living, the man certainly knew his way around the jungle.

Grant ducked under the shelter, too, relieving his shoulders of the weight of his own backpack. He had apparently decided that while they were waiting out the rain they might as well eat, because he dug out a couple of cans of field rations.

Jane sat up straight and leaned closer, staring at the cans. "What's that?"

"Food."

"What kind of food?"

He shrugged. "I've never looked at it long enough to identify it. Take my advice: don't think about it. Just eat it."

She put her hand on his as he started to open the cans. "Wait. Why don't we save those for have-to situations?"

"This *is* a have-to situation," he grunted. "We *have* to eat."

"Yes, but we don't have to eat *that*!"

Exasperation tightened his hard features. "Honey, we either eat this, or two more cans exactly like them!"

"Oh, ye of little faith," she scoffed, dragging her own backpack closer. She began delving around in it, and in a moment produced a small packet wrapped in a purloined towel. With an air of triumph she unwrapped it to expose two badly smashed but still edible sandwiches, then returned to the backpack to dig around again. Her face flushed with success, she pulled out two cans of orange juice. "Here!" she said cheerfully, handing him one of the cans. "A peanut butter and jelly sandwich, and a can of orange juice. Protein, carbohydrates and vitamin C. What more could we ask for?"

Grant took the sandwich and the pop-top can she offered him, staring at them in disbelief. He blinked once, then an amazing thing happened: he laughed. It wasn't much of a laugh. It was rather rusty sounding, but it revealed his straight white teeth and made his amber eyes crinkle at the corners. The rough texture of that laugh gave her a funny little feeling in her chest. It was obvious that he rarely laughed, that life didn't hold much humor for him, and she felt both happy that she'd made him laugh and sad that he'd had so little to laugh about. Without laughter she would never have kept her sanity, so she knew how precious it was.

Chewing on his sandwich, Grant relished the gooiness of the peanut butter and the sweetness of the jelly. So what if the bread was a little stale? The unexpected treat made such a detail unimportant. He leaned back and propped himself against his backpack, stretching his long legs out before him. The first drops of rain began to patter against the upper canopy. It would be impossible for anyone to track them through the downpour that was coming, even if those guerrillas had an Indian tracker with them, which he doubted. For the first time since he'd seen the helicopter that morning, he relaxed, his highly developed sense of danger no longer nagging him.

He finished the sandwich and poured the rest of the orange juice down his throat, then glanced over at Jane to see her daintily licking the last bit of jelly from her fingers. She looked up, caught his gaze, and gave him a cheerful smile that made her dimples flash, then returned to the task of cleaning her fingers.

Against his will, Grant felt his body tighten with a surge of lust that surprised him with its strength. She was a charmer, all right, but not at all what he'd expected. He'd expected a spoiled, helpless, petulant debutante, and instead she had had the spirit, the pure guts, to hurl herself into the jungle with two peanut butter sandwiches and some orange juice as provisions. She'd also dressed in common-sense clothing, with good sturdy boots and green khaki pants, and a short-sleeved black blouse. Not right out of the fashion pages, but he'd had a few distracting moments crawling behind her, seeing those pants molded to her shapely bottom. He hadn't been able to prevent a deep masculine appreciation for the soft roundness of her buttocks.

She was a mass of contradictions. She was a jet-setter, so wild that her father had disinherited her, and she'd been George Persall's mistress, yet he couldn't detect any signs of hard living in her face. If anything, her face was as open and innocent as a child's, with a child's enthusiasm for life shining out of her dark brown eyes. She had a look of perpetual mischievousness on her face, yet it was a face of honest sensuality. Her long hair was so dark a brown that

it was almost black, and it hung around her shoulders in
snarls and tangles. She had pushed it away from her face
with total unconcern. Her dark brown eyes were long and
a little narrow, slanting in her high-cheekboned face in a
way that made him think she might have a little Indian
blood. A smattering of small freckles danced across those
elegant cheekbones and the dainty bridge of her nose. Her
mouth was soft and full, with the upper lip fuller than the
lower one, which gave her an astonishingly sensual look.
All in all, she was far from beautiful, but there was a
freshness and zest about her that made all the other women
he'd known suddenly seem bland.

Certainly he'd never been as intimate with any other
woman's knee.

Even now, the thought of it made him angry. Part of it
was chagrin that he'd left himself open to the blow; he'd
been bested by a lightweight! But another part of it was an
instinctive, purely male anger, sexually based. He'd watch
her knee now whenever she was within striking distance.
Still, the fact that she'd defended herself, and the moves
she'd made, told him that she'd had professional training,
and that was another contradiction. She wasn't an expert,
but she knew what to do. Why would a wild, spoiled play-
girl know anything about self-defense? Some of the pieces
didn't fit, and Grant was always uneasy when he sensed
details that didn't jibe.

He felt pretty grim about the entire operation. Their
situation right now was little short of desperate, regard-
less of the fact that they were, for the moment, rather secure. They had probably managed to shake the soldiers,
whoever they worked for, but Turego was a different story.
The microfilm wasn't the only issue now. Turego had been
operating without the sanction of the government, and if
Jane made it back and filed a complaint against him, the

repercussions would cost him his position, and possibly his freedom.

It was Grant's responsibility to get her out, but it was no longer the simple in-and-out situation he'd planned. From the moment he'd seen Pablo leaning so negligently against the helicopter, waiting for them, he'd known that the deal had gone sour. Pablo wasn't the type to be waiting for them so casually; in all the time Grant had know him, Pablo had been tense, ready to move, always staying in the helicopter with the rotors turning. The elaborate pose of relaxation had tipped Grant off as clearly as if Pablo had hung a sign around his neck. Perhaps Pablo had been trying to warn him. There was no way he'd ever know for certain.

Now he had to get her through the jungle, out of the mountains, and south through a swamp, with Turego in hot pursuit. With luck, in a day or so, they'd find a village and be able to hitch a ride, but even that depended on how close behind Turego was.

And on top of that, he couldn't trust her. She'd disarmed that soldier far too casually, and hadn't turned a hair at anything that had happened. She was far too matter-of-fact about the whole situation. She wasn't what she seemed, and that made her dangerous.

He was wary of her, but at the same time he found that he was unable to stop watching her. She was too damned sexy, as lush and exotic as a jungle orchid. What would it be like to lie with her? Did she use the rich curves of her body to make a man forget who he was? How many men had been taken in by that fresh, open expression? Had Turego found himself off balance with her, wanting her, knowing that he could force her at any time—but being eaten alive by the challenge of trying to win her, of making her give herself freely? How else had she managed to control him? None of it added up to what she should have been, unless she played with men as some sort of ego trip, where the more dangerous the man, the greater the thrill at controlling him.

Grant didn't want her to have that much influence over him; she wasn't worth it. No matter how beguiling the expression in her dark, slanted eyes, she simply wasn't worth it. He didn't need the sort of complication she offered; he just wanted to get her out, collect his money from her father, and get back to the solitude of the farm. Already he'd felt the jungle pulling at him, the heated, almost sexual excitement of danger. The rifle felt like an extension of his body, and the knife fit his palm as if he'd never put it down. All the old moves, the old instincts, were still there, and blackness rose in him as he wondered bitterly if he'd ever really be able to put this life behind him. The blood lust had been there in him, and perhaps he'd have killed that soldier if she hadn't kicked the rifle up when she had.

Was it part of the intoxication of battle that made him want to pull her beneath him and drive himself into her body, until he was mindless with intolerable pleasure? Part of it was, and yet part of it had been born hours ago, on the floor of her bedroom, when he'd felt the soft, velvety roundness of her breasts in his hands. Remembering that, he wanted to know what her breasts looked like, if they thrust out conically or had a full lower slope, if her nipples were small or large, pink or brown. Desire made him harden, and he reminded himself caustically that it had been a while since he'd had a woman, so it was only natural that he would be turned on. If nothing else, he should be glad of the evidence that he could still function!

She yawned, and blinked her dark eyes at him like a sleepy cat. "I'm going to take a nap," she announced, and curled up on the ground. She rested her head on her arm, closed her eyes and yawned again. He watched her, his eyes narrowed. This utter adaptability she displayed was another piece of the puzzle that didn't fit. She should have been moaning and bitching about how uncomfortable she was, rather than calmly curling up on the ground for a nap. But a nap sounded pretty damned good right now, he thought.

Grant looked around. The rain had become a fullfledged downpour, pounding through the canopy and turning the jungle floor into a river. The constant, torrential rains leeched the nutrients out of the soil, making the jungle into a contradiction, where the world's greatest variety of animal and plant life existed on some of the poorest soil. Right now the rain also made it almost impossible for them to be found. They were safe for the time being, and for the first time he allowed himself to feel the weariness in his muscles. He might as well take a nap, too; he'd wake when the rain stopped, alerted by the total cessation of noise.

Reaching out, he shook her shoulder, and she roused to stare at him sleepily. "Get against the back of the lean-to," he ordered. "Give me a little room to stretch out, too."

She crawled around as he'd instructed and stretched out full length, sighing in ecstasy. He pushed their backpacks to one side, then lay down beside her, his big body between her and the rain. He lay on his back, one brawny arm thrown behind his head. There was no twitching around, no yawning or sighing, for him. He simply lay down, closed his eyes and went to sleep. Jane watched him sleepily, her gaze lingering on the hawklike line of his profile, noting the scar that ran along his left cheekbone. How had he gotten it? His jaw was blurred with several days' growth of beard, and she noticed that his beard was much darker than his hair. His eyebrows and lashes were dark, too, and that made his amber eyes seem even brighter, almost as yellow as an eagle's.

The rain made her feel a little chilled after the intense heat of the day; instinctively she inched closer to the heat she could feel emanating from his body. He was so warm . . . and she felt so safe . . . safer than she'd felt since she was nine years old. With one more little sigh, she slept.

Sometime later the rain ceased abruptly, and Grant woke immediately, like a light switch being flipped on. His senses were instantly alert, wary. He started to surge to his feet, only to realize that she was lying curled against his side, with her head pillowed on his arm and her hand lying on his chest. Disbelief made him rigid. How could she have gotten that close to him without waking him? He'd always slept like a cat, alert to the smallest noise or movement—but this damned woman had practically crawled all over him and he hadn't even stirred. She must've been disappointed, he thought furiously. The fury was directed as much at himself as at her, because the incident told him how slack he had become in the past year. That slackness might cost them their lives.

He lay still, aware of the fullness of her breasts against his side. She was soft and lush, and one of her legs was thrown up over his thigh. All he had to do was roll over and he'd be between her legs. The mental image made moisture break out on his forehead. God! She'd be hot and tight, and he clenched his teeth at the heavy surge in his loins. She was no lady, but she was all woman, and he wanted her naked and writhing beneath him with an intensity that tied his guts into knots.

He had to move, or he'd be taking her right there on the rocky ground. Disgusted at himself for letting her get to him the way she had, he eased his arm from beneath her head, then shook her shoulder. "Let's get moving," he said curtly.

She muttered something, her forehead puckering, but she didn't open her eyes, and in a moment her forehead smoothed as she lapsed back into deep sleep. Impatiently, Grant shook her again. "Hey, wake up."

She rolled over on her stomach and sighed deeply, burrowing her head against her folded arm as she sought a more comfortable position. "Come on, we've got to get going," he said, shaking her more vigorously. "Wake up!"

She aimed a drowsy swat at him, as if he were a pesky fly, brushing his hand aside. Exasperated, Grant caught her shoulders and pulled her to a sitting position, shaking her once again. "Damn it, would you get up? On your feet, honey; we've got some walking to do." Her eyes finally opened, and she blinked at him groggily, but she made no move to get up.

Swearing under his breath, Grant hauled her to her feet. "Just stand over there, out of the way," he said, turning her around and starting her on her way with a swat on her bottom before he turned his attention to taking down their shelter.

J ane stopped, her hand going to her bottom. Awakened now, and irritated by his light, casual slap, she turned. "You didn't have to do that!"

"Do what?" he asked with total disinterest, already busy removing the tarp from the top of the lean-to and rolling it up to replace it in his backpack.

"Hit me! A simple 'wake-up' would have sufficed!"

Grant looked at her in disbelief. "Well, pardon me all to hell," he drawled in a sarcastic tone that made her want to strangle him. "Let me start over. Excuse me, Priscilla, but nappy time is over, and we really do have to—hey! Damn it!" He ducked in time, throwing his arm up to catch the force of her fist. Swiftly he twisted his arm to lock his fingers around her wrist, then caught her other arm before she could swing at him with it. She'd exploded into fury, hurling herself at him like a cat pouncing. Her fist had hit his arm with enough strength that she might have broken his nose if the blow had landed on target. "Woman, what in *hell* is wrong with you?"

"I told you not to call me that!" Jane raged at him, spitting the words out in her fury. She struggled wildly, trying to free her arm so she could hit him again.

Panting, Grant wrestled her to the ground and sat astride her, holding her hands above her head, and this time making damned certain that her knee wouldn't come anywhere near him. She kept wriggling and heaving, and he felt as if he were trying to hold an octopus, but finally he had her subdued.

Glaring at her, he said, "You told me not to call you Pris."

"Well, don't call me Priscilla, either!" she fumed, glaring right back.

"Look, I'm not a mind reader! What am I supposed to call you?"

"Jane!" she shouted at him. "My name is Jane! *Nobody* has *ever* called me Priscilla!"

"All right! All you had to do was tell me! I'm getting damned tired of you snapping at my ankles, understand? I may hurt you before I can stop myself, so you'd better think twice before you attack again. Now, if I let you up, are you going to behave?"

Jane still glared at him, but the weight of his knees on her bruised arms was excruciating. "All right," she said sullenly, and he slowly got up, then surprised her by offering his hand to help her up. She surprised herself by taking it.

A sudden twinkle lit the dark gold of his eyes. "Jane, huh?" he asked reflectively, looking at the surrounding jungle.

She gave him a threatening look. "No 'Me Tarzan, you Jane' stuff," she warned. "I've heard it since grade school." She paused, then said grudgingly, "But it's still better than Priscilla."

He grunted in agreement and turned away to finish dismantling their shelter, and after a moment Jane began helping. He glanced at her, but said nothing. He wasn't much of a talker, she'd noticed, and he didn't improve any on closer acquaintance. But he'd risked his own life to help her, and he hadn't left her behind, even though Jane knew he could have moved a lot faster, and with a lot less risk to himself, on his own. And there was something in his eyes, an expression that was weary and cynical and a little empty, as if he'd seen far too much to have any faith or trust left. That made Jane want to put her arms around him and shield him. Lowering her head so he wouldn't be able to read her expression, she chided herself for feeling protective of a man who was so obviously capable of handling himself. There had been a time in her own life when she had been afraid to trust anyone except her parents, and it had been a horrible, lonely time. She knew what fear was, and loneliness, and she ached for him.

All signs of their shelter obliterated, he swung his backpack up and buckled it on, then slung the rifle over his shoulder, while Jane stuffed her hair up under her cap. He leaned down to pick up her pack for her, and a look of astonishment crossed his face; then his dark brows snapped together. "What the—" he muttered. "What all do you have in this damned thing? It weighs a good twenty pounds more than my pack!"

"Whatever I thought I'd need," Jane replied, taking the pack from him and hooking her arm through the one good shoulder strap, then buckling the waist strap to secure it as well as she could.

"Like what?"

"Things," she said stubbornly. Maybe her provisions weren't exactly proper by military standards, but she'd take her peanut butter sandwiches over his canned whatever any time. She thought he would order her to dump the pack on the ground for him to sort through and decide what to keep, and she was determined not to allow it. She set her jaw and looked at him.

He put his hands on his hips and surveyed her funny, exotic face, her lower lip pouting out in a mutinous expression, her delicate jaw set. She looked ready to light into him again, and he sighed in resignation. Damned if she wasn't the stubbornest, scrappiest woman he'd ever met. "Take it off," he growled, unbuckling his own pack. "I'll carry yours, and you can carry mine."

If anything, the jaw went higher. "I'm doing okay with my own."

"Stop wasting time arguing. That extra weight will slow you down, and you're already tired. Hand it over, and I'll fix that strap before we start out."

Reluctantly she slipped the straps off and gave him the pack, ready to jump him if he showed any sign of dumping it. But he took a small folder from his own pack, opened it to extract a needle and thread, and deftly began to sew the two ends of the broken strap together.

Astounded, Jane watched his lean, calloused hands wielding the small needle with a dexterity that she had to envy. Reattaching a button was the limit of her sewing skill, and she usually managed to prick her finger doing that. "Do they teach sewing in the military now?" she asked, crowding in to get a better look.

He gave her another one of his glances of dismissal. "I'm not in the military."

"Maybe not now," she conceded. "But you were, weren't you?"

"A long time ago."

"Where did you learn how to sew?"

"I just picked it up. It comes in handy." He bit the thread off, then replaced the needle in its package. "Let's get moving; we've wasted too much time as it is."

Jane took his backpack and fell into step behind him; all she had to do was follow him. Her gaze drifted over the width of his shoulders, then eased downward. Had she ever known anyone as physically strong as this man? She didn't think so. He seemed to be immune to weariness, and he ignored the steamy humidity that drained her strength and drenched her clothes in perspiration. His long, powerful legs moved in an effortless stride, the flexing of his thigh muscles pulling the fabric of his pants tight across them. Jane found herself watching his legs and matching her own stride to his. He took a step, and she took a step automatically. It was easier that way; she could separate her mind from her body, and in doing so ignore her protesting muscles.

He stopped once and took a long drink from the canteen, then passed it to Jane without comment. Also without comment, and without wiping the mouth of the canteen, she tipped it up and drank thirstily. Why worry about drinking after him? Catching cold was the least of her concerns. After capping the canteen, she handed it back to him, and they began walking again.

There was madness to his method, or so it seemed to her. If there was a choice between two paths, he invariably chose the more difficult one. The route he took was through the roughest terrain, the thickest vegetation, up the highest, most rugged slope. Jane tore her pants sliding down a bluff, that looked like pure suicide from the top, and not much better than that from the bottom, but she followed without complaining. It wasn't that she didn't think of plenty of complaints, but that she was too tired to voice them. The benefits of her short nap had long since been dissipated. Her legs ached, her back ached, her bruised arms were so painful she could barely move them, and her eyes felt as if they were burning out of their sockets. But she didn't ask him to stop. Even if the pace killed her, she wasn't going to slow him down any more than she already had, because she had no doubt that he could travel much faster without her. The easy movements of his long legs told her that his stamina was far greater than hers; he could probably walk all night long again without a noticeable slowing of his stride. She felt a quiet awe of that sort of strength and conditioning, something that had been completely outside her experience before she'd met him. He wasn't like other men; it was evident in his superb body, in the awesome competence with which he handled everything, in the piercing gold of his eyes.

As if alerted by her thoughts, he stopped and looked back at her, assessing her condition with that sharp gaze that missed nothing. "Can you make it for another mile or so?"

On her own, she couldn't have, but when she met his eyes she knew there was no way she'd admit to that. Her chin lifted, and she ignored the increasingly heavy ache in her legs as she said, "Yes."

A flicker of expression crossed his face so swiftly that she couldn't read it. "Let me have that pack," he growled, coming back to her and jerking the straps free of the buckles, then slipping the pack from her shoulders.

"I'm handling it okay," she protested fiercely, grabbing for the pack and wrapping both arms around it. "I haven't complained, have I?"

His level dark brows drawing together in a frown, he forcefully removed the pack from her grasp. "Use your head," he snapped. "If you collapse from exhaustion, then I'll have to carry you, too."

The logic of that silenced her. Without another word he turned and started walking again. She was better able to keep up with him without the weight of the pack, but she felt frustrated with herself for not being in better shape, for being a burden to him. Jane had fought fiercely for her independence, knowing that her very life depended on it. She'd never been one to sit and wait for someone else to do

things for her. She'd charged at life head-on, relishing the
challenges that came her way because they reaffirmed her
acute sense of the wonder of life. She'd shared the joys,
but handled the problems on her own, and it unsettled her
now to have to rely on someone else.

They came to another stream, no wider than the first
one they had crossed, but deeper. It might rise to her knees
in places. The water rushing over the rocks sounded cool,
and she thought of how heavenly it would be to refresh her
sweaty body in the stream. Looking longingly at it, she
stumbled over a root and reached out to catch her balance. Her palm came down hard against a tree trunk, and
something squished beneath her fingers.

"Oh, yuk!" she moaned, trying to wipe the dead insect
off with a leaf.

Grant stopped. "What is it?"

"I smashed a bug with my hand." The leaf didn't clean
too well; a smear still stained her hand, and she looked at
Grant with disgust showing plainly on her face. "Is it all
right if I wash my hand in the stream?"

He looked around, his amber eyes examining both sides
of the stream. "Okay. Come over here."

"I can get down here," she said. The bank was only a
few feet high, and the underbrush wasn't that thick. She
carefully picked her way over the roots of an enormous
tree, bracing her hand against its trunk to steady herself as
she started to descend to the stream.

"Watch out!" Grant said sharply, and Jane froze in her
tracks, turning her head to look askance at him.

Suddenly something incredibly heavy dropped onto her
shoulders, something long and thick and alive, and she
gave a stifled scream as it began to coil around her body.
She was more startled than frightened, thinking a big vine
had fallen; then she saw the movement of a large triangu-

lar head and she gave another gasping cry. "Grant! Grant, *help me*!"

Terror clutched at her throat, choking her, and she began to claw at the snake, trying to get it off. It was a calm monster, working its body around her, slowly tightening the lethal muscles that would crush her bones. It twined around her legs and she fell, rolling on the ground. Dimly she could hear Grant cursing, and she could hear her own cries of terror, but they sounded curiously distant. Everything was tumbling in a mad kaleidoscope of brown earth and green trees, of Grant's taut, furious face. He was shouting something at her, but she couldn't understand him; all she could do was struggle against the living bonds that coiled around her. She had one shoulder and arm free, but the boa was tightening itself around her rib cage, and the big head was coming toward her face, its mouth open. Jane screamed, trying to catch its head with her free hand, but the snake was crushing the breath out of her and the scream was almost soundless. A big hand, not hers, caught the snake's head, and she dimly saw a flash of silver.

The snake's coils loosened about her as it turned to meet this new prey, seeking to draw Grant into its deadly embrace, too. She saw the flash of silver again, and something wet splashed into her face. Vaguely she realized that it was his knife she'd seen. He was swearing viciously as he wrestled with the snake, mostly astride her as she writhed on the ground, struggling to free herself. "Damn it, hold still!" he roared. "You'll make me cut you!"

It was impossible to be still; she was wrapped in the snake, and it was writhing with her in its coils. She was too crazed by fear to realize that the snake was in its death throes, not even when she saw Grant throw something aside and begin forcibly removing the thick coils from around her body. It wasn't until she actually felt herself coming free of the constrictor's horrible grasp that she understood it was over, that Grant had killed the snake. She stopped fighting and lay limply on the ground. Her face was utterly white except for the few freckles across her nose and cheekbones; her eyes were fixed on Grant's face.

"It's over," he said roughly, running his hands over her arms and rib cage. "How do you feel? Anything broken?"

Jane couldn't say anything; her throat was frozen, her voice totally gone. All she could do was lie there and stare at him with the remnants of terror in her dark eyes. Her lips trembled like a child's, and there was something pleading in her gaze. He automatically started to gather her into his arms, the way one would a frightened child, but before he could do more than lift his hand, she dragged her gaze away from his with a visible effort. He could see what it cost her in willpower, but somehow she found the inner strength to still the trembling of her lips, and then her chin lifted in that characteristic gesture.

"I'm all right," she managed to say. Her voice was jerky, but she said the words, and in saying them, believed it. She slowly sat up and pushed her hair away from her face. "I feel a little bruised, but there's nothing bro—"

She stopped abruptly, staring at her bloody hand and arm. "I'm all bloody," she said in a bewildered tone, and her voice shook. She looked back at Grant, as if for confirmation. "I'm all bloody," she said again, extending her wildly trembling hand for him to see. "Grant, there's blood all over me!"

"It's the snake's blood," he said, thinking to reassure her, but she stared at him with uncontrolled revulsion.

"Oh, *God*!" she said in a thin, high voice, scrambling to her feet and staring down at herself. Her black blouse was wet and sticky, and big reddish splotches stained her khaki pants. Both her arms had blood smeared down them. Bile rose in her throat as she remembered the wetness that had splashed her face. She raised exploring fingers and found the horrible stickiness on her cheeks, as well as smeared in her hair.

She began to shake even harder, and tears dripped down her cheeks. "Get it off," she said, still in that high, wavering voice of utter hysteria. "I have to get it off. There's blood all over me, and it isn't mine. It's all over me; it's even in my hair... It's in my *hair*!" she sobbed, plunging for the stream.

Cursing, Grant grabbed for her, but in her mad urgency to wash the blood away she jerked free of him, stumbling over the body of the snake and crashing to the ground. Before she could scramble away again, Grant pounced on her, holding her in an almost painful grip while she fought and sobbed, pleading and swearing at him all at once.

"Jane, stop it!" he said sharply. "I'll get the blood off you. Just hold still and let me get our boots off, okay?"

He had to hold her still with one arm and pull her boots off with his free hand, but by the time he started to remove his own boots she was crying so hard that she lay limply on the ground. His face was grim as he looked at her. She'd stood up to so much without turning a hair that he hadn't expected her to fall apart like this. She'd been pulling herself together until she'd seen the blood on herself, and that had evidently been more than she could bear. He jerked his boots off, then turned to her and roughly undid her pants and pulled them off. Lifting her into his arms as easily as he would have lifted a child, he climbed down the bank and waded out into the stream, disregarding the fact that his own pants were being soaked.

When the water reached the middle of his calves, he stood her in the stream and bent to begin splashing water on her legs, rubbing the blood stains from her flesh. Next, cupping water in his palms, he washed her arms and hands clean, dripping the cooling water over her and soaking her blouse. All the while he tended to her, she stood docile, with silent tears still running down her face and making tracks in the blood smeared across her cheeks.

"Everything's all right, honey," he crooned soothingly to her, coaxing her to sit down in the stream so he could wash the blood from her hair. She let him splash water on her head and face, blinking her eyes to protect them from the stinging water, but otherwise keeping her gaze fixed on his hard, intent features. He took a handkerchief from his back pocket and wet it, then gently cleaned her face. She was calmer now, no longer crying in that silent, gut-wrenching way, and he helped her to her feet.

"There, you're all cleaned up," he started to say, then noticed the pink rivulets of water running down her legs. Her blouse was so bloody that he'd have to take it off to get her clean. Without hesitation, he began to unbutton it. "Let's get this off so we can wash it," he said, keeping his voice calm and soothing. She didn't even glance down as he unbuttoned her blouse and pulled it off her shoulders, then tossed it to the bank. She kept her eyes on his face, as if he were her lifeline to sanity and to look away meant a return to madness.

Grant looked down, and his mouth went dry as he stared at her naked breasts. He'd wondered how she looked and now he knew, and it was like being punched in the stomach. Her breasts were round and a little heavier than he'd expected, tipped by small brown nipples, and he wanted to bend down and put his mouth to them, taste them. She might as well have been naked; all she had on was a pair of gossamer panties that had turned transparent in the water. He could see the dark curls of hair beneath the wisp of fabric, and he felt his loins tighten and swell. She was beautifully made, long-legged and slim-hipped, with the sleek muscles of a dancer. Her shoulders were straight, her arms slim but strong, her breasts rich; he wanted to spread her legs and take her right there, driving deeply into her body until he went out of his mind with pleasure. He couldn't remember ever wanting a woman so badly. He'd wanted sex, but that had been simply a physical pleasure, and any willing female body had been acceptable. Now he wanted Jane, the essence of her; it was her legs he wanted wrapped around him, her breasts in his hands, her mouth under his, her body sheathing him.

He jerked his gaze away from her, bending to dip the handkerchief in the water again. That was even worse; his eyes were level with the top of her thighs, and he straightened abruptly. He washed her breasts with a gentle touch, but every moment of it was torture to him, feeling her silky flesh under his fingers, watching her nipples tighten into reddened little nubs as he touched them.

"You're clean," he said hoarsely, tossing the handkerchief to the bank to join her blouse.

"Thank you," she whispered, then fresh tears glittered in her eyes, and with a little whimper she flung herself against him. Her arms went around him and clung to his back. She buried her face against his chest, feeling reassured by the steady beat of his heart and the warmth of his body. His very presence drove the fear away; with him, she was safe. She wanted to rest in his arms and forget everything.

His hands moved slowly over her bare back, his calloused palms stroking her skin as if he relished the texture of it. Her eyes slid shut, and she nestled closer to him, inhaling the distinctly male scent of his strong body. She felt oddly drunk, disoriented; she wanted to cling to him as the only steady presence in the world. Her body was awash in strange sensations, from the rushing water swirling about her feet to the faint breeze that fanned her wet, naked skin, while he was so hard and warm. An unfamiliar heat swept along her flesh in the path of his hands as they moved from her back to her shoulders. Then one hand stroked up her throat to cup her jaw, his thumb under her chin and his fingers in her hair, and he turned her face up to him.

Taking his time about it, he bent and fitted his mouth to hers, slanting his head to make the contact deep and firm. His tongue moved leisurely into her mouth, touching hers and demanding a response, and Jane found herself helplessly giving him what he wanted. She'd never been kissed like that before, with such complete confidence and expertise, as if she were his for the taking, as if they had reverted to more primitive times when the dominant male had his pick of the women. Vaguely alarmed, she made a small effort to free herself from his grasp. He subdued her with gentle force and kissed her again, holding her head still for the pressure of his mouth. Once again Jane found herself opening her mouth for him, forgetting why she'd struggled to begin with. Since her divorce a lot of men had kissed her and tried to make her respond. They'd left her cold. Why should this rough...mercenary, or whatever he was, make shivers of pleasure chase over her body, when some of the most sophisticated men in the world had only bored her with their passion? His lips were warm and hard, the taste of his mouth heady, his tongue bold in its exploration, and his kisses caused an unfamiliar ache to tighten within her body.

A mindless little whimper of delight escaped her throat, the soft female sound making his arms tighten around her.

Her hands slid up to his shoulders, then locked around his neck, hanging on to him for support. She couldn't get close enough to him, though he was crushing her against him. The buttons of his shirt dug into her bare breasts, but she wasn't aware of any pain. His mouth was wild, hungry with a basic need that had flared out of control, bruising her lips with the force of his kisses, and she didn't care. Instead she gloried in it, clinging to him. Her body was suddenly alive with sensations and needs that she didn't recognize, never having felt them before. Her skin actually ached for his touch, yet every stroke of his hard fingers made the ache intensify.

Boldly cupping her breast in his palm, he rubbed the rough pad of his thumb across her tightly puckered nipple, and Jane almost cried aloud at the surge of heat that washed through her. It had never been like this for her before; the urgency of the pure, brazen sensuality of her own body took her by surprise. She'd long ago decided that she simply wasn't a very physical person, then forgotten about it. Sex hadn't been something that interested her very much. The way Grant was making her feel completely shattered her concept of herself. She was a female animal in his arms, grinding against him, feeling and glorying in the swollen response of his body, and hurting with the emptiness deep inside her.

Time disappeared as they stood in the water, the late afternoon sun dappling them with the shifting patterns of light created by the sheltering trees. His hands freely roamed her body. She never even thought of resisting him. It was as if he had every right to her flesh, as if she were his to touch and taste. He bent her back over his arm, making her breasts jut enticingly, and his lips traveled hotly down her throat to the warm, quivering mounds. He took her nipple into his mouth and sucked strongly, and she surged against him like a wild creature, on fire and dying and wanting more.

His hand swept downward, his fingers curving between her legs to caress her through the silk of her panties. The boldness of his touch shocked her out of her sensual frenzy; automatically she stiffened in his grasp and brought her arms down from around his neck to wedge them between their bodies and push against him. A low, gutteral sound rattled in his throat, and for a brief, terrified moment she thought there wouldn't be any stopping him. Then, with a curse, he thrust her away from him.

Jane staggered a little, and his hand shot out to catch her, hauling her back to face him. "Damn you, is this how you get your kicks?" he asked, infuriated. "Do you like seeing how far you can push a man?"

Her chin came up, and she swallowed. "No, that's not it at all. I'm sorry. I know I shouldn't have thrown myself at you like that—"

"Damned right, you shouldn't," he interrupted savagely. He *looked* savage; his eyes were narrowed and bright with rage, his nostrils flared, and his mouth a thin, grim line. "Next time, you'd better make sure you want what you're asking for, because I'm damned sure going to give it to you. Is that clear?"

He turned and began wading to the bank, leaving her standing in the middle of the stream. Jane crossed her arms over her bare breasts, suddenly and acutely aware of her nakedness. She hadn't meant to tease him, but she'd been so frightened, and he'd been so strong and calm that it had seemed the most natural thing in the world to cling to him. Those frenzied kisses and caresses had taken her by surprise, shaken her off balance. Still, she wasn't about to have sex with a man she barely knew, especially when she didn't quite know if she liked what little she did know about him.

He reached the bank and turned to look at her. "Are you coming or not?" he snapped, so Jane waded toward him, still keeping her arms over her breasts.

"Don't bother," he advised in a curt voice. "I've already seen, and touched. Why pretend to be modest?" He gestured to her blouse lying on the ground. "You might want to wash the blood out of that, since you're so squeamish about it."

Jane looked at the blood-stained blouse, and she went a little pale again, but she was under control now. "Yes, I will," she said in a low voice. "Will you...will you get my pants and boots for me, please?"

He snorted, but climbed up the bank and tossed her pants and boots down to her. Keeping her back turned to him, Jane pulled on her pants, shuddering at the blood that stained them, too, but at least they weren't soaked the way her blouse was. Her panties were wet, but there wasn't anything she could do about that now, so she ignored the clammy discomfort. When she was partially clad again, she squatted on the gravel at the edge of the stream and began trying to wash her blouse. Red clouds drifted out of the fabric, staining the water before being swept downstream. She scrubbed and scrubbed before she was satisfied, then wrung out as much water as possible and shook the blouse. As she started to put the blouse on, he said irritably, "Here," and held his shirt in front of her. "Wear this until yours gets dry."

She wanted to refuse, but she knew false pride wouldn't gain her anything. She accepted the shirt silently and put it on. It was far too big, but it was dry and warm and not too dirty, and it smelled of sweat, and the musky odor of his skin. The scent was vaguely comforting. There were rust colored stains on it, too, reminding her that he'd saved her life. She tied the tails in a knot at her waist and sat down on the gravel to put on her boots.

When she turned, she found him standing right behind her, his face still grim and angry. He helped her up the bank, then lifted their packs to his shoulders. "We're not going much farther. Follow me, and for God's sake don't touch anything that I don't touch, or step anywhere except in my footprints. If another boa wants you, I just may let him have you, so don't push your luck."

Jane pushed her wet hair behind her ears and followed obediently, walking where he walked. For a while, she stared nervously at every tree limb they passed under, then made herself stop thinking about the snake. It was over; there was no use dwelling on it.

Instead she stared at his broad back, wondering how her father had found a man like Grant Sullivan. They obviously lived in two different worlds, so how had they met?

Then something clicked in her mind, and a chill went down her spine. *Had* they met? She couldn't imagine her father knowing anyone like Sullivan. She also knew what her own position was. Everyone wanted to get their hands on her, and she had no way of knowing whose side Grant Sullivan was on. He'd called her Priscilla, which was her first name. If her father had sent him, wouldn't he have known that she was never called Priscilla, that she'd been called Jane from birth? *He hadn't known her name!*

Before he died, George had warned her not to trust anyone. She didn't want to think that she was alone in the middle of the jungle with a man who would casually cut her throat when he had no further use for her. Still, the fact remained that she had no proof that her father had sent him. He'd simply knocked her out, put her over his shoulder and hauled her off into the jungle.

Then she realized that she had to trust this man; she had no alternative. He was all she had. It was dangerous, trusting him, but not as dangerous as trying to make it out of the jungle on her own. He had shown flashes of kindness. She felt a funny constriction in her chest as she remembered the way he'd cared for her after he'd killed the snake. Not just cared for her, kissed her—she was still shaken by the way he'd kissed her. Mercenary or not, enemy or not, he made her want him. Her mind wasn't certain about him, but her body was.

She would have found it funny, if she hadn't been so frightened.

They moved directly away from the stream at a forty-five-degree angle, and it wasn't long before he stopped, looked around and unslung the packs from his shoulders. "We'll camp here."

Jane stood in silence, feeling awkward and useless, watching as he opened his pack and took out a small, rolled bundle. Under his skilled hands, the bundle was rapidly transformed into a small tent, complete with a polyethylene floor and a flap that could be zipped shut. When the tent was up he began stripping vines and limbs from the nearby trees to cover it, making it virtually invisible. He hadn't so much as glanced in her direction, but after a moment she moved to help him. He did look at her then, and allowed her to gather more limbs while he positioned them over the tent.

When the job was completed, he said, "We can't risk a fire, so we'll just eat and turn in. After today, I'm ready for some sleep."

Jane was, too, but she dreaded the thought of the night to come. The light was rapidly fading, and she knew that it would soon be completely dark. She remembered the total blackness of the night before and felt a cold finger of fear trace up her backbone. Well, there was nothing she could do about it; she'd have to tough it out.

She crouched beside her pack and dug out two more cans of orange juice, tossing one to him; he caught it deftly, and eyed her pack with growing irritation. "How many more cans of this do you have in that traveling supermarket?" he asked sarcastically.

"That's it. We'll have to drink water from now on. How about a granola bar?" She handed it to him, refusing to let herself respond to the irritation in his voice. She was tired, she ached, and she was faced with a long night in total darkness. Given that, his irritation didn't seem very important. He'd get over it.

She ate her own granola bar, but was still hungry, so she rummaged for something else to eat. "Want some cheese and crackers?" she offered, dragging the items out of the depths of the pack.

She looked up to find him watching her with an expression of raw disbelief on his face. He held out his hand, and she divided the cheese and crackers between them. He looked at her again, shook his head and silently ate his share.

Jane saved a little of her orange juice, and when she finished eating she took a small bottle from the pack. Opening it, she shook a pill into the palm of her hand, glanced at Grant, then shook out another one. "Here," she said.

He looked at it, but made no move to take it. "What the hell's that?"

"It's a yeast pill."

"Why should I want to take a yeast pill?"

"So the mosquitoes and things won't bite you."

"Sure they won't."

"They won't! Look at me. I don't have any insect bites, and it's because I take yeast pills. It does something to your skin chemistry. Come on, take it. It won't hurt you."

He took the pill from her hand and held it with a pained expression on his face while she took her own, washing it down with a sip of the orange juice she'd saved. She passed the can to him, and he muttered something obscene before he tossed the pill into his mouth and slugged down the rest of the juice.

"Okay, bedtime," he said, rising to his feet. He jerked his head toward a tree. "There's your bathroom, if you want to go before we turn in."

Jane stepped behind the tree. He was crude, he was rude, he was a little cruel—and he had saved her life. She didn't know what to expect from him. No matter how rough he was, he would eventually disarm her with an unexpected act of kindness. On the other hand, when things were going smoothly between them, he would say things that stung, as if deliberately trying to start a quarrel.

He was waiting for her by the opening of the tent. "I've already put the blanket down. Crawl in."

She knelt down and crawled into the small tent. He had spread the blanket over the floor, and she sat on it. He shoved their packs inside. "Put these out of the way," he instructed. "I'm going to take a quick look around."

She shoved the packs into the far corners of the tent, then lay down on her back and stared tensely at the thin walls. The light was almost gone; only a glimmer entered through the translucent fabric. It wasn't quite as dark outside yet, but the limbs he'd used as camouflage made it darker inside. The flap parted, and he crawled in, then zipped the opening shut.

"Take your boots off and put them in the corner next to your feet."

Sitting up, she did as he said, then lay down again. Her eyes strained open so widely that they burned. Her body stiff with dread, she listened to him stretch and yawn and make himself comfortable.

Moments later the silence became nearly as unbearable as the darkness. "A collapsible tent comes in handy, doesn't it?" she blurted nervously. "What is it made out of?"

"Nylon," he replied, yawning again. "It's nearly indestructible."

"How much does it weigh?"

"Three pounds and eight ounces."

"Is it waterproof?"

"Yes, it's waterproof."

"And bug proof?"

"Bug proof, too," he muttered.

"Do you think a jaguar could—"

"Look, it's *jaguar* proof, *mildew* proof, *fire* proof and *snake* proof. I personally guarantee you that it's proof against everything except elephants, and I don't think we're going to be stomped on by an elephant in Costa Rica! Is there any other damned thing you're worried about?" he exploded. "If not, why don't you be quiet and let me get some sleep?"

Jane lay tensely, and silence fell again. She clenched her fists in an effort to control her nervousness, listening to the growing cacophony of the jungle night. Monkeys howled and chattered; insects squeaked their calls; underbrush rustled. She was exhausted but she had no real hope of sleeping, at least not until dawn, and at dawn this devil beside her would want to start another day of marathon travel.

He was totally silent in that unnerving way of his. She couldn't even hear him breathe. The old fear began to rise in her chest, making her own breathing difficult. She might as well be alone, and that was the one thing she absolutely couldn't bear.

"Where are you from?"

He heaved a sigh. "Georgia."

That explained his drawl. She swallowed, trying to ease the constriction of her dry throat. If she could just keep him talking, then she wouldn't feel so alone. She'd know he was there.

"What part of Georgia?"

"South. Ever hear of the Okefenokee?"

"Yes. It's a swamp."

"I grew up in it. My folks own a farm just on the edge of it." It had been a normal boyhood, except for the skills he'd learned automatically in the swamp, those skills, which had eventually changed his life by shaping him into something not quite human. He willed the memories away, pulling a mental shade down over them, isolating himself. There was no use in thinking about what had been.

"Are you an only child?"

"Why all the questions?" he snapped, edgy at revealing any information about himself.

"I'm just interested, that's all."

He paused, suddenly alert. There was something in her voice, a tone that he couldn't quite place. It was dark, so he couldn't see her face; he had to go entirely by what his ears told him. If he kept her talking, he might be able to figure it out.

"I've got a sister," he finally said reluctantly.

"I'll bet she's younger. You're so bossy, you must be an older brother."

He let the dig pass and said only, "She's four years younger."

"I'm an only child," she volunteered.

"I know."

She searched frantically for something else to say, but the darkness was making her panic. She felt herself move to grab for him, then remembered what he'd said about startling him, and about not making offers she didn't mean. She ground her teeth together and stilled her reaching hands, the effort so intense that tears actually welled in her eyes. She blinked them away. "Grant," she said in a shaking voice.

"What?" he growled.

"I don't want you to think I'm throwing myself at you again because I'm really not, but would you mind very much if I . . . just held your hand?" she whispered. "I'm sorry, but I'm afraid of the dark, and it helps if I know I'm not alone."

He was still for a moment; then she heard his clothing rustle as he rolled onto his side. "You're really that afraid of the dark?"

Jane tried for a laugh, but the sound was so shaky that it was close to a sob. "The word 'terrified' only begins to describe how afraid I am. I can't sleep in the dark. All the time I was at that wretched plantation I was awake all night long, never sleeping until dawn. But at least I could use that time to watch the guards and figure out their routine. Besides, it wasn't as totally dark there as it is here."

"If you're so all-fired scared of the dark, why were you getting ready to hit the jungle on your own?"

A dark, handsome, incredibly cruel face swam before her mind's eye. "Because even dying in the jungle would be better than Turego," she said quietly.

Grant grunted. He could understand that choice, but the fact that she had so correctly summed up the situation illustrated once again that she was more than what she seemed. Then again, perhaps she already had reason to know just how vile Turego could be. Had Turego raped her, or would it have been rape? With this woman, who knew? "Did you have sex with him?"

The blunt question made her shudder. "No. I'd been holding him off, but when he left yesterday... it *was* just yesterday, wasn't it? It seems like a year ago. Anyway, I knew that, when he came back, I wouldn't be able to stop him any longer. My time had run out."

"What makes you so certain of that?"

Jane paused, wondering just how much to tell him, wondering how much he already knew. If he was involved, he would be familiar with Luis's name; if he wasn't, the name would mean nothing to him. She wanted to tell him; she didn't want to be alone in this nightmare any longer. But she remembered George telling her once that secrecy was synonymous with security, and she quelled the need to turn into Grant's arms and tell him how afraid and alone she had been. If he wasn't involved already, he was safer not knowing anything about it. On the other hand, if he was involved, *she* might be safer if he didn't realize how deeply she was a part of things. Finally, to answer his question, she said, "I wasn't certain. I was just afraid to stay, afraid of Turego."

He grunted, and that seemed to be the end of the conversation. Jane clenched her jaw against the sudden chattering of her teeth. It was hot and steamy inside the dark tent, but chills were running up and down her body. Why didn't he say something else, anything, rather than lying there so quietly? She might as well have been alone. It was unnatural for anyone to be that soundless, that utterly controlled.

"How was Dad?"

"Why?"

"I just wondered." Was he being deliberately evasive? Why didn't he want to talk about her father? Perhaps he hadn't been hired by her father at all and didn't want to be drawn into a conversation about someone he was supposed to have met, but hadn't.

After a measured silence, as if he had carefully considered his answer, he said, "He was worried sick about you. Surprised?"

"No, of course not," she said, startled. "I'd be surprised if he weren't."

"It doesn't surprise you that he'd pay a small fortune to get you out of Turego's hands, even though you don't get along with him?"

He was confusing her; she felt left out of the conversation, as if he were talking about someone else entirely. "What are you talking about? We get along perfectly, always have."

She couldn't see him, couldn't hear him, but suddenly there was something different about him, as if the very air had become electrically charged. A powerful sense of danger made the fine hairs on her body stand up. The danger was coming from him. Without knowing why, she shrank back from him as far as she could in the confines of the small tent, but there was no escape. With the suddenness of a snake striking, he rolled and pinned her down, forcing her hands over her head and holding them shackled there in a grip that hurt her wrists. "All right, Jane, or Priscilla, or whoever you are, we're going to talk. I'm going to ask the questions and you're going to answer them, and you'd better have the right answers or you're in trouble, sugar. Who are you?"

Had he gone mad? Jane struggled briefly against the grip on her wrists, but there was no breaking it. His weight bore down heavily on her, controlling her completely. His muscled legs clasped hers, preventing her from even kicking. "W—what...?" she stammered. "Grant, you're hurting me!"

"Answer me, damn you! Who are you?"

"Jane Greer!" Desperately, she tried to put some humor in her voice, but it wasn't a very successful effort.

"I don't like being lied to, sugar." His voice was velvety soft, and the sound of it chilled her to her marrow. Not even Turego had affected her like this; Turego was a dangerous, vicious man, but the man who held her now was the most lethal person she'd ever seen. He didn't have to reach for a weapon to kill her; he could kill her with his bare hands. She was totally helpless against him.

"I'm not lying!" she protested desperately. "I'm Priscilla Jane Hamilton Greer."

"If you were, you'd know that James Hamilton cut you out of his will several years ago. So you get along with him just perfectly, do you?"

"Yes, I do!" She strained against him, and he deliberately let her feel more of his weight, making it difficult for her to breathe. "He did it to protect me!"

For a long, silent moment in which she could hear the roaring of her blood in her ears, she waited for his reaction. His silence scraped along her nerves. Why didn't he say something? His warm breath was on her cheek, telling her how close he was to her, but she couldn't see him at all in that suffocating darkness. "That's a good one," he finally responded, and she flinched at the icy sarcasm of his tone. "Too bad I don't buy it. Try again."

"I'm telling you the truth! He did it to make me a less attractive kidnap target. It was my idea, damn it!"

"Sure it was," he crooned, and that low, silky sound made her shudder convulsively. "Come on, you can do better than that."

Jane closed her eyes, searching desperately for some way of convincing him of her identity. None came to mind, and she had no identification with her. Turego had taken her passport, so she didn't have even that. "Well, what about you?" she blurted in sudden fury. She'd taken a lot from him, endured without complaining, and now he'd frightened her half out of her mind. She'd had her back to the wall before, and had learned to strike back. "Who are you? How do I know that Dad hired you? If he did why didn't you know that no one ever calls me Priscilla? You were sloppy with your homework!"

"In case you haven't noticed, honey, I'm the one on top. *You* answer *my* questions."

"I did, and you didn't believe me," she snapped. "Sorry, but I don't have my American Express card with me. For God's sake, do I look like a terrorist? You nearly broke my arm; then you knocked me out. You've bounced me on the ground like a rubber ball, and you've got the utter gall to act like *I'm* dangerous? My goodness, you'd better search me, too, so you'll be able to sleep tonight. Who knows? I might have a bazooka strapped to my leg, since I'm such a dangerous character!" Her voice had risen furiously, and he cut her off by resting all his weight on her ribcage. When she gasped, he eased up again.

"No, you're unarmed. I've already had your clothes off, remember?" Even in the darkness, Jane blushed at the memory, thinking of the way he'd kissed her and touched her, and how his hands on her body had made her feel. He moved slowly against her, stopping her breath this time with the suggestive intimacy of his movements. His warm breath stirred her hair as he dipped his head closer to her. "But I wouldn't want to disappoint a lady. If you want to be searched, I'll oblige you. I wouldn't mind giving you a body search."

Fuming, Jane tried again to free her hands, but finally fell back in disgust at the futile action. Raw frustration finally cleared her mind, giving her an idea, and she said harshly, "Did you go in the house when Dad hired you?"

He was still, and she sensed his sudden increase of interest. "Yes."

"Did you go in the study?"

"Yes."

"Then a hotshot like you would have noticed the portrait over the mantle. You're trained to notice things, aren't you? The portrait is of my grandmother, Dad's mother. She was painted sitting down, with a single rose on her lap. Now, you tell me what color her gown was," she challenged.

"Black," he said slowly. "And the rose was blood red."

Thick silence fell between them; then he released her hands and eased his weight from her. "All right," he said finally. "I'll give you the benefit of the doubt—"

"Well, gee, thanks!" Huffily she rubbed her wrists, trying to keep her anger alive in the face of the enormous relief that filled her. Evidently her father had hired him, for otherwise how could he have seen the portrait in the study? She wanted to remain mad at him, but she knew she would forgive him because it was still dark. In spite of everything she was terribly glad he was there. Besides, she told herself cautiously, it was definitely better to stay on this man's good side.

"Don't thank me," he said tiredly. "Just be quiet and go to sleep."

Sleep! If only she could! Consciously, she knew she wasn't alone, but her subconscious mind required additional affirmation from her senses. She needed to see him, hear him, or touch him. Seeing him was out of the question; she doubted he'd leave a flashlight burning all night, even assuming he had one. Nor would he stay awake all night talking to her. Perhaps, if she just barely touched him, he'd think it was an accident and not make a big deal out of it. Stealthily she moved her right hand until the backs of her fingers just barely brushed his hairy forearm—and immediately her wrist was seized in that bruising grip again.

"Ouch!" she yelped, and his fingers loosened.

"Okay, what is it this time?" His tone showed plainly that he was at the end of his patience.

"I just wanted to touch you," Jane admitted, too tired now to care what he thought, "so I'll know I'm not alone."

He grunted. "All right. It looks like that's the only way I'm going to get any sleep." He moved his hand, sliding his rough palm against hers, and twined their fingers together. "*Now* will you go to sleep?"

"Yes," she whispered. "Thank you."

She lay there, enormously and inexplicably comforted by the touch of that hard hand, so warm and strong. Her eyes slowly closed, and she gradually relaxed. The night terrors didn't come. He kept them firmly at bay with the strong, steady clasp of his hand around hers. Everything was going to be all right. Another wave of exhaustion swept over her, and she was asleep with the suddenness of a light turning off.

Grant woke before dawn, his senses instantly alert. He knew where he was, and he knew what time it was; his uncanny sixth sense could pinpoint the time within a few minutes. The normal night sounds of the jungle told him that they were safe, that there was no other human nearby. He knew immediately the identity of the other person in the tent with him. He knew that he couldn't move, and he even knew why: Jane was asleep on top of him.

He really didn't mind being used as a bed. She was soft and warm, and there was a female smell to her that made his nostrils flare in appreciation. The softness of her breasts against him felt good. That special, unmistakable softness never left a man's mind, hovering forever in his memory once he'd felt the fullness of a woman against him. It had been a long time since he'd slept with a woman, and he'd forgotten how good it could feel. He'd had sex— finding an available woman was no problem—but those encounters had been casual, just for the sake of the physical act. Once it was finished, he hadn't been inclined to linger. This past year, especially, he'd been disinclined to tolerate anyone else's presence. He'd spent a lot of time alone, like an injured animal licking its wounds; his mind and his soul had been filled with death. He'd spent so much time in the shadows that he didn't know if he'd ever find the sunlight again, but he'd been trying. The sweet, hot Tennessee sun had healed his body, but there was still an icy darkness in his mind.

Given that, given his acute awareness of his surroundings, even in sleep, how had Jane gotten on top of him without waking him? This was the second time she'd gotten close to him without disturbing him, and he didn't like it. A year ago, she couldn't have twitched without alerting him.

She moved then, sighing a little in her sleep. One of her arms was around his neck, her face pressed into his chest, her warm breath stirring the curls of hair in the low neckline of his undershirt. She lay on him as bonelessly as a cat, her soft body conforming to the hard contours of his. Her legs were tangled with his, her hair draped across his bare shoulder and arm. His body hardened despite his almost savage irritation with himself, and slowly his arms came up to hold her, his hands sliding over her supple back. He could have her if he wanted her. The highly specialized training he'd received had taught him how to deal excruciating pain to another human being, but a side benefit to that knowledge was that he also knew how to give pleasure. He knew all the tender, sensitive places of her body, knew how to excite nerves that she probably didn't even know she had. Beyond that, he knew how to control his own responses, how to prolong a sensual encounter until his partner had been completely satisfied.

The sure knowledge that he could have her ate at him, filling his mind with images and sensations. Within ten minutes he could have her begging him for it, and he'd be inside her, clasped by those long, sleek, dancer's legs. The only thing that stopped him was the almost childlike trust with which she slept curled on top of him. She slept as if she felt utterly safe, as if he could protect her from anything. Trust. His life had been short on trust for so many years that it startled him to find someone who could trust so easily and completely. He was uncomfortable with it, but at the same time it felt good, almost as good as her body in his arms. So he lay there staring into the darkness, holding her as she slept, the bitter blackness of his thoughts contrasting with the warm, elusive sweetness of two bodies pressed together in quiet rest.

When the first faint light began to filter through the trees, he shifted his hand to her shoulder and shook her lightly. "Jane, wake up."

She muttered something unintelligible and burrowed against him, hiding her face against his neck. He shifted gently to his side, easing her onto the blanket. Her arms still hung around his neck, and she tightened her grip as if afraid of falling. "Wait! Don't go," she said urgently, and the sound of her own voice woke her. She opened her eyes, blinking owlishly at him. "Oh. Is it morning?"

"Yes, it's morning. Do you think you could let me up?"

Confused, she stared at him, then seemed to realize that she was still clinging around his neck. She dropped her arms as if scalded, and though the light was too dim for him to be certain, he thought that her cheeks darkened with a blush. "I'm sorry," she apologized.

He was free, yet oddly reluctant to leave the small enclosure of the tent. His left arm was still under her neck, pillowing her head. The need to touch her was overwhelming, guiding his hand under the fabric of her shirt, which was actually his. He flattened his hand against her bare stomach. His fingers and palm luxuriated in the warm silkiness of her skin, tantalized by the knowledge that even richer tactile pleasures waited both above and below where his hand now rested.

Jane felt her breathing hasten in rhythm, and her heartbeat lurched from the slow, even tempo of sleep to an almost frantic pace. "Grant?" she asked hesitantly. His hand simply rested on her stomach, but she could feel her breasts tightening in anticipation, her nipples puckering. A restless ache stirred to life inside her. It was the same empty need that she'd felt when she'd stood almost naked in his arms, in the middle of the stream, and let him touch her with a raw sensuality that she'd never before experienced. She was a little afraid of that need, and a little afraid of the man who created it with his touch, who leaned over her so intently.

Her only sexual experience had been with her husband. The lack of success in that area of their marriage had severely limited what she knew, leaving her almost completely unawakened, even disinterested. Chris had given her no useful standard, for there was no comparison at all between her ex-husband—a kind, cheerful man, slender and only a few inches taller than she was—and this big, rough, muscular warrior. Chris was totally civilized; Grant wasn't civilized at all. If he took her, would he control his fearsome strength, or would he dominate her completely? Perhaps that was what frightened her most of all, because the greatest struggle of her life had been for independence: for freedom from fear, and from the overprotectiveness of her parents. She'd fought so hard and so long for control of her life that it was scary now to realize that she was totally at Grant's mercy. None of the training she'd had in self-defense was of any use against him; she had no defense at all. All she could do was trust him.

"Don't be afraid," he said evenly. "I'm not a rapist."

"I know." A killer, perhaps, but not a rapist. "I trust you," she whispered, and laid her hand against his stubbled jaw.

He gave a small, cynical laugh. "Don't trust me too much, honey. I want you pretty badly, and waking up with you in my arms is straining my good intentions to the limit." But he turned his head and pressed a quick kiss into the tender palm of the hand that caressed his cheek. "Come on, let's get moving. I feel like a sitting duck in this tent, now that it's daylight."

He heaved himself into a sitting position and reached for his boots, tugging them on and lacing them up with quick, expert movements. Jane was slower to sit up, her entire body protesting. She yawned and shoved her tangled hair back from her face, then put on her own boots. Grant had already left the tent by the time she finished, and she crawled after him. Once on her feet, she stretched her aching muscles, then touched her toes several times to limber up. While she was doing that, Grant swiftly dismantled the tent. He accomplished that in so short a time that she could only blink at him in amazement. In only a moment the tent was once more folded into an impossibly small bundle and stored in his backpack, with the thin blanket rolled up beside it.

"Any more goodies in that bottomless pack of yours?" he asked. "If not, we eat field rations."

"That yukky stuff you have?"

"That's right."

"Well, let's see. I know I don't have any more orange juice...." She opened the pack and peered into it, then thrust her hand into its depths. "Ah! Two more granola bars. Do you mind if I have the one with coconut? I'm not that crazy about raisins."

"Sure," he agreed lazily. "After all, they're yours."

She gave him an irritated glance. "They're *ours*. Wait—here's a can of..." She pulled the can out and read the label, then grinned triumphantly. "Smoked salmon! And some crackers. Please take a seat, sir, and we'll have breakfast."

He obediently sat, then took his knife from his belt and reached for the can of salmon. Jane drew it back, her brows lifted haughtily. "I'll have you know that this is a high class eating establishment. We do not open our cans with knives!"

"We don't? What do we use, our teeth?"

She lifted her chin at him and searched in the backpack again, finally extracting a can opener. "Listen," she said, giving the opener to him, "when I escape, I do it in style."

Taking the opener, he began to open the can of salmon. "So I see. How did you manage to get all of this stuff? I can just see you putting in an order with Turego, collecting what you wanted for an escape."

Jane chuckled, a rich, husky sound that made him lift his dark gold head from his task. Those piercing yellow eyes lit on her face, watching her as if examining a treasure. She was busy fishing crackers out of the backpack, so she missed the fleeting expression. "It was almost like that. I kept getting these 'cravings,' though I seldom mentioned them to Turego. I'd just have a word with the cook, and he generally came up with what I wanted. I raided the kitchen or the soldiers' quarters for a little something almost every night."

"Like that pack?" he queried, eyeing the object in question.

She patted it fondly. "Nice one, isn't it?"

He didn't reply, but there was a faint crinkling at the corners of his eyes, as if he were thinking of smiling. They ate the salmon and crackers in companionable silence, with the food washed down by water from Grant's canteen. He ate his granola bar, but Jane decided to save hers for later.

Squatting beside the pack, she took her brush and restored order to her tangled mane of hair, then cleaned her face and hands with a premoistened towelette. "Would you like one?" she asked Grant politely, offering him one of the small packets.

He had been watching her with a stunned sort of amazement, but he took the packet from her hand and tore it open. The small, wet paper had a crisp smell to it, and he felt fresher, cooler, after cleaning his face with it. To his surprise, some of the face black he'd put on before going in after Jane had remained on his skin; he'd probably looked like a devil out of hell, with those streaks on his face.

A familiar sound caught his attention and he turned to look at Jane. A tube of toothpaste lay on the ground beside her, and she was industriously brushing her teeth. As he watched, she spat out the toothpaste, then took a small bottle and tilted it to her mouth, swishing the liquid around, then spitting it out, too. His stunned gaze identified the bottle. For five whole seconds he could only gape at her; then he sat back and began to laugh helplessly. Jane was rinsing her mouth with Perrier water.

Chapter Six

J ane pouted for a moment, but it was so good to hear him laugh that after a few seconds she sat back on her heels and simply watched him, smiling a little herself. When he laughed that harsh, scarred face became younger, even beautiful, as the shadows left his eyes. Something caught in her chest, something that hurt and made a curious melting feeling. She wanted to go over and hold him, to make sure that the shadows never touched him again. She scoffed at herself for her absurd sense of protectiveness. If anyone could take care of himself, it was Grant Sullivan. Nor would he welcome any gesture of caring; he'd probably take it as a sexual invitation.

To hide the way she felt, she put her things back into her pack, then turned to eye him questioningly. "Unless you want to use the toothpaste?" she offered.

He was still chuckling. "Thanks, honey, but I have tooth powder and I'll use the water in the canteen. God! Perrier water!"

"Well, I had to have water, but I wasn't able to snitch a canteen," she explained reasonably. "Believe me, I'd much rather have had a canteen. I had to wrap all the bottles in cloth so they wouldn't clink against each other or break."

It seemed completely logical to her, but it set him off again. He sat with his shoulders hunched and shaking, holding his head between his hands and laughing until tears streamed down his face. After he had stopped, he brushed his own teeth, but he kept making little choking noises that told Jane he was still finding the situation extremely funny. She was lighthearted, happy that she had made him laugh.

She felt her blouse and found it stiff, but dry. "You can have your shirt back," she told him, turning her back to take it off. "Thanks for the loan."

"Is yours dry?"

"Completely." She pulled his shirt off and dropped it on her backpack, and hurriedly began to put her blouse on. She had one arm in a sleeve when he swore violently. She jumped, startled, and looked over her shoulder at him.

His face was grim as he strode rapidly over to her. His expression had been bright with laughter only a moment before, but now he looked like a thundercloud. "What happened to your arm?" he snapped, catching her elbow and holding her bruised arm out for his inspection. "Why didn't you tell me you'd hurt yourself?"

Jane tried to grab the blouse and hold it over her bare breasts with her free arm, feeling horribly vulnerable and exposed. She had been trying for a nonchalant manner while changing, but her fragile poise was shattered by his closeness and his utter disregard for her modesty. Her cheeks reddened, and in self-defense she looked down at her badly bruised arm.

"Stop being so modest," he growled irritably when she fumbled with the blouse. "I told you, I've already seen you without any clothes." That was embarrassingly true, but it didn't help. She stood very still, her face burning, while he gently examined her arm.

"That's a hell of a bruise, honey. How does your arm feel?"

"It hurts, but I can use it," she said stiffly.

"How did it happen?"

"In a variety of ways," she said, trying to hide her embarrassment behind a bright manner. "This bruise right here is where you hit me on the arm after sneaking into my bedroom and scaring me half to death. The big, multicolored one is from falling down that bluff yesterday morning. This little interesting welt is where a limb swung back and caught me—"

"Okay, I get the idea." He thrust his fingers through his hair. "I'm sorry I bruised you, but I didn't know who you were. I'd say we were more than even on that score, anyway, after that kick you gave me."

Jane's dark chocolate eyes widened with remorse. "I didn't mean to, not really. It was just a reflex. I'd done it before I thought. Are you okay? I mean, I didn't do any permanent damage, did I?"

A small, unwilling grin tugged at his lips as he remembered the torment of arousal he'd been enduring on her account. "No, everything's in working order," he assured her. His gaze dropped to where she clutched her blouse to her chest, and his clear amber eyes darkened to a color like melted gold. "Couldn't you tell that when we were standing in the stream kissing?"

Jane looked down automatically, then jerked her gaze back up in consternation when she realized where she was looking. "Oh," she said blankly.

Grant slowly shook his head, staring at her. She was a constant paradox, an unpredictable blend of innocence and contrariness, of surprising prudery and amazing boldness. In no way was she what he'd expected. He was beginning to enjoy every moment he spent with her, but acknowledging that made him wary. It was his responsibility to get her out of Costa Rica, but he would compro-

mise his own effectiveness if he allowed himself to become
involved with her. Worrying over her could cloud his
judgment. But, damn, how much could a man stand? He
wanted her, and the wanting increased with every moment. In some curious way he felt lighter, happier. She
certainly kept him on his toes! He was either laughing at
her or contemplating beating her, but he was never bored
or impatient in her company. Funny, but he couldn't remember ever laughing with a woman before. Laughter,
especially during the past few years, had been in short
supply in his life.

A chattering monkey caught his attention, and he
looked up. The spots of sunlight darting through the
shifting layers of trees reminded him that they were losing
traveling time. "Get your blouse on," he said tersely,
swinging away from her to sling his backpack on. He
buckled it into place, then swung her pack onto his right
shoulder. The rifle was slung over his left shoulder. By that
time, Jane had jerked her blouse on and buttoned it up.
Rather than stuffing it in her pants, she tied the tails in a
knot at her waist as she had with Grant's shirt. He was already starting off through the jungle.

"Grant! Wait!" she called to his back, hurrying after
him.

"You'll have to stay with me," he said unfeelingly, not
slackening his pace.

Well, did he think she couldn't? Jane fumed, panting
along in his path. She'd show him! And he could darn well
act macho and carry both packs if he wanted; she wasn't
going to offer to help! But he wasn't acting macho, she realized, and that deflated some of her indignation. He actually was that strong and indefatigable.

Compared to the harrowing day before, the hours
passed quietly, without sight of another human being. She

followed right on his heels, never complaining about the punishing pace he set, though the heat and humidity were even worse than the day before, if that were possible. There wasn't any hint of a breeze under the thick, smothering canopy. The air was still and heavy, steamy with an almost palpable thickness. She perspired freely, soaking her clothes and making her long for a real bath. That dousing in the stream the day before had felt refreshing, but didn't really qualify as bathing. Her nose wrinkled. She probably smelled like a goat.

Well, so what, she told herself. If she did, then so did he. In the jungle it was probably required to sweat.

They stopped about midmorning for a break, and Jane tiredly accepted the canteen from him. "Do you have any salt tablets?" she asked. "I think I need one."

"You don't need salt, honey, you need water. Drink up."

She drank, then passed the canteen back to him. "It's nearly empty. Let's pour the Perrier into it and chuck the empty bottles."

He nodded, and they were able to discard three bottles. As he got ready to start out again, Jane asked, "Why are you in such a hurry? Do you think we're being followed?"

"Not followed," he said tersely. "But they're looking for us, and the slower we move, the better chance they have of finding us."

"In this?" Jane joked, waving her hand to indicate the enclosing forest. It was difficult to see ten feet in any direction.

"We can't stay in here forever. Don't underrate Turego; he can mobilize a small army to search for us. The minute we show our faces, he'll know it."

"Something should be done about him," Jane said strongly. "Surely he's not operating with the sanction of the government?"

"No. Extortion and terrorism are his own little sidelines. We've known about him, of course, and occasionally fed him what we wanted him to know."

"We?" Jane asked casually.

His face was immediately shuttered, as cold and blank as a wall. "A figure of speech." Mentally, he swore at himself for being so careless. She was too sharp to miss anything. Before she could ask any more questions, he began walking again. He didn't want to talk about his past, about what he had been. He wanted to forget it all, even in his dreams.

About noon they stopped to eat, and this time they had to resort to the field rations. After a quick glance at what she was eating, Jane didn't look at it at all, just put it in her mouth and swallowed without allowing herself to taste it too much. It wasn't really that bad; it was just so awfully bland. They each drank a bottle of Perrier, and Jane insisted that they take another yeast pill. A roll of thunder announced the daily downpour, so Grant quickly found them shelter under a rocky outcropping. The opening was partially blocked by bushes, making it a snug little haven.

They sat watching the deluge for a few minutes; then Grant stretched out his long legs, leaning back to prop himself on his elbow. "Explain this business of how your father disinherited you as a form of protection."

Jane watched a small brown spider pick its way across the ground. "It's very simple," she said absently. "I wouldn't live with around-the-clock protection the way he wanted, so the next best thing was to remove the incentive for any kidnappers."

"That sounds a little paranoid, seeing kidnappers behind every tree."

"Yes," she agreed, still watching the spider. It finally minced into a crevice in the rock, out of sight, and she sighed. "He *is* paranoid about it, because he's afraid that next time he wouldn't get me back alive again."

"Again?" Grant asked sharply, seizing on the implication of her words. "You've been kidnapped before?"

She nodded. "When I was nine years old."

She made no other comment and he sensed that she wasn't going to elaborate, if given a choice. He wasn't going to allow her that choice. He wanted to know more about her, learn what went on in that unconventional brain. It was new to him, this overwhelming curiosity about a woman; it was almost a compulsion. Despite his relaxed position, tension had tightened his muscles. She was being very matter-of-fact about it, but instinct told him that the kidnapping had played a large part in the formation of the woman she was now. He was on the verge of discovering the hidden layers of her psyche.

"What happened?" he probed, keeping his voice casual.

"Two men kidnapped me after school, took me to an abandoned house and locked me in a closet until Dad paid the ransom."

The explanation was so brief as to be ridiculous; how could something as traumatic as a kidnapping be condensed into one sentence? She was staring at the rain now, her expression pensive and withdrawn.

Grant knew too much about the tactics of kidnappers, the means they used to force anxious relatives into paying the required ransom. Looking at her delicate profile, with the lush provocativeness of her mouth, he felt something savage well up in him at the thought that she might have been abused.

"Did they rape you?" He was no longer concerned about maintaining a casual pose. The harshness of his tone made her glance at him, vague surprise in her exotically slanted eyes.

"No, they didn't do anything like that," she assured him. "They just left me in that closet...alone. It was dark."

And to this day she was afraid of the dark, of being alone in it. So that was the basis for her fear. "Tell me about it," he urged softly.

She shrugged. "There isn't a lot more to tell. I don't know how long I was in the closet. There were no other houses close by, so no one heard me scream. The two men just left me there and went to some other location to negotiate with my parents. After awhile I became convinced that they were never coming back, that I was going to die there in that dark closet, and that no one would ever know what had happened to me."

"Your father paid the ransom?"

"Yes. Dad's not stupid, though. He knew that he wasn't likely to get me back alive if he just trusted the kidnappers, so he brought the police in on it. It's lucky he did. When the kidnappers came back for me, I overheard them making their plans. They were just going to kill me and dump my body somewhere, because I'd seen them and could identify them." She bent her head, studying the ground with great concentration, as if to somehow divorce herself from what she was telling him. "But there were police sharpshooters surrounding the house. When the two men realized that they were trapped, they decided to use me as a hostage. One of them grabbed my arm and held his pistol to my head, forcing me to walk in front of them when they left the house. They were going to take me with them, until it was safe to kill me.''

Jane shrugged, then took a deep breath. ''I didn't plan it, I swear. I don't remember if I tripped, or just fainted for a second. Anyway, I fell, and the guy had to let go of me or be jerked off balance. For a second the pistol wasn't pointed at me, and the policemen fired. They killed both men. The...the man who had held me was shot in the chest and the head, and he fell over on me. His blood splattered all over me, on my face, my hair....'' Her voice trailed away.

For a moment there was something naked in her face, the stark terror and revulsion she'd felt as a child; then, as he had seen her do when he'd rescued her from the snake, she gathered herself together. He watched as she defeated the fear, pushed the shadows away. She smoothed her expression and even managed a glint of humor in her eyes as she turned to look at him. ''Okay, it's your turn. Tell me something that happened to you.''

Once he'd felt nothing much at all; he'd accepted the chilled, shadowed brutality of his life without thought. He still didn't flinch from the memories. They were part of him, as ingrained in his flesh and blood, in his very being, as the color of his eyes and the shape of his body. But when he looked into the uncommon innocence of Jane's eyes, he knew that he couldn't brutalize her mind with even the mildest tale of the life he'd known. Somehow she had kept a part of herself as pure and crystalline as a mountain stream, a part of childhood forever unsullied. Nothing that had happened to her had touched the inner woman, except to increase the courage and gallantry that he'd seen twice now in her determined efforts to pull herself together and face forward again.

''I don't have anything to tell,'' he said mildly.

"Oh, sure!" she hooted, shifting herself on the ground until she was sitting facing him, her legs folded in a boneless sort of knot that made him blink. She rested her chin in her palm and surveyed him, so big and controlled and capable. If this man had led a normal life, she'd eat her boots, she told herself, then quickly glanced down at the boots in question. Right now they had something green and squishy on them. Yuk. They'd have to be cleaned before even a goat would eat them. She returned her dark gaze to Grant and studied him with the seriousness of a scientist bent over a microscope. His scarred face was hard, a study of planes and angles, of bronzed skin pulled tautly over the fierce sculpture of his bones. His eyes were those of an eagle, or a lion; she couldn't quite decide which. The clear amber color was brighter, paler, than topaz, almost like a yellow diamond, and like an eagle's, the eyes saw everything. They were guarded, expressionless; they hid an almost unbearable burden of experience and weary cynicism.

"Are you an agent?" she asked, probing curiously. Somehow, in those few moments, she had discarded the idea that he was a mercenary. Same field she thought, but a different division.

His mouth quirked. "No."

"Okay, let's try it from another angle. *Were* you an agent?"

"What sort of agent?"

"Stop evading my questions! The cloak-and-dagger sort of agent. You know, the men in overcoats who have forty sets of identification."

"No. Your imagination is running wild. I'm too easily identifiable to be any good undercover."

That was true. He stood out like a warrior at a tea party. Something went quiet within her, and she knew. "Are you retired?"

He was quiet for so long that she thought he wasn't going to answer her. He seemed to be thinking of something else entirely. Then he said flatly, "Yeah, I'm retired. For a year now."

His set, blank face hurt her, on the inside. "You were a . . . weapon, weren't you?"

There was a terrible clarity in his eyes as he slowly shifted his gaze to her. "Yes," he said harshly. "I was a weapon."

They had aimed him, fired him, and watched him destroy. He would be matchless, she realized. Before she'd even known him, when she'd seen him gliding into her darkened bedroom like a shadow, she'd realized how lethal he could be. And there was something else, something she could see now. He had retired himself, turned his back and walked away from that grim, shadowed life. Certainly his superiors wouldn't have wanted to lose his talents.

She reached out and placed her hand on his, her fingers slim and soft, curling around the awesome strength of his. Her hand was much smaller made with a delicacy that he could crush with a careless movement of his fingers, but implicit in her touch was the trust that he wouldn't turn that strength against her. A deep breath swelled the muscled planes of his chest. He wanted to take her right then, in the dirt. He wanted to stretch her out and pull her clothes off, bury himself in her. He wanted more of her touch, all of her touch, inside and out. But the need for her satiny female flesh was a compulsion that he couldn't satisfy with a quick possession, and there wasn't time for more. The rain was slowing and would stop entirely at any moment. There was a vague feeling marching up and down his spine that told him they couldn't afford to linger any longer.

But it was time she knew. He removed his hand from hers, lifting it to cup her chin. His thumb rubbed lightly over her lips. "Soon," he said, his voice guttural with need, "you're going to lie down for me. Before I take you back to your daddy, I'm going to have you, and the way I feel now, I figure it's going to take a long time before I'm finished with you."

Jane sat frozen, her eyes those of a startled woodland animal. She couldn't even protest, because the harsh desire in his voice flooded her mind and her skin with memories. The day before, standing in the stream, he'd kissed her and touched her with such raw sexuality that, for the first time in her life, she'd felt the coiling, writhing tension of desire in herself. For the first time she'd wanted a man, and she'd been shocked by the unfamiliarity of her own body. Now he was doing it to her again, but this time he was using words. He'd stated his intentions bluntly, and images began forming in her mind of the two of them lying twined together, of his naked, magnificent body surging against her.

He watched the shifting expressions that flitted across her face. She looked surprised, even a little shocked, but she wasn't angry. He'd have understood anger, or even amusement; that blank astonishment puzzled him. It was as if no man had ever told her that he wanted her. Well, she'd get used to the idea.

The rain had stopped, and he picked up the packs and the rifle, settling them on his shoulders. Jane followed him without a word when he stepped out from beneath the rocky outcropping into the already increasing heat. Steam rose in wavering clouds from the forest floor, immediately wrapping them in a stifling, humid blanket.

She was silent for the rest of the afternoon, lost in her thoughts. He stopped at a stream, much smaller than the one they'd seen the day before, and glanced at her. "Care for a bath? You can't soak, but you can splash."

Her eyes lit up, and for the first time that afternoon a smile danced on her full lips. He didn't need an answer to know how she felt about the idea. Grinning, he searched out a small bar of soap from his pack and held it out to her. "I'll keep watch, then you can do the same for me. I'll be up there."

Jane looked up the steep bank that he'd indicated. That was the best vantage point around; he'd have a clear view of the stream and the surrounding area. She started to ask if he was going to watch her, too, but bit back the question. As he'd already pointed out, it was too late for modesty. Besides, she felt infinitely safer knowing that he'd be close by.

He went up the bank as sure-footedly as a cat, and Jane turned to face the stream. It was only about seven feet wide, and wasn't much more than ankle-deep. Still, it looked like heaven. She hunted her lone change of underwear out of her pack, then sat down to pull off her boots. Glancing nervously over her shoulder to where Grant sat, she saw that he was in profile to her, but she knew that he would keep her in his peripheral vision. She resolutely undid her pants and stepped out of them. Nothing was going to keep her from having her bath...except maybe another snake, or a jaguar, she amended.

Naked, she gingerly picked her way over the stony bottom to a large flat rock and sat down in the few inches of water. It was deliciously cool, having run down from a higher altitude, but even tepid water would have felt good

on her over-heated skin. She splashed it on her face and
head until her hair was soaked. Gradually she felt the
sweaty stickiness leave her hair, until the strands were once
more silky beneath her fingers. Then she took the small bar
of soap out from under her leg, where she'd put it for
safekeeping, and rubbed it over her body. The small lux-
ury made her feel like a new woman, and a sense of peace
crept into her. It was only a simple pleasure, to bathe in a
clear, cool stream, but added to it was her sense of nakedness, of being totally without restrictions. She knew that
he was there, knew that he was watching her, and felt her
breasts grow tight.

What would it be like if he came down from that bank
and splashed into the water with her? If he took the blanket from his pack and laid her down on it? She closed her
eyes, shivering in reaction, thinking of his hard body
pressing down on her, thrusting into her. It had been so
many years, and the few experiences she'd had with Chris
hadn't taught her that she could be a creature of wanting,
but with Grant she wasn't the same woman.

Her heart beat heavily in her breast as she rinsed herself
by cupping water in her palms and pouring it over her.
Standing up, she twisted the water out of her hair, then
waded out. She was trembling as she pulled on her clean
underwear, then dressed distastefully in her stained pants
and shirt. "I'm finished," she called, lacing up her boots.

He appeared soundlessly beside her. "Sit in the same
place where I sat," he instructed, placing the rifle in her
hands. "Do you know how to use this?"

The weapon was heavy, but her slim hands looked capable as she handled it. "Yes. I'm a fairly good shot." A
wry smile curved her lips. "With paper targets and clay
pigeons, anyway."

"That's good enough." He began unbuttoning his shirt, and she stood there in a daze, her eyes on his hands. He paused. "Are you going to guard me from down here?"

She blushed. "No. Sorry." Quickly she turned and scrambled up the bank, then took a seat in the exact spot where he'd sat. She could see both banks, but at the same time there was a fair amount of cover that she could use if the need arose. He'd probably picked this out as the best vantage point without even thinking about it, just automatically sifting through the choices and arriving at the correct one. He might be retired, but his training was ingrained.

A movement, a flash of bronze, detected out of the corner of her eye, told her that he was wading into the stream. She shifted her gaze a fraction so she wouldn't be able to see him at all, but just the knowledge that he was as naked as she had been kept her heart pounding erratically. She swallowed, then licked her lips, forcing herself to concentrate on the surrounding jungle, but the compulsion to look at him continued.

She heard splashing and pictured him standing there like a savage, bare and completely at home.

She closed her eyes, but the image remained before her. Slowly, totally unable to control herself, she opened her eyes and turned her head to look at him. It was only a small movement, a fraction of an inch, until she was able to see him, but that wasn't enough. Stolen glances weren't enough. She wanted to study every inch of him, drink in the sight of his powerful body. Shifting around, she looked fully at him, and froze. He was beautiful, so beautiful that she forgot to breathe. Without being handsome, he had the raw power and grace of a predator, all the terrible beauty of a hunter. He was bronzed all over, his tan a deep, even brown. Unlike her, he didn't keep his back turned in case she looked; he had a complete disregard for modesty. He was taking a bath; she could look or not look, as she wished.

His skin was sleek and shiny with water, and the droplets caught in the hair on his chest glittered like captured diamonds. His body hair was dark, despite the sun-streaked blondness of his head. It shadowed his chest, ran in a thin line down his flat, muscled stomach, and bloomed again at the juncture of his legs. His legs were as solid as tree trunks, long and roped with muscle; every movement he made set off ripples beneath his skin. It was like watching a painting by one of the old masters come to life.

He soaped himself all over, then squatted in the water to rinse in the same manner she had, cupping his palms to scoop up the water. When he was rinsed clean, he stood and looked up at her, probably to check on her, and met her gaze head on. Jane couldn't look away, couldn't pretend that she hadn't been staring at him with an almost painful appreciation. He stood very still in the stream, watching her as she watched him, letting her take in every detail of his body. Under her searching gaze, his body began to stir, harden, growing to full, heavy arousal.

"Jane," he said softly, but still she heard him. She was so attuned to him, so painfully sensitive to every move and sound he made, that she would have heard him if he'd whispered. "Do you want to come down here?"

Yes. Oh, God, yes, more than she'd ever wanted anything. But she was still a little afraid of her own feelings, so she held back. This was a part of herself that she didn't know, wasn't certain she could control.

"I can't," she replied, just as softly. "Not yet."

"Then turn around, honey, while you still have a choice."

She quivered, almost unable to make the required movement, but at last her muscles responded and she turned away from him, listening as he waded out of the water. In less than a minute he appeared noiselessly at her side and took the rifle from her hands. He had both packs with him. Typically, he made no further comment on what had just happened. "We'll get away from the water and set up camp. It'll be night pretty soon."

Night. Long hours in the dark tent, lying next to him. Jane followed him, and when he stopped she helped him do the work they had done the night before, setting up the tent and hiding it. She didn't protest at the cold field rations, but ate without really tasting anything. Soon she was crawling into the tent and taking off her boots, waiting for him to join her.

When he did, they lay quietly side by side, watching as the remaining light dimmed, then abruptly vanished.

Tension hummed through her, making her muscles tight. The darkness pressed in on her, an unseen monster that sucked her breath away. No list of compulsive questions leaped to her lips tonight; she felt oddly timid, and it had been years since she'd allowed herself to be timid about anything. She no longer knew herself.

"Are you afraid of me?" he asked, his voice gentle.

Just the sound of his voice enabled her to relax a little. "No," she whispered.

"Then come here and let me keep the dark away from you."

She felt his hand on her arm, urging her closer, then she was enfolded in arms so strong that nothing could ever make her afraid while they held her. He cradled her against his side, tucking her head into the hollow of his shoulder. With a touch so light that it could have been the brush of a butterfly's wings, he kissed the top of her head. "Good night, honey," he whispered.

"Good night," she said in return.

Long after he was asleep, Jane lay in his arms with her eyes open, though she could see nothing. Her heart was pounding in her chest with a slow, heavy rhythm, and her insides felt jittery. It wasn't fear that kept her awake, but a churning emotion that shifted everything inside her. She knew exactly what was wrong with her. For the first time in too many years, everything was right with her.

She'd learned to live her life with a shortage of trust. No matter that she'd learned to enjoy herself and her freedom; there had always been that residual caution that kept her from letting a man get too close. Until now she'd never been strongly enough attracted to a man for the attraction to conquer the caution.... Until now. Until Grant. And now the attraction had become something much stronger. The truth stunned her, yet she had to accept it: she loved him. She hadn't expected it, though for two days she had felt it tugging at her. He was harsh and controlled, badtempered, and his sense of humor was severely underdeveloped, but he had gently washed the snake's blood from her, held her hand during the night, and had gone out of his way to make their trek easier for her. He wanted her, but he hadn't taken her because she wasn't ready. She was afraid of the dark, so he held her in his arms. Loving him was at once the easiest and most difficult thing she'd ever done.

Chapter Seven

Once again he awoke to find her cuddled on top of him, but this time it didn't bother him that he had slept peacefully through the night. Sliding his hands up her back, he accepted that his normally keen instincts weren't alarmed by her because there was absolutely no danger in her except perhaps the danger of her driving him crazy. She managed to do that with every little sway of her behind. Reveling in the touch of her all along his body, he moved his hands down, feeling her slenderness, the small ribs, the delicate spine, the enticing little hollow at the small of her back, then the full, soft mounds of her buttocks. He cupped his palms over them, kneading her with his fingers. She muttered and shifted against him, brushing at a lock of hair that had fallen into her face. Her eyelashes fluttered, then closed completely once more.

He smiled, enjoying the way she woke up. She did it by slow degrees, moaning and grousing while still more asleep than awake, frowning and pouting, and moving against him as if trying to sink herself deeper into him so she wouldn't have to wake up at all. Then her eyes opened, and she blinked several times, and as quickly as that the pout faded from her lips and she gave him a slow smile that would have melted stone.

"Good morning," she said, and yawned. She stretched, then abruptly froze in place. Her head came up, and she stared at him in stupefaction. "I'm on top of you," she said blankly.

"Again," he confirmed.

"Again?"

"You slept on top of me the night before last, too. Evidently my holding you while you sleep isn't enough; you think you have to hold me down."

She slithered off him, sitting up in the tent and straightening her twisted, wrinkled clothing. Color burned in her face. "I'm sorry. I know it can't have been very comfortable for you."

"Don't apologize. I've enjoyed it," he drawled. "If you really want to make it up to me, though, we'll reverse positions tonight."

Her breath caught and she stared at him in the dim light, her eyes soft and melting. Yes. Everything in her agreed. She wanted to belong to him; she wanted to know everything about his body and let him know everything about hers. She wanted to tell him, but she didn't know how to put it into words. A crooked smile crossed his face; then he sat up and reached for his boots, thrusting his feet into them and lacing them up. Evidently he took her silence for a refusal, because he dropped the subject and began the task of breaking camp.

"We have enough food for one more meal," he said as they finished eating. "Then I'll have to start hunting."

She didn't like that idea. Hunting meant that he'd leave her alone for long stretches of time. "I don't mind a vegetarian diet," she said hopefully.

"Maybe it won't come to that. We've been gradually working our way out of the mountains, and unless I miss my guess we're close to the edge of the forest. We'll probably see fields and roads today. But we're going to avoid people until I'm certain it's safe, okay?"

She nodded in agreement.

Just as he'd predicted, at midmorning they came abruptly to the end of the jungle. They stood high on a steep cliff, and stretched out below them was a valley with cultivated fields, a small network of roads, and a cozy village situated at the southern end. Jane blinked at the suddenly brilliant sunlight. It was like stepping out of one century into another. The valley looked neat and prosperous, reminding her that Costa Rica was the most highly developed country in Central America, despite the thick tangle of virgin rain forest at her back.

"Oh," she breathed. "Wouldn't it be nice to sleep in a bed again?"

He grunted an absent reply, his narrowed eyes sweeping the valley for any sign of abnormal activity. Jane stood beside him, waiting for him to make his decision.

It was made for them. Abruptly he grabbed her arm and jerked her back into the sheltering foliage, dragging her to the ground behind a huge bush just as a helicopter suddenly roared over their heads. It was flying close to the ground, following the tree line; she had only a glimpse of it before it was gone, hidden by the trees. It was a gunship, and had camouflage paint.

"Did you see any markings?" she asked sharply, her nails digging into his skin.

"No. There weren't any." He rubbed his stubbled jaw. "There's no way of telling who it belonged to, but we can't take any chances. Now we know that we can't just walk across the valley. We'll work our way down, and try to find more cover."

If anything, the terrain was even more difficult now. They were at the edge of a volcanic mountain range, and the land had been carved with a violent hand. It seemed to be either straight up, or straight down. Their pace was ag-

onizingly slow as they worked their way down rocky bluffs
and up steep gorges. When they stopped to eat, they had
covered less than one-fourth the length of the valley, and
Jane's legs ached as they hadn't since the wild run through
the jungle the first day.

Right on schedule, just as they finished eating, they
heard the boom of thunder. Grant looked around for
shelter, considering every outcropping of rock. Then he
pointed. "I think that's a cave up there. If it is we'll be in
high cotton."

"What?" Jane asked, frowning.

"Sitting pretty," he explained. "Luxurious accommo-
dations, in comparison to what we've had."

"Unless it's already occupied."

"That's why you're going to wait down here while I
check it out." He moved up the fern covered wall of the
gorge, using bushes and vines and any other toehold he
could find. The gorge itself was narrow and steep, enclosing them on all four sides. Its shape gave a curious clarity
to the calls of the innumerable birds that flitted among the
trees like living Christmas decorations, all decked out in
their iridescent plumage. Directly overhead was a streak of
sky, but it consisted of rolling black clouds instead of the
clear blue that she'd seen only moments before.

Grant reached the cave, then immediately turned and
waved to her. "Come on up; it's clear! Can you make it?"

"Have I failed yet?" she quipped, starting the climb, but
she'd had to force the humor. The desolation had been
growing in her since they'd seen the valley. Knowing that
they were so close to civilization made her realize that their
time together was limited. While they had been in the forest, the only two people locked in a more primitive time,
she'd had no sense of time running out. Now she couldn't
ignore the fact that soon, in a few days or less, their time

together would end. She felt as if she'd already wasted so much time, as if the golden sand had been trickling through her fingers and she'd only just realized what she held. She felt panic-stricken at the thought of discovering love only to lose it, because there wasn't enough time to let it grow.

He reached his hand down and caught hers, effortlessly lifting her the last few feet. "Make yourself comfortable; we could be here a while. This looks like the granddaddy of all storms."

Jane surveyed their shelter. It wasn't really a cave; it was little more than an indentation in the face of the rock, about eight feet deep. It had a steeply slanting ceiling that soared to ten or eleven feet at the opening of the cave, but was only about five feet high at the back. The floor was rocky, and one big rock, as large as a love seat and shaped like a peanut, lay close to the mouth of the cave. But it was dry, and because of its shallowness it wasn't dark, so Jane wasn't inclined to find fault with it.

Given Grant's eerie sense of timing, she wasn't surprised to hear the first enormous raindrops begin filtering through the trees just as he spread out the tarp at the back of the cave. He placed it behind the big rock, using its bulk to shelter them. She sat down on the tarp and drew her legs up, wrapping her arms around them and resting her chin on her knees, listening to the sound of the rain as it increased in volume.

Soon it was a din and the solid sheets of water that obscured their vision heightened the impression that they were under a waterfall. She could hear the crack of lightning, feel the earth beneath her shake from the enormous claps of thunder. It was dark now, as the rain blotted out what light came through the thick canopy. She could barely see Grant, who was standing just inside the mouth of the cave with his shoulder propped against the wall, occasionally puffing on a cigarette.

Chills raced over her body as the rain cooled the air. Hugging her legs even tighter for warmth, Jane stared through the dimness at the broad, powerful shoulders outlined against the gray curtain of rain. He wasn't an easy man to get to know. His personality was as shadowy as the jungle, yet just the sight of that muscular back made her feel safe and protected. She knew that he stood between her and any danger. He had already risked his life for her on more than one occasion, and was as matter-of-fact about it as if being shot at were an everyday occurrence. Perhaps it was for him, but Jane didn't take it so lightly.

He finished his cigarette and field-stripped it. Jane doubted that anyone would track them here through the rain, but it was second nature to him to be cautious. He went back to his calm perusal of the storm, standing guard while she rested.

Something shifted inside her and coiled painfully in her chest. He was so alone. He was a hard, lonely man, but everything about him drew her like a magnet, pulling at her heart and body.

Her eyes clouded as she watched him. When this was over he'd walk away from her as if these days in the jungle had never existed. This was all routine for him. What she could have of him, all that she could ever have of him, was the present, too few days before this was over. And that just wasn't enough.

She was cold now, chilled to her bones. The unceasing, impenetrable curtain of rain carried a damp coldness with it, and her own spirits chilled her from the inside. Instinctively, like a sinuous cat seeking heat, she uncoiled from the tarp and went up to him, gravitating to his certain warmth and comfort. Silently she slid her arms around his taut waist and pressed her face into the marvelous heat of his chest. Glancing down at her, he lifted an eyebrow in mild inquiry. "I'm cold," she muttered, leaning her head on him and staring pensively at the rain.

He looped his arm around her shoulder, holding her closer to him and sharing his warmth with her. A shiver ran over her; he rubbed his free hand up her bare arm, feeling the coolness of her skin. Of its own accord his hand continued upward, stroking her satiny jaw, smoothing the dark tangle of hair away from her face. She was in a melancholy mood, this funny little cat, staring at the rain as if it would never stop, her eyes shadowed and that full, passionate mouth sad.

Cupping her chin in his hand, he tilted her face up so he could study her quiet expression. A small smile curved the corners of his hard mouth. "What's wrong, honey? Rain making you feel blue?" Before she could answer, he bent his head and kissed her, using his own cure.

Jane's hands went to his shoulders, clinging to him for support. His mouth was hard and demanding and oh so sweet. The taste of him, the feel of him, was just what she wanted. Her teeth parted, allowing the slow probing of his tongue. Deep inside her, fire began to curl, and she curled too, twining against him in an unconscious movement that he read immediately.

Lifting his mouth from hers just a little, he muttered, "Honey, this feels like an offer to me."

Her dark eyes were a little dazed as she looked up at him. "I think it is," she whispered.

He dropped his arms to her waist and wrapped them around her, lifting her off her feet, bringing her level with him. She wound her arms around his neck and kissed him fervently, lost in the taste and feel of his mouth, not even aware he'd moved until he set her down to stand on the tarp. The dimness at the back of the cave hid any expression that was in his eyes, but she could feel his intent amber gaze on her as he began calmly unbuttoning her shirt. Jane's mouth went dry, but her own shaking fingers moved to his chest and began opening his shirt in turn.

When both garments were hanging open, he shrugged out of his and tossed it on the tarp, never taking his eyes from her. Tugging his undershirt free of his pants, he caught the bottom of it and peeled it off over his head. He tossed it aside, too, completely baring his broad, hairy chest. As it had the day before, the sight of his half-naked body mesmerized her. Her chest hurt; breathing was incredibly difficult. Then his hard, hot fingers were inside her shirt, on her breasts, molding them to fit his palms. The contrast of his heated hands on her cool skin made her gasp in shocked pleasure. Closing her eyes, she leaned into his hands, rubbing her nipples against his calloused palms. His chest lifted on a deep, shuddering breath.

She could feel the sexual tension emanating from him in waves. Like no other man she'd known, he made her acutely aware of his sexuality, and equally aware of her own body and its uses. Between her legs, an empty throb began to torment her, and she instinctively pressed her thighs together in an effort to ease the ache.

As slight as it was, he felt her movement. One of his hands left her breast and drifted downward, over her stomach and hips to her tightly clenched thighs. "That won't help," he murmured. "You'll have to open your legs, not close them." His fingers rubbed insistently at her and pleasure exploded along her nerves. A low moan escaped from her lips; then she swayed toward him. She felt her legs parting, allowing him access to her tender body. He explored her through her pants, creating such shock waves of physical pleasure that her knees finally buckled and she fell against him, her bare breasts flattening against the raspy, hair-covered expanse of his chest.

Quickly he set her down on the tarp and knelt over her, unzipping her pants and pulling them down her legs, his hands rough and urgent. He had to pause to remove her boots, but in only moments she was naked except for the shirt that still hung around her shoulders. The damp air made her shiver, and she reached for him. "I'm cold," she complained softly. "Get me warm."

She offered herself to him so openly and honestly that he wanted to thrust into her immediately, but he also wanted more. He'd had her nearly naked in his arms before. In the stream, that wisp of wet silk had offered no protection, but he hadn't had the time to explore her as he'd wanted. Her body was still a mystery to him; he wanted to touch every inch of her, taste her and enjoy the varying textures of her skin.

Jane's eyes were wide and shadowed as he knelt over her, holding himself away from her outstretched arms. "Not just yet, honey," he said in a low, gravelly voice. "Let me look at you first." Gently he caught her wrists and pressed them down to the tarp above her head, making her round, pretty breasts arch as if they begged for his mouth. Anchoring her wrists with one hand, he slid his free hand to those tempting, gently quivering mounds.

A small, gasping sound escaped from Jane's throat. Why was he holding her hands like that? It made her feel incredibly helpless and exposed, spread out for his delectation, yet she also felt unutterably safe. She could sense him savoring her with his eyes, watching intently as her nipples puckered in response to the rasp of his fingertips. He was so close to her that she could feel the heat of his body, smell the hot, musky maleness of his skin. She arched, trying to turn her body into that warmth and scent, but he forced her flat again.

Then his mouth was on her, sliding up the slope of her breast and closing hotly on her nipple. He sucked strongly at her, making waves of burning pleasure sweep from her breast to her loins. Jane whimpered, then bit her lip to hold back the sound. She hadn't known, had never realized, what a man's mouth on her breasts could do to her. She was on fire, her skin burning with an acute sensitivity that was both ecstatic and unbearable. She squirmed, clenching her legs together, trying to control the ache that threatened to master her.

His mouth went to her other breast, the rasp of his tongue on her nipple intensifying an already unbearable sensation. He swept his hand down to her thighs, his touch demanding that she open herself to him. Her muscles slowly relaxed for him, and he spread her legs gently. His fingers combed through the dark curls that had so enticed him before, making her body jerk in anticipation; then he covered her with his palm and thoroughly explored the soft, vulnerable flesh between her legs. Beneath his touch, Jane began to tremble wildly. "Grant," she moaned, her voice a shaking, helpless plea.

"Easy," he soothed, blowing his warm breath across her flesh. He wanted her so badly that he felt he would explode, but at the same time he couldn't get enough of touching her, of watching her arch higher and higher as he aroused her. He was drunk on her flesh, and still trying to satiate himself. He took her nipple in his mouth and began sucking again, wringing another cry from her.

Between her legs a finger suddenly penetrated, searching out the depths of her readiness, and shock waves battered her body. Something went wild inside her, and she could no longer hold her body still. It writhed and bucked against his hand, and his mouth was turning her breasts into pure flame. Then his thumb brushed insistently over her straining, aching flesh, and she exploded in his arms, blind with the colossal upheaval of her senses, crying out unconsciously. Nothing had ever prepared her for this, for the total, mind-shattering pleasure of her own body.

When it was over, she lay sprawled limply on the tarp. He undid his pants and shoved them off, his eyes glittering and wild. Jane's eyes slowly opened and she stared up at him dazedly. Grasping her legs, he lifted them high and spread them; then he braced himself over her and slowly sank his flesh into hers.

Jane's hands clenched on the tarp, and she bit her lips to keep from crying out as her body was inexorably stretched and filled. He paused, his big body shuddering, allowing her the time to accept him. Then suddenly it was she who couldn't bear any distance at all between them, and she surged upward, taking all of him, reaching up her arms to pull him close.

She never noticed the tears that ran in silvered streaks down her temples, but Grant gently wiped them away with his rough thumbs. Supporting his weight on his arms, sliding his entire body over her in a subtle caress, he began moving with slow, measured strokes. He was so close to the edge that he could feel the feathery sensation along his spine, but he wanted to make it last. He wanted to entice her again to that satisfying explosion, watch her go crazy in his arms.

"Are you all right?" he asked in a raw, husky tone, catching another tear with his tongue as it left the corner of her eye. If he were hurting her, he wouldn't prolong the loving, though he felt it would tear him apart to stop.

"Yes, I'm fine," she breathed, stroking her hands up the moving, surging muscles of his back. Fine... What a word for the wild magnificence of belonging to him. She'd never dreamed it could feel like this. It was as if she'd found a half of herself that she hadn't even known was missing. She'd never dreamed that *she* could feel like this. Her fingers clutched mindlessly at his back as his long, slow movements began to heat her body.

He felt her response and fiercely buried his mouth against the sensitive little hollow between her throat and collarbone, biting her just enough to let her feel his teeth, then licking where he'd bitten. She whimpered, that soft, uncontrollable little sound that drove him crazy, and he lost control. He began driving into her with increasing power, pulling her legs higher around him so he could have more of her, all of her, deeper and harder, hearing her little cries and going still crazier. There was no longer any sense of time, or of danger, only the feel of the woman beneath him and around him. While he was in her arms he could no longer feel the dark, icy edges of the shadows in his mind and soul.

In the aftermath, like that after a storm of unbelievable violence, they lay in exhausted silence, each reluctant to speak for fear it would shatter the fragile peace. His massive shoulders crushed her, making it difficult for her to breathe, but she would gladly have spent the rest of her life lying there. Her fingers slowly stroked the sweat-darkened gold of his hair, threading through the heavy, live silk. Their bodies were reluctant to leave each other, too. He hadn't withdrawn from her; instead, after easing his weight down onto her, he'd nestled closer and now seemed to be lightly dozing.

Perhaps it had happened too quickly between them, but she couldn't regret it. She was fiercely happy that she'd given herself to him. She'd never been in love before, never wanted to explore the physical mysteries of a man and a woman. She'd even convinced herself that she just wasn't a physical person, and had decided to enjoy her solitary life. Now her entire concept of herself had been changed, and it was as if she'd discovered a treasure within herself. After the kidnapping she had withdrawn from people, except for the trusted precious few who she had loved before: her parents, Chris, a couple of other friends. And even though she had married Chris, she had remained essentially alone, emotionally withdrawn. Perhaps that was why their marriage had failed, because she hadn't been willing to let him come close enough to be a real husband. Oh, they had been physically intimate, but she had been unresponsive, and eventually he had stopped bothering her. That was exactly what it had been for her: a bother. Chris had deserved better. He was her best friend, but only a friend, not a lover. He was much better off with the warm, responsive, adoring woman he'd married after their divorce.

She was too honest with herself to even pretend that any blame for their failed marriage belonged to Chris. It had been entirely her fault, and she knew it. She'd thought it was a lack in herself. Now she realized that she did have the warm, passionate instincts of a woman in love—because she was in love for the first time. She hadn't been able to respond to Chris, simply because she hadn't loved him as a woman should love the man she marries.

She was twenty-nine. She wasn't going to pretend to a shyness she didn't feel for the sake of appearance. She loved the man who lay in her arms, and she was going to enjoy to the fullest whatever time she had with him. She hoped to have a lifetime; but if fate weren't that kind, she would not let timidity cheat her out of one minute of the time they did have. Her life had been almost snuffed out twenty years ago, before it had really begun. She knew that life and time were too precious to waste.

Perhaps it didn't mean to Grant what it did to her, to be able to hold and love like this. She knew intuitively that his life had been much harder than hers, that he'd seen things that had changed him, that had stolen the laughter from his eyes. His experiences had hardened him, had left him extraordinarily cautious. But even if he were only taking the shallowest form of comfort from her, that of sexual release, she loved him enough to give him whatever he needed from her, without question. Jane loved as she did everything else, completely and courageously.

He stirred, lifting his weight onto his forearms and staring down at her. His golden eyes were shadowed, but there was something in them that made her heart beat faster, for he was looking at her the way a man looks at the woman who belongs to him. "I've got to be too heavy for you."

"Yes, but I don't care." Jane tightened her arms about his neck and tried to pull him back down, but his strength was so much greater than hers that she couldn't budge him.

He gave her a swift, hard kiss. "It's stopped raining. We have to go."

"Why can't we stay the night here? Aren't we safe?"

He didn't answer, just gently disengaged their bodies and sat up, reaching for his clothes, and that was answer enough. She sighed, but sat up to reach for her own clothes. The sigh became a wince as she became aware of the various aches she'd acquired by making love on the ground.

She could have sworn that he wasn't looking at her, but his awareness of his surroundings was awesome. His head jerked around, and a slight frown pulled his dark brows together. "Did I hurt you?" he asked abruptly.

"No, I'm all right." He didn't look convinced by her reassurance. When they descended the steep slope to the floor of the gorge, he kept himself positioned directly in front of her. He carried her down the last twenty feet, hoisting her over his shoulder despite her startled, then indignant, protests.

It was a waste of time for her to protest, though; he simply ignored her. When he put her down silently and started walking, she had no choice but to follow.

Twice that afternoon they heard a helicopter, and both times he pulled her into the thickest cover, waiting until the sound had completely faded away before emerging. The grim line of his mouth told her that he didn't consider it just a coincidence. They were being hunted, and only the dense cover of the forest kept them from being caught. Jane's nerves twisted at the thought of leaving that cover; she wasn't afraid for just herself now, but for Grant, too. He put himself in jeopardy just by being with her. Turego wanted her alive, but Grant was of no use to him at all.

If it came to a choice between Grant's life and giving Turego what he wanted, Jane knew that she would give in. She'd have to take her chances with Turego, though it would be impossible now to catch him off guard the way she had the first time. He knew now that she wasn't a rich man's flirtatious, charming plaything. She'd made a fool of him, and he wouldn't forget.

Grant stepped over a large fallen tree and turned back to catch her around the waist and lift her over it with that effortless strength of his. Pausing, he pushed her tangled hair back from her face, his touch surprisingly gentle. She knew how lethal those hands could be. "You're too quiet," he muttered. "It makes me think you're up to something, and that makes me nervous."

"I was just thinking," she defended herself.

"That's what I was afraid of."

"If Turego catches us . . ."

"He won't," Grant said flatly. Staring down at her, he saw more now than just an appealing, sloe-eyed woman. He knew her now, knew her courage and strength, her secret fears and her sunny nature. He also knew her temper, which could flare or fade in an instant. Sabin's advice had been to kill her quickly rather than let Turego get his hands on her; Grant had seen enough death to accept that as a realistic option at the time. But that was before he had known her, tasted her and felt the silky texture of her skin, watched her go wild beneath him. Things had changed now. He had changed—in ways that he neither welcomed nor trusted, but had to acknowledge. Jane had become important to him. He couldn't allow that, but for the time being he had to accept it. Until she was safe, she could be his, but no longer. There wasn't any room in his life for permanency, for roots, because he still wasn't certain that he'd ever live in the sunshine again. Like Sabin, he'd been in the shadows too long. There were still dark spots on his soul that were revealed in the lack of emotion in his eyes. There was still the terrible, calm acceptance of things that were too terrible to be accepted.

If things had gone as originally planned, they would have gotten on that helicopter and she would be safely home by now. He would never have really known her; he would have delivered her to her father and walked away. But instead, they had been forced to spend days with only each other for company. They had slept side by side, eaten together, shared moments of danger and of humor. Perhaps the laughter was the more intimate, to him; he'd known danger many times with many people, but humor was rare in his life. She had made him laugh, and in doing so had captured a part of him.

Damn her for being the woman she was, for being lively and good-natured and desirable, when he'd expected a spoiled, sulky bitch. Damn her for making men want her, for making *him* want her. For the first time in his life he felt a savage jealousy swelling in his heart. He knew that he would have to leave her, but until then he wanted her to be his and only his. Remembering the feel of her body under his, he knew that he would have to have her again. His golden eyes narrowed at the feeling of intense possessiveness that gripped him. An expression of controlled violence crossed his face, an expression that the people who knew him had learned to avoid provoking. Grant Sullivan was dangerous enough in the normal way of things; angered, he was deadly. She was his now, and her life was being threatened. He'd lost too much already; his youth, his laughter, his trust in others, even part of his own humanity. He couldn't afford to lose anything else. He was a desperate man trying to recapture his soul. He needed to find again even a small part of the boy from Georgia who had walked barefoot in the warm dirt of plowed fields, who had learned survival in the mysterious depths of the great swamp. What Vietnam had begun, the years of working in intelligence and operations had almost completed, coming close to destroying him as a man.

Jane and her screwball brand of gallantry were the source of the only warmth he'd felt in years.

He reached out and caught her by the nape of her neck, his strong fingers halting her. Surprised, she turned an inquiring glance at him, and the small smile that had begun forming on her lips faded at the fierce expression he couldn't hide.

"Grant? Is something wrong?"

Without thinking, he used the grip he had on her neck to pull her to him, and kissed her full lips, still faintly swollen from the lovemaking they'd shared in the cave. He took his time about it, kissing her with slow, deep movements of his tongue. With a small sound of pleasure she wound her arms around his neck and lifted herself on tiptoe to press more fully against him. He felt the soft juncture of her thighs and ground himself against her, his body jolting with desire at the way she automatically adjusted herself to his hardness.

She was his, as she'd never belonged to any other man.

Her safety hinged on how swiftly he could get her out of the country, for he sensed Turego closing in on them. That man would never give up, not while the microfilm was still missing. There was no way in hell, Grant vowed, that he would allow Turego ever to touch Jane again. Lifting his mouth from hers, he muttered in a harsh tone, "You're mine now. I'll take care of you."

Jane rested her head against his chest. "I know," she whispered.

Chapter Eight

That night changed forever the way Jane thought of the darkness. The fear of being alone in the dark would probably always remain with her, but when Grant reached out for her, it stopped being an enemy to be held at bay. It became instead a warm blanket of safety that wrapped around them, isolating them from the world. She felt his hands on her and forgot about the night.

He kissed her until she was clinging to him, begging him wordlessly for release from the need he'd created in her. Then he gently stripped her and himself, then rolled to his back, lifting her astride him. "I hurt you this morning," he said, his voice low and rough. "You control it this time; take only as much as you're comfortable with."

Comfort didn't matter; making love with him was a primitive glory, and she couldn't place any limits on it. She lost control, moving wildly on him, and her uninhibited delight snapped the thin thread of control he was trying to maintain. He made a rough sound deep in his throat and clasped her to him, rolling once again until she was beneath him. The wildly soaring pleasure they gave each other wiped her mind clear of everything but him and the love that swelled inside of her. There was no darkness. With his passion, with the driving need of his body, he took her out of the darkness. When she fell asleep in his arms, it was without once having thought of the impenetrable darkness that surrounded them.

The next morning, as always, she awoke slowly, moving and murmuring to herself, snuggling against the wonderfully warm, hard body beneath her, knowing even in her sleep that it was Grant's. His hands moved down her back to cup and knead her buttocks, awakening her fully. Then he shifted gently onto his side, holding her in his arms and depositing her on her back. Her eyes fluttered open, but it was still dark, so she closed them again and turned to press her face against his neck.

"It's almost dawn, honey," he said against her hair, but he couldn't force himself to stop touching her, to sit up and put on his clothing. His hands slipped over her bare, silky skin, discovering anew all the places he'd touched and kissed during the night. Her response still overwhelmed him. She was so open and generous, wanting him and offering herself with a simplicity that took his breath away.

She groaned, and he eased her into a sitting position, then reached out to unzip the flap of the tent and let in a faint glimmer of light. "Are you awake?"

"No," she grumbled, leaning against him and yawning.

"We have to go."

"I know." Muttering something under her breath, she found what she presumed to be her shirt and began trying to untangle it. There was too much cloth, so she stopped in frustration and handed it to him. "I think this is yours. It's too big to be mine."

He took the shirt, and Jane scrambled around until she found her own under the blanket they'd been lying on. "Can't you steal a truck or something?" she asked, not wanting even to think about another day of walking.

He didn't laugh, but she could almost feel the way the corners of his lips twitched. "That's against the law, you know."

"Stop laughing at me! You've had a lot of specialized training, haven't you? Don't you know how to hot-wire an ignition?"

He sighed. "I guess I can hot-wire anything we'd be likely to find, but stealing a vehicle would be like advertising our position to Turego."

"How far can we be from Limon? Surely we could get there before Turego would be able to search every village between here and there?"

"It'd be too risky, honey. Our safest bet is still to cut across to the east coast swamps, then work our way down the coast. We can't be tracked in the swamp." He paused. "I'll have to go into the village for food but you're going to stay hidden in the trees."

Jane drew back. "Like hell."

"Damn it, don't you realize that it's too dangerous for you to show your face?"

"What about *your* face? At least I have dark hair and eyes like everyone else. Don't forget, that soldier saw you, and your pilot friend no doubt told them all about you, so they know we're together. That long blond mane of yours is pretty unusual around here."

He ran his hand through his shaggy hair, faintly surprised at how long it was. "It can't be helped."

She folded her arms stubbornly. "You're not going anywhere without me."

Silence lay between them for a moment. She was beginning to think she'd won a surprisingly easy victory when he spoke, and the even, almost mild tone of his voice made chills go up her spine, because it was the most implacable voice she'd ever heard. "You'll do what I say, or I'll tie and gag you and leave you here in the tent."

Now it was her turn to fall silent. The intimacy that had been forged between them had made her forget that he was a warrior first, and her lover second. Despite the gentle passion with which he made love to her, he was still the same man who had knocked her out and thrown her over his shoulder, carrying her away into the jungle. She hadn't held a grudge against him for that, after the reception she'd given him, but this was something else entirely. She felt as if he were forcibly reminding her of the original basis of their relationship, making her acknowledge that their physical intimacy had not made her an equal in his eyes. It was as if he'd used her body, since she had so willingly offered it, but saw no reason to let that give her any influence over him.

Jane turned away from him, fumbling with her shirt and finally getting it straight. She wouldn't let him see any hint of hurt in her eyes; she'd known that the love she felt was completely one-sided.

His hand shot out and pulled the shirt away from her. Startled, she looked at him. "I have to get dressed. You said we need to—"

"I know what I said," he growled, easing her down onto the blanket. The lure of her soft body, the knowledge that he'd hurt her and her characteristic chin-up attempt to keep him from seeing it, all made it impossible for him to remember the importance of moving on. The core of ice deep inside his chest kept him from whispering to her how much she meant to him. The remoteness bred into him by years of living on the edge of death hadn't yet been overcome; perhaps it never would be. It was still vital to him to keep some small significant part of himself sealed away, aloof and cold. Still, he couldn't let her draw away from him with that carefully blank expression on her face. She was his, and it was time she came to terms with the fact.

Putting his hands on her thighs, he spread them apart and mounted her. Jane caught her breath, her hands going up to grab at his back. He slowly pushed into her, filling her with a powerful movement that had her body arching on the blanket.

He went deep inside her, holding her tightly to him. Her inner tightness made him almost groan aloud as wild shivers of pleasure ran up his spine. Shoving his hand into her hair, he turned her head until her mouth was under his, then kissed her with a violence that only hinted at the inferno inside him. She responded to him immediately. Her mouth molded to his and her body rose to meet his thrusts in increasingly ecstatic undulations. He wanted to immerse himself in her, go deeper and deeper until they were bonded together, their flesh fused. He held her beneath him, their bodies locked together in total intimacy. He reveled in the waves of intensifying pleasure that made them clutch at each other, straining together in an effort to reach the peak of their passion. When he was inside her, he no longer felt the need to isolate himself. She was taking a part of him that he hadn't meant to offer, but he couldn't stop it. It was as if he'd gotten on a roller coaster and there was no way to get off until it reached the end of the line. He'd just have to go along for the ride, and he meant to wring every moment of pleasure he could from the short time that he had her all to himself.

Jane clung to his shoulders, driven out of her senses by the pounding of his body. He seemed to have lost all control; he was wild, almost violent, his flesh so heated that his skin burned her palms. She was caught up in the depth of his passion, writhing against him and begging for more. Then, abruptly, her pleasure crested, and he ground his mouth against hers to catch her mindless cries. Her hot flare of ecstasy caught him in its explosion, and he began shuddering as the final shock waves jolted through his body. Now it was she who held him, and when it was over he collapsed on her, his eyes closed and his chest heaving, his body glistening with sweat.

Her fingers gently touched the shaggy, dark gold threads of his hair, pushing them away from his forehead. She didn't know what had triggered his sudden, violent possession, but it didn't matter. What mattered was that, despite everything, he needed her in a basic way that he didn't welcome, but couldn't deny. That wasn't what she wanted, but it was a start. Slowly she trailed her hand down his back, feeling the powerful muscles that lay under his supple bronzed skin. The muscles twitched then relaxed under her touch, and he grew heavier as the tension left him.

"Now we *really* have to go," he murmured against her breast.

"Ummm." She didn't want to stir; her limbs were heavy, totally relaxed. She could happily have lain there for the rest of the day, dozing with him and waking to make love again. She knew that the peace wouldn't last; in a moment he stirred and eased their bodies apart.

They dressed in silence, except for the rustling of their clothing, until she began lacing her boots on her feet. He reached out and tilted her chin then, his thumb rubbing over her bottom lip. "Promise me," he demanded, making her look at him. "Tell me that you're going to do what I say, without an argument. Don't make me tie you up."

Was he asking for obedience, or trust? Jane hesitated, then went with her instincts. "All right," she whispered. "I promise."

His pupils dilated, and his thumb probed at the corner of her lips. "I'll take care of you," he said, and it was more than a promise.

They took down the tent; then Jane got out the meager supply of remaining food. She emptied the last of the Perrier into his canteen, disposed of the bottles, and broke in two the granola bar that she'd been saving. That and a small can of grapefruit was their breakfast, and the last of their food.

The morning was almost gone, and the heat and humidity had risen to almost unbearable levels, when Grant stopped and looked around. He wiped his forehead on his sleeve. "We're almost even with the village. Stay here, and I'll be back in an hour or so."

"How long is 'or so'?" she asked politely, but the sound of her teeth snapping together made him grin.

"Until I get back." He took the pistol out of its holster and extended it to her. "I take it you know how to use this, too?"

Jane took the weapon from his hand, a grim expression on her mouth. "Yes. After I was kidnapped, Dad insisted that I learn how to protect myself. That included a course in firearms, as well as self-defense classes." Her slim hand handled the gun with respect, and reluctant expertise. "I've never seen one quite like this. What is it?"

"A Bren 10 millimeter," he grunted.

Her eyebrows lifted. "Isn't it still considered experimental?"

He shrugged. "By some people. I've used it for a while; it does what I want." He watched her for a moment, then a frown drew his brows together. "Could you use it, if you had to?"

"I don't know." A smile wobbled on her mouth. "Let's hope it doesn't come to that."

He touched her hair, hoping fervently that she never had to find the answer to his question. He didn't want anything ever to dim the gaiety of her smile. Bending, he kissed her roughly, thoroughly, then without a word blended into the forest in that silent, unnerving way of his. Jane stared at the gun in her hand for a long moment, then walked over to a fallen tree and carefully inspected it for animal life before sitting down.

She couldn't relax. Her nerves were jumpy, and though she didn't jerk around at every raucous bird call or chattering monkey, or even the alarming rustles in the underbrush, her senses were acutely, painfully attuned to the noises. She had become used to having Grant close by, his mere presence making her feel protected. Without him, she felt vulnerable and more alone than she had ever felt before.

Fear ate at her, but it was fear for Grant, not herself. She had walked into this with her eyes open, accepting the danger as the price to be paid, but Grant was involved solely because of her. If anything happened to him, she knew she wouldn't be able to bear it, and she was afraid. How could he expect to walk calmly into a small village and not be noticed. Everything about him drew attention, from his stature to his shaggy blond hair and those wild, golden eyes. She *knew* how single-mindedly Turego would search for her, and since Grant had been seen with her, his life was on the line now just as much as hers.

By now Turego must know that she had the microfilm. He'd be both furious and desperate; furious because she'd played him for a fool, and desperate because she could destroy his government career. Jane twisted her fingers together, her dark eyes intent. She thought of destroying the microfilm, to ensure that it would never fall into the hands of Turego or any hostile group or government—but she didn't know what was on it, only that it was supremely important. She didn't want to destroy information that her own country might need. Not only that, but she might need it as a negotiating tool. George had taught her well, steeped her in his cautious, quicksilver tactics, the tactics that had made him so shadowy that few people had known of his existence. If she had her back to the wall, she would use every advantage she had, do whatever she had to—but she hoped it wouldn't come to that kind of desperation. The best scenario would be that Grant would be able to smuggle her out of the country. Once she was safe in the States, she'd make contact and turn the microfilm over to the people who should have it. Then she could concentrate on chasing Grant until he realized that he couldn't live without her. The worst scenario she could imagine would be for something to happen to Grant. Everything in her shied away even from the thought.

He'd been hurt too much already. He was a rough, hardened warrior, but he bore scars, invisible ones inside as well as the ones that scored his body. He'd retired, trying to pull himself away, but the wasteland mirrored in his eyes told her that he still lived partially in the shadows, where sunlight and warmth couldn't penetrate.

A fierce protectiveness welled up inside her. She was strong; she'd already lived through so much, overcome a childhood horror that could have crippled her emotionally. She hadn't allowed that to clip her wings, had learned instead to soar even higher, reveling in her freedom. But she wasn't strong enough to survive a world without Grant. She had to know that he was alive and well, or there would be no more sunshine for her. If anyone dared harm him...

Perspiration curled the hair at her temples and trickled between her breasts. Sighing, she wondered how long she had been waiting. She wiped her face and twisted her hair into a knot on top of her head to relieve herself of its hot weight on the back of her neck. It was so hot! The air was steamy, lying on her skin like a wet, warm blanket, making it difficult to breathe. It had to rain soon; it was nearing the time of day when the storms usually came.

She watched a line of ants for a time, then tried to amuse herself by counting the different types of birds that flitted and chirped in the leafy terraces above her head. The jungle teemed with life, and she'd come to learn that, with caution, it was safe to walk through it—not that she wanted to try it without Grant. The knowledge and the experience were his. But she was no longer certain that death awaited her behind every bush. The animal life that flourished in the green depths was generally shy, and skittered away from the approach of man. It was true that the most dangerous animal in the jungle was man himself.

Well over an hour had passed, and a sense of unease was prickling her spine. She sat very still, her green and black clothing mingling well with the surrounding foliage, her senses alert.

She saw nothing, heard nothing out of the ordinary, but the prickling sensation along her spine increased. Jane sat still for a moment longer, then gave in to the screaming of her instincts. Danger was near, very near. Slowly she moved, taking care not to rustle even a leaf, and crawled behind the shelter of the fallen tree's roots. They were draped in vines and bushes that had sprung to life already, feeding off the death of the great plant. The heaviness of the pistol she held reminded her that Grant had had a reason for leaving it with her.

A flash of movement caught her attention, but she turned only her eyes to study it. It was several long seconds before she saw it again, a bit of tanned skin and a green shape that was not plant or animal, but a cap. The man was moving slowly, cautiously, making little noise. He carried a rifle, and he was headed in the general direction of the village.

Jane's heart thudded in her breast. Grant could well meet him face to face, but Grant might be surprised, while this man, this guerrilla, was expecting to find him. Jane didn't doubt that normally Grant would be the victor, but if he were overtaken from behind he could be shot before he had a chance to act.

The distinctive beating of helicopter blades assaulted the air, still distant, but signaling the intensified search. Jane waited while the noise of the helicopter faded, hoping that its presence had alerted Grant. Surely it had; he was far too wary not to be on guard. For that, if nothing else, she was grateful for the presence of the helicopters.

She had to find Grant before he came face to face with one of the guerrillas and before they found her. This lone man wouldn't be the only one searching for her.

She had learned a lot from Grant these past few days, absorbing the silent manner in which he walked, his instinctive use of the best shelter available. She slid into the jungle, moving slowly, keeping low, and always staying behind and to the side of the silent stalker. Terror fluttered in her chest, almost choking her, but she reminded herself that she had no choice.

A thorny vine caught her hair, jerking it painfully, and tears sprang to her eyes as she bit her lip to stifle a reflexive cry of pain. Trembling, she freed her hair from the vine. Oh, God, where was Grant? Had he been caught already?

Her knees trembled so badly that she could no longer walk at a crouch. She sank to her hands and knees and began crawling, as Grant had taught her, keeping the thickest foliage between herself and the man, awkwardly clutching the pistol in her hand as she moved.

Thunder rumbled in the distance, signaling the approach of the daily rains. She both dreaded and prayed for the rain. It would drown out all sound and reduce visibility to a few feet, increasing her chances for escape—but it would also make it almost impossible for Grant to find her.

A faint crackle in the brush behind her alerted her, but she whirled a split second too late. Before she could bring the pistol around, the man was upon her, knocking the gun from her grip and twisting her arm up behind her, then pushing her face into the ground. She gasped, her breath almost cut off by the pressure of his knee on her back. The moist, decaying vegetation that littered the forest floor was ground into her mouth. Twisting her head to one side, Jane spat out the dirt. She tried to wrench her arm free; he cursed and twisted her arm higher behind her back, wringing an involuntary cry of pain from her.

Someone shouted in the distance, and the man answered, but Jane's ears were roaring and she couldn't understand what they said. Then he roughly searched her, slapping his free hand over her body and making her face turn red with fury. When he was satisfied that she carried no other weapons, he released her arm and flipped her onto her back.

She started to surge to her feet, but he swung his rifle around so close that the long, glinting barrel was only a few inches from her face. She glanced at it, then lifted her eyes to glare at her captor. Perhaps she could catch him off guard. "Who are you?" she demanded in a good imitation of a furious, insulted woman, and swatted the barrel away as if it were an insect. His flat, dark eyes briefly registered surprise, then wariness. Jane scrambled to her feet and thrust her face up close to his, letting him see her narrowed, angry eyes. Using all the Spanish she knew, she proceeded to tell him what she thought of him. For good measure she added all the ethnic invective she'd learned in college, silently wondering at the meaning of everything she was calling the soldier, who looked more stunned by the moment.

She poked him repeatedly in the chest with her finger, advancing toward him, and he actually fell back a few paces. Then the other soldier, the one she'd spotted before, joined them, and the man pulled himself together.

"Be quiet!" he shouted.

"I won't be quiet!" Jane shouted in return, but the other soldier grabbed her arms and tied her wrists. Incensed, Jane kicked out behind her, catching him on the shin with her boot. He gave a startled cry of pain, then whirled her around and drew his fist back, but at the last moment stayed his blow. Turego probably had given orders that she wasn't to be hurt, at least until he'd gotten the information he wanted from her.

Shaking her tangled hair away from her eyes, Jane glared at her captors. "What do you want? Who are you?"

They ignored her, and pushed her roughly ahead of them. With her arms tied behind her, her balance was off, and she stumbled over a tangled vine. She couldn't catch herself, and pitched forward with a small cry. Instinctively one of the soldiers grabbed for her. Trying to make it look accidental, she flung out one of her legs and tangled it through his, sending him crashing into a bush. She landed with a jolt on a knotted root, which momentarily stunned her and made her ears ring.

He came out of nowhere. One moment he wasn't there; the next he was in the midst of them. Three quick blows with the side of his hand to the first soldier's face and neck had the man crumpling like a broken doll. The soldier who Jane had tripped yelled and tried to swing his rifle around, but Grant lashed out with his boot, catching the man on the chin. There was a sickening thud; the man's head jerked back, and he went limp.

Grant wasn't even breathing hard, but his face was set and coldly furious as he hauled Jane to her feet and roughly turned her around. His knife sliced easily through the bonds around her wrists. "Why didn't you stay where I left you?" he grated. "If I hadn't heard you yelling—"

She didn't want to think about that. "I did stay," she protested. "Until those two almost walked over me. I was trying to hide, and to find you before you ran straight into them!"

He gave her an impatient glance. "I would've handled them." He grabbed her wrist and began dragging her after him. Jane started to defend herself, then sighed. Since he so obviously *had* handled them, what could she say? She concentrated instead on keeping her feet under her and dodging the limbs and thorny vines that swung at her.

"Where are we going?"

"Be quiet."

There was a loud crack, and Grant knocked her to the ground, covering her with his body. Winded, at first Jane thought that the thunder of the approaching storm had startled him; then her heart convulsed in her chest as she realized what the noise had been. Someone was shooting at them! The two soldiers hadn't been the only ones nearby. Her eyes widened to dark pools; they were shooting at Grant, not at her! They would have orders to take her alive. Panic tightened her throat, and she clutched at him.

"Grant! Are you all right?"

"Yeah," he grunted, slipping his right arm around her and crawling with her behind the shelter of a large mahogany tree, dragging her like a predator carrying off its prey. "What happened to the Bren?"

"He knocked it out of my hand...over there." She waved her hand to indicate the general area where she'd lost the gun. Grant glanced around, measuring the shelter available to him and swearing as he decided it was too much of a risk.

"I'm sorry," Jane said, her dark eyes full of guilt.

"Forget it." He unslung the rifle from his shoulder, his motions sure and swift as he handled the weapon. Jane hugged the ground, watching as he darted a quick look around the huge tree trunk. There was a glitter in his amber eyes that made her feel a little in awe of him; at this moment he was the quintessential warrior, superbly trained and toned, coolly assessing the situation and determining what steps to take.

Another shot zinged through the trees, sending bark flying only inches from Grant's face. He jerked back, then swiped at a thin line of blood that trickled down from his cheekbone, where a splinter had caught him.

"Stay low," he ordered, his tone flat and hard. "Crawl on your belly through those bushes right behind us, and keep going no matter what. We've got to get out of here."

She'd gone white at the sight of the blood ribboning down his face, but she didn't say anything. Controlling the shaking of her legs and arms, she got down on her stomach and obeyed, snaking her way into the emergent shrubs. She could feel him right behind her, directing her with his hand on her leg. He was deliberately keeping himself between her and the direction from which the shots had come, and the realization made her heart squeeze painfully.

Thunder rumbled, so close now that the earth shuddered from the shock waves. Grant glanced up. "Come on, rain," he muttered. "Come on."

It began a few minutes later, filtering through the leaves with a dripping sound, then rapidly intensifying to the thunderous deluge that she'd come to expect. They were soaked to the skin immediately, as if they'd been tossed into a waterfall. Grant shoved her ahead of him, heedless now of any noise they made, because the roar of the rain obliterated everything else. They covered about a hundred yards on their hands and knees, then he pulled her upright and brought his mouth close to her ear. "Run!" he yelled, barely making himself heard over the din of the pummeling rain.

Jane didn't know how she could run but she did. Her legs were trembling, she was dizzy and disoriented, but somehow her feet moved as Grant pulled her through the forest at breakneck speed. Her vision was blurred; she could see only a confused jumble of green, and the rain, always the rain. She had no idea where they were going, but trusted Grant's instincts to guide them.

Suddenly they broke free of the jungle's edge, where man had cut back the foliage in an attempt to bring civilization to a small part of the tropical rain forest. Staggering across fields turned into a quagmire by the rain, Jane was held upright only by Grant's unbreakable grip on her wrist. She fell to her knees once and he dragged her for a few feet before he noticed. Without a word he scooped her up and tossed her over his shoulder, carrying her as effortlessly as ever, showing no trace of the exhaustion she felt.

She closed her eyes and hung on, already dizzy and now becoming nauseated as her stomach was jolted by his hard shoulder. Their surroundings had become a nightmare of endless gray water slapping at them, wrapping them in a curtain that obliterated sight and sound. Terror lay in her stomach in a cold, soggy lump, triggered by the sight of the blood on Grant's face. She couldn't bear it if anything happened to him, she simply couldn't....

He lifted her from his shoulder, propping her against something hard and cold. Jane's fingers spread against the support, and dimly she recognized the texture of metal. Then he wrenched open the door of the ancient pickup truck and picked her up to thrust her into the shelter of the cab. With a lithe twist of his body he slid under the wheel, then slammed the door.

"Jane," he bit out, grabbing her shoulder in a tight grip and shaking her. "Are you all right? Are you hit?"

She was sobbing, but her eyes were dry. She stretched out a trembling hand to touch the red streak that ran down his rain-wet face. "You're hurt," she whispered; he couldn't hear her over the thunder of the rain pounding on the metal top of the old truck, but he read her lips and gathered her in his arms, pressing hard, swift kisses to her dripping hair.

"It's just a scratch, honey," he reassured her. "What about you? Are you okay?"

She managed a nod, clinging to him, feeling the incredible warmth of his body despite the soggy condition of his clothes. He held her for a moment, then pulled her arms from around his neck and put her on the other side of the truck. "Sit tight while I get this thing going. We've got to get out of here before the rain stops and everyone comes out."

He bent down and reached under the dash of the truck, pulling some wires loose.

"What are you doing?" Jane asked numbly.

"Hot-wiring this old crate," he replied, and gave her a quick grin. "Pay close attention, since you've been so insistent that I do this. You may want to steal a truck someday."

"You can't see to drive in this," she said, still in that helpless, numb tone of voice, so unlike her usual cheerful matter-of-fact manner. A frown drew his brows together, but he couldn't stop to cradle her in his arms and reassure her that everything was going to be all right. He wasn't too sure of that himself; all hell had broken loose, reminding him how much he disliked being shot at—and now Jane was a target as well. He hated this whole set-up so much that a certain deadly look had come into his eyes, the look that had become legend in the jungles and rice paddies of Southeast Asia.

"I can see well enough to get us out of here."

He put two wires together, and the engine coughed and turned over, but didn't start. Swearing under his breath, he tried it again, and the second time the engine caught. He put the old truck in gear and let up on the clutch. They lurched into motion with the old vehicle groaning and protesting. The rain on the windshield was so heavy that the feeble wipers were almost useless, but Grant seemed to know where he was going.

Looking around, Jane saw a surprisingly large number of buildings through the rain, and several streets seemed to branch away from the one they were on. The village was a prosperous one, with most of the trappings of civilization, and it looked somehow incongruous existing so close to the jungle.

"Where are we going?" she asked.

"South, honey. To Limon, or at least as far as this crate will carry us down the road."

_____ *Chapter Nine*

Limon. The name sounded like heaven, and as she clung to the tattered seat of the old truck, the city seemed just as far away. Her dark eyes were wide and vulnerable as she stared at the streaming windshield, trying to see the road. Grant gave her a quick look, all he could safely spare when driving took so much of his attention. Keeping his voice calm, he said, "Jane, scoot as far into the corner as you can. Get your head away from the back window. Do you understand?"

"Yes." She obeyed, shrinking into the corner. The old truck had a small window in back and smaller windows on each side, leaving deep pockets of protection in the corners. A broken spring dug into the back of her leg, making her shift her weight. The upholstery on this side of the seat was almost nonexistent, consisting mostly of miscellaneous pieces of cloth covering some of the springs. Grant was sitting on a grimy patch of burlap. Looking down, she saw a large hole in the floorboard beside the door.

"This thing has character," she commented, regaining a small portion of her composure.

"Yeah, all of it bad." The truck skewed sideways on a sea of mud, and Grant gave all his attention to steering the thing in a straight line again.

"How can you tell where we're going?"

"I can't. I'm guessing." A devilish grin twisted his lips, a sign of the adrenaline that was racing through his system. It was a physical high, an acute sensitivity brought on by pitting his wits and his skills against the enemy. If it hadn't been for the danger to Jane, he might even have enjoyed this game of cat and mouse. He risked another quick glance at her, relaxing a little as he saw that she was calmer now, gathering herself together and mastering her fear. The fear was still there, but she was in control.

"You'd better be a good guesser," she gasped as the truck lurched sickeningly to the side. "If you drive us off a cliff, I swear I'll never forgive you!"

He grinned again and shifted his weight uncomfortably. He leaned forward over the wheel. "Can you get these packs off? They're in the way. And keep down!"

She slithered across the seat and unbuckled the backpacks, pulling them away from him so he could lean back. How could she have forgotten her pack? Stricken that she'd been so utterly reckless with it, she drew the buckles through the belt loops of her pants and fastened the straps.

He wasn't paying any attention to her now, but was frowning at the dash. He rapped at a gauge with his knuckle. "Damn it!"

Jane groaned. "Don't tell me. We're almost out of gas!"

"I don't know. The damned gauge doesn't work. We could have a full tank, or it could quit on us at any time."

She looked around. The rain wasn't as torrential as it had been, though it was still heavy. The forest pressed closely on both sides of the road, and the village was out of sight behind them. The road wasn't paved, and the truck kept jouncing over the uneven surface, forcing her to cling to the seat to stay in it—but it was a road and the truck was still running along it. Even if it quit that minute, they were still better off than they had been only a short while before. At least they weren't being shot at now. With any luck Turego would think they were still afoot and continue searching close by, at least for a while. Every moment was precious now, putting distance between them and their pursuers.

Half an hour later the rain stopped, and the temperature immediately began to climb. Jane rolled down the window on her side of the truck, searching for any coolness she could find. "Does this thing have a radio?" she asked.

He snorted. "What do you want to listen to, the top forty? No, it doesn't have a radio."

"There's no need to get snippy," she sniffed.

Grant wondered if he'd ever been accused of being "snippy" before. He'd been called a lot of things, but never that; Jane had a unique way of looking at things. If they *had* met up with a jaguar, she probably would have called it a "nice kitty"! The familiar urge rose in him, making him want to either throttle her or make love to her. His somber expression lightened as he considered which would give him the most pleasure.

The truck brushed against a bush that was encroaching on the narrow road. Jane ducked barely in time to avoid being slapped in the face by the branches that sprang through the open window, showering them with the raindrops that had been clinging to the leaves.

"Roll that window up," he ordered, concern making his voice sharp. Jane obeyed and sat back in the corner again. Already she could feel perspiration beading on her face, and she wiped her sleeve across her forehead. Her hand touched her hair, and she pushed the heavy mass away from her face, appalled at the tangled ringlets she found. What she wouldn't give for a bath! A real bath, with hot water and soap and shampoo, not a rinsing in a rocky stream. And clean clothes! She thought of the hairbrush in her pack, but she didn't have the energy to reach for it right now.

Well, there was no sense in wasting her time wishing for something she couldn't have. There were more important issues at hand. "Did you get any food?"

"In my pack."

She grabbed the pack and opened it, pulling out a towel-wrapped bundle of bread and cheese. That was all there was, but she wasn't in the mood to quibble about the limited menu. Food was food. Right now, even field rations would have been good.

Leaning over, she took his knife from his belt and swiftly sliced the bread and cheese. In less than a minute, she'd made two thick cheese sandwiches and returned the knife to its sheath. "Can you hold the sandwich and drive, or do you want me to feed you?"

"I can manage." It was awkward, wrestling with the steering wheel and holding the sandwich at the same time, but she would have to slide closer to him to feed him, and that would expose her head in the back window. The road behind them was still empty, but he wasn't going to take any chances with her welfare.

"I could lie down with my head in your lap and feed you," she suggested softly, and her dark eyes were sleepy and tender.

He jerked slightly, his entire body tensing. "Honey, if you put your head in my lap, I might drive this crate up a tree. You'd better stay where you are."

Was it only yesterday that he'd taken her so completely in that cave? He'd made her his, possessed her and changed her, until she found it difficult to remember what it had been like before she'd known him. The focus of her entire life had shifted, redirected itself onto him.

What she was feeling was plainly revealed in her eyes, in her expressive face. A quick glance at her had him swallowing to relieve an abruptly dry throat, and his hands clenched on the wheel. He wanted her, immediately; he wanted to stop the truck and pull her astride him, then bury himself in her inner heat. The taste and scent of her lingered in his mind, and his body still felt the silk of her skin beneath his. Perhaps he wouldn't be able to get enough of her to satisfy him in the short time they had remaining, but he was going to try, and the trying would probably drive him crazy with pleasure.

They wolfed down the sandwiches, then Jane passed him the canteen. The Perrier was flat, but it was still wet, and he gulped it thirstily. When he gave the canteen back to her, she found herself gulping, too, in an effort to replenish the moisture her body was losing in perspiration. It was so hot in the truck! Somehow, even trekking through the jungle hadn't seemed this hot, though there hadn't been even a hint of breeze beneath the canopy. The metal shell of the truck made her feel canned, like a boiled shrimp. She forced herself to stop drinking before she emptied the canteen, and capped it again.

Ten minutes later the truck began sputtering and coughing; then the engine stopped altogether, and Grant coasted to a stop, as far to one side of the narrow road as he could get. "It lasted almost two hours," he said, opening the door and getting out.

Jane scrambled across the truck and got out on his side, since he'd parked so close to the edge that her door was blocked by a tree. "How far do you think we got?"

"Thirty miles or so." He wound a lock of her hair around his forefinger and smiled down at her. "Feel up to a walk?"

"A nice afternoon stroll? Sure, why not?"

He lowered his head and took a hard kiss from her mouth. Before she could respond he'd drawn away and pushed her off the road and into the shelter of the forest again. He returned to the truck, and she looked back to see him obliterating their footprints; then he leaped easily up the low bank and came to her side. "There's another village down the road a few more miles; I hoped we'd make it so we could buy more gas, but—" He broke off and shrugged at the change of plans. "We'll follow the road and try to get to the village by nightfall, unless they get too close to us. If they do, we'll have to go back into the interior."

"We're not going to the swamp?"

"We can't," he explained gently. "There's too much open ground to cover, now that they know we're in the area."

A bleak expression came and went in her eyes so fast that he wasn't certain he'd seen it. "It's my fault. If I'd just hidden from them, instead of trying to find you..."

"It's done. Don't worry about it. We just have to adjust our plans, and the plan now is to get to Limon as fast as we can, any way we can."

"You're going to steal another truck?"

"I'll do whatever has to be done."

Yes, he would. That knowledge was what made her feel so safe with him; he was infinitely capable, in many different areas. Even wearily following him through the overgrown tangle of greenery made her happy, because she was with him. She didn't let herself think of the fact that they would soon part, that he'd casually kiss her goodbye and walk away, as if she were nothing more than another job finished. She'd deal with that when it happened; she wasn't going to borrow trouble. She had to devote her energies now to getting out of Costa Rica, or at least to some trustworthy authorities, where Grant wouldn't be in danger of being shot while trying to protect her. When she'd seen the blood on his face, some vital part inside of her had frozen knowing that she couldn't survive if anything happened to him. Even though she'd been able to see that he wasn't badly hurt, the realization of his vulnerability had frightened her. As strong as he was, as vital and dangerous, he was a man, and therefore mortal.

They heard only one vehicle on the road, and it was moving toward the village where they'd stolen the truck. The sun edged downward, and the dim light in the forest began to fade. Right before the darkness became total, they came to the edge of a field, and down the road about half a mile they could see the other village spread out. It was really more of a small town than a village; there were bright electric lights, and cars and trucks were parked on the streets. After days spent in the jungle, it looked like a booming metropolis, a cornerstone of civilization.

"We'll stay here until it's completely dark, then go into town," Grant decided, dropping to the ground and stretching out flat on his back. Jane stared at the twinkling lights of the town, torn between a vague uneasiness and an eagerness to take advantage of the comforts a town offered. She wanted a bath, and to sleep in a bed, but after so much time spent alone with Grant, the thought of once more being surrounded by other people made her wary. She couldn't relax the way Grant did, so she remained on her feet, her face tense and her hands clenched.

"You might as well rest, instead of twitching like a nervous cat."

"I am nervous. Are we going on to Limon tonight?"

"Depends on what we find when we get into town."

She glared down at him in sudden irritation. He was a master at avoiding straight answers. It was so dark that she couldn't make out his features; he was only a black form on the ground, but she was certain that he was aware of her anger, and that the corner of his mouth was turning up in that almost-smile of his. She was too tired to find much humor in it, though, so she walked away from him a few paces and sat down, leaning her head on her drawn-up knees and closing her eyes.

There wasn't even a whisper of sound to warn her, but suddenly he was behind her, his strong hands massaging the tight muscles of her shoulders and neck. "Would you like to sleep in a real bed tonight?" he murmured in her ear.

"And take a real bath. And eat real food. Yes, I'd like that," she said, unaware of how wistful her tone was.

"A town this size probably has a hotel of some sort, but we can't risk going there, not looking the way we do. I'll try to find someone who takes in boarders and won't ask many questions."

Taking her hand, he pulled her to her feet and draped his arm over her shoulder. "Let's go, then. A bed sounds good to me, too."

Walking across the field, ever closer to the beckoning lights, Jane became more conscious of how she looked, and she pushed her fingers through her tangled hair. She knew that her clothes were filthy, and that her face was probably dirty. "No one is going to let us in," she predicted.

"Money has a way of making people look past the dirt."

She glanced up at him in surprise. "You have money?"

"A good Boy Scout is always prepared."

In the distance, the peculiarly mournful wail of a train whistle floated into the air, reinforcing the fact that they'd left the isolation of the rain forest behind. Oddly, Jane felt almost nakedly vulnerable, and she moved closer to Grant. "This is stupid, but I'm scared," she whispered.

"It's just a mild form of culture shock. You'll feel better when you're in a tub of hot water."

They kept to the fringes of the town, in the shadows. It appeared to be a bustling little community. Some of the streets were paved, and the main thoroughfare was lined with prosperous looking stores. People walked and laughed and chatted, and from somewhere came the unmistakable sound of a jukebox, another element of civilization that jarred her nerves. The universally-known red and white sign of a soft drink swung over a sidewalk, making her feel as if she had emerged from a time warp. This was definitely culture shock.

Keeping her pushed behind him, Grant stopped and carried on a quiet conversation with a rheumy-eyed old man who seemed reluctant to be bothered. Finally Grant thanked him and walked away, still keeping a firm grip on Jane's arm. "His sister-in-law's first cousin's daughter takes in boarders," he told her, and Jane swallowed a gasp of laughter.

"Do you know where his sister-in-law's first cousin's daughter lives?"

"Sure. Down this street, turn left, then right, follow the alley until it dead ends in a courtyard."

"If you say so."

Of course he found the boarding house easily, and Jane leaned against the white adobe wall that surrounded the courtyard while he rang the bell and talked with the small, plump woman who answered the door. She seemed reluctant to admit such exceedingly grimy guests. Grant passed her a wad of bills and explained that he and his wife had been doing field research for an American pharmaceutical company, but their vehicle had broken down, forcing them to walk in from their camp. Whether it was the money or the tale of woe that swayed Señora Trejos, her face softened and she opened the grill, letting them in.

Seeing the tautness of Jane's face, Señora Trejos softened even more. "Poor lamb," she cooed, ignoring Jane's dirty state and putting her plump arm around the young woman's sagging shoulders. "You are exhausted, no? I have a nice cool bedroom with a soft bed for you and the *señor*, and I will bring you something good to eat. You will feel better then?"

Jane couldn't help smiling into the woman's kind dark eyes. "That sounds wonderful, all of it," she managed in her less-than-fluent Spanish. "But most of all, I need a bath. Would that be possible?"

"But of course!" Señora Trejos beamed with pride. "Santos and I, we have the water heated by the tank. He brings the fuel for the heating from San Jose."

Chatting away, she led them inside her comfortable house, with cool tiles on the floors and soothing white walls. "The upstairs rooms are taken," she said apologetically. "I have only the one room below the stairs, but it is nice and cool, and closer to the conveniences."

"Thank you, Señora Trejos," Grant said. "The downstairs room will more than make us happy."

It did. It was small, with bare floors and plain white walls, and there was no furniture except for the wood framed double bed, a cane chair by the lone, gracefully arched window, and a small wooden washstand that held a pitcher and bowl. Jane gazed at the bed with undisguised longing. It looked so cool and comfortable, with fat fluffy pillows.

Grant thanked Señora Trejos again; then she went off to prepare them something to eat, and they were alone. Jane glanced at him and found that he was watching her steadily. Somehow, being alone with him in a bedroom felt different from being alone with him in a jungle. There, their seclusion had been accepted. Here there was the sensation of closing out the world, of coming together in greater intimacy.

"You take the first turn at the bath," he finally said. "Just don't go to sleep in the tub."

Jane didn't waste time protesting. She searched the lower floor, following her nose, until she found Señora Trejos happily puttering about the kitchen. "Pardon, *señora*," she said haltingly. She didn't know all the words needed to explain her shortage of a robe or anything to wear after taking a bath, but Señora Trejos caught on immediately. A few minutes later Jane had a plain white nightgown thrust into her hands and was shown to the *señora's* prized bathroom.

The bathroom had cracked tile and a deep, old-fashioned tub with curved claw feet, but when she turned on the water it gushed out in a hot flood. Sighing in satisfaction, Jane quickly unbuckled the backpack from her belt and set it out of the way, then stripped off her clothes and got into the tub, unwilling to wait until it was full. The heat seeped into her sore muscles and a moan of pleasure escaped her. She would have liked to soak in the tub for hours, but Grant was waiting for his own bath, so she didn't allow herself to lean against the high back and relax. Quickly she washed away the layers of grime, unable to believe how good it felt to be clean again. Then she washed her hair, sighing in relief as the strands came unmatted and once again slipped through her fingers like wet silk.

Hurrying, she wrapped her hair in a towel and got her safety razor out of the backpack. Sitting on the edge of the tub, she shaved her legs and under her arms, then smoothed moisturizer into her skin. A smile kept tugging at her mouth as she thought of spending the night in Grant's arms again. She was going to be clean and sweet-smelling, her skin silky. After all, it wasn't going to be easy to win a warrior's love, and she was going to use all the weapons at her disposal.

She brushed her teeth, then combed out her wet hair and pulled the white nightgown over her head, hoping that she wouldn't meet any of Señora Trejos's other boarders on the short trip back to her room. The *señora* had told her to leave her clothes on the bathroom floor, that she would see that they were washed, so Jane got the backpack and hurried down the hall to the room where Grant waited.

He had closed the shutters over the arched window and was leaning with one shoulder propped against the wall, declining to sit in the single chair. He looked up at her entrance, and the inky pupils at the center of his golden irises expanded until there was only a thin ring of amber circling the black. Jane paused, dropping the pack beside the bed, feeling abruptly shy, despite the tempestuous lovemaking she'd shared with this man. He looked at her as if he were about to pounce on her, and she found herself crossing her arms over her breasts, aware that her nakedness was fully apparent beneath the thin nightgown. She cleared her throat, her mouth suddenly dry. "The bathroom is all yours."

He straightened slowly, not taking his eyes from her. "Why don't you go on to bed?"

"I'd rather wait for you," she whispered.

"I'll wake you up when I come to bed." The intensity of his gaze promised her that she wasn't going to sleep alone that night.

"My hair... I have to dry my hair."

He nodded and left the room, and Jane sat down on the chair weakly, shaking inside from the way he'd looked at her. Bending over, she rubbed her hair briskly, then began to brush it dry. It was so thick and long that it was still damp when Grant came back into the room and stood silently, watching her as she sat bent over, her slender arms curving as she drew the brush through the dark mass. She sat up, tossing her head to fling her hair back over her shoulders, and for a moment they simply stared at each other.

They had made love before, but now sensual awareness was zinging between them like an electric current. Without even touching each other, they were both becoming aroused, their heartbeats quickening, their skin growing hot.

He had shaved, probably using the razor she'd left in the bathroom. It was the first time she'd seen him without several days' growth of beard, and the clean, hard lines of his scarred face made her breath catch. He was naked except for a towel knotted around his lean waist, and as she watched he pulled the towel free and dropped it to the floor. Reaching behind him, he locked the door. "Are you ready for bed?"

"My hair... isn't quite dry."

"Leave it," he said, coming toward her.

The brush dropped to the floor as he caught her hand and pulled her up. Instantly she was in his arms, lifted off her feet by his fierce embrace. Their mouths met hungrily, and her fingers tangled in his water-darkened hair, holding him to her. His mouth was fresh and hot, his tongue thrusting deep into her mouth in a kiss that made her whimper as currents of desire sizzled her nerves.

He was hard against her, his manhood pushing against her softness, his hands kneading her hips and rubbing her over him. Jane pulled her mouth free, gasping, and dropped her head to his broad shoulder. She couldn't contain the wild pleasure he was evoking, as if her body were out of control, already reaching for the peak that his arousal promised. She'd been quite content to live celibately for years, the passion in her unawakened until she met Grant. He was as wild and beautiful and free as the majestic jaguars that melted silently through the tangled green jungle. The wildness in him demanded a response, and she was helpless to restrain it. He didn't have to patiently build her passion; one kiss and she trembled against him, empty and aching and ready for him, her breasts swollen and painful, her body growing wet and soft.

"Let's get this thing off you," he whispered, pulling at the nightgown and easing it up. Reluctantly she released him, and he pulled the gown over her head, dropping it over the chair; then she was back in his arms, and he carried her to the bed.

Their naked bodies moved together, and there was no more waiting. He surged into her, and she cried out a little from the delicious shock of it. Catching the small cry with his mouth, he lifted her legs and placed them around his waist, then began to move more deeply into her.

It was like the night before. She gave no thought to anything but the man with shoulders so broad that they blocked out the light. The bed was soft beneath them, the sheets cool and smooth, and the rhythmic creak of the springs in time with his movements was accompanied by the singing of insects outside the window. Time meant nothing. There was only his mouth on hers, his hands on her body, the slow thrusts that went deep inside her and touched off a wildfire of sensation, until they strained together in frenzied pleasure and the sheets were no longer cool, but warm from their damp, heated flesh.

Then it was quiet again, and he lay heavily on her, drawing in deep breaths while her hands moved over his powerful back. Her lips trembled with the words of love that she wanted to give him, but she held them back. All her instincts told her that he wouldn't want to know, and she didn't want to do anything to spoil their time together.

Perhaps he had given her something anyway, if not his love, something at least as infinitely precious. As her sensitive fingertips explored the deep valley of his spine, she wondered if he had given her his baby. A tremor of pleasure rippled down her body, and she held him closer, hoping that her body would be receptive to his seed.

He stirred, reaching out to turn off the lamp, and in the darkness he moved to lie beside her. She curled against his side, her head on his shoulder, and after a moment he gave a low chuckle.

"Why don't you just save time and get on top of me now?" he suggested, scooping her up and settling her on his chest.

Jane gave a sigh of deep satisfaction, stretching out on him and looping her arm around his neck. With her face pressed against his throat she was comfortable and safe, as if she'd found a sheltering harbor. "I love you," she said silently, moving her lips without sound against his throat.

They woke with the bright early morning sun coming through the slats of the shutters. Leaving Jane stretching and grousing on the bed, Grant got up and opened the shutters, letting the rosy light pour into the room. When he turned, he saw the way the light glowed on her warm-toned skin, turning her nipples to apricot, catching the glossy lights in her dark hair. Her face was flushed, her eyes still heavy with sleep.

Suddenly his body throbbed, and he couldn't bear to be separated from her by even the width of the small room. He went back to the bed and pulled her under him, then watched the way her face changed as he slowly eased into her, watched the radiance that lit her. Something swelled in his chest, making it difficult for him to breathe, and as he lost himself in the soft depths of her body he had one last, glaringly clear thought: she'd gotten too close to him, and letting her go was going to be the hardest thing he'd ever done.

He dressed, pulling on the freshly washed clothes that one of Señora Trejos's daughters had brought, along with a tray of fruit, bread and cheese. Jane flushed wildly when she realized that Señora Trejos must have brought a tray to them the night before, then discreetly left when she heard the sounds they had been making. A quick glance at Grant told her that he'd had the same thought, because the corner of his mouth was twitching in amusement.

The *señora* had also sent along a soft white off-the-shoulder blouse, and Jane donned it with pleasure, more than glad to discard her tattered black shirt. After selecting a piece of orange from the tray, she bit into the juicy fruit as she watched him pull his dark green undershirt over his head.

"You're going to be pretty noticeable in those camouflage fatigues," she said, poking a bit of the orange into his mouth.

"I know." He quickly kissed her orange-sticky lips. "Put the shirt in your pack and be ready to go when I get back."

"Get back? Where are you going?"

"I'm going to try to get some sort of transport. It won't be as easy this time."

"We could take the train," she pointed out.

"The rifle would be a mite conspicuous, honey."

"Why can't I go with you?"

"Because you're safer here."

"The last time you left me, I got into trouble," she felt obliged to remind him.

He didn't appreciate the reminder. He scowled down at her as he reached for a spear of melon. "If you'll just keep your little butt where I tell you to, you'll be fine."

"I'm fine when I'm with you."

"Damn it, stop arguing with me!"

"I'm not arguing. *I'm* pointing out some obvious facts! *You're* the one who's arguing!"

His eyes were yellow fire. He bent down until they were almost nose to nose, his control under severe stress. His teeth were clenched together as he said, evenly spacing the words out, "If you make it home without having the worst spanking of your life, it'll be a miracle."

"I've never had a spanking in my life," she protested.

"It shows!"

She flounced into the chair and pouted. Grant's hands clenched; then he reached for her and pulled her out of the chair, hauling her up to him for a deep, hard kiss. "Be good, for a change," he said, aware that he was almost pleading with her. "I'll be back in an hour—"

"Or so!" she finished in unison with him. "All right, I'll wait! But I don't like it!"

He left before he completely lost his temper with her, and Jane munched on more of the fruit, terribly grateful for something fresh to eat. Deciding that he'd meant only for her to stay in the house, not in the room, she first got everything ready for them to leave, as he'd instructed, then sought out the *señora* and had a pleasant chat with her. The woman was bustling around the kitchen preparing food for her boarders, while two of her daughters diligently cleaned the house and did a mountain of laundry. Jane had her arms deep in a bowl of dough when Grant returned.

He'd gone first to their room, and when he found her in the kitchen there was a flicker of intense relief in his eyes before he masked it. Jane sensed his presence and looked up, smiling. "Is everything arranged?"

"Yes. Are you ready?"

"Just as soon as I wash my hands."

She hugged the *señora* and thanked her, while Grant leaned in the doorway and watched her. Did she charm everyone so effortlessly? The *señora* was beaming at her, wishing her a safe journey and inviting her back. There would always be a room for the lovely young *señora* and her husband in the Trejos house!

They collected their packs, and Grant slung the rifle over his shoulder. They risked attracting attention because of it, but he didn't dare leave it behind. With any luck they would be on a plane out of Costa Rica by nightfall, but until they were actually on their way he couldn't let his guard down. The close call the day before had been proof of that. Turego wasn't giving up; he stood to lose too much.

Out in the alley, Jane glanced up at him. "What exactly did you arrange?"

"A farmer is going into Limon, and he's giving us a ride."

After the adventure of the last several days that seemed almost boringly tame, but Jane was happy to be bored. A nice, quiet ride, that was the ticket. How good it would be not to feel hunted!

As they neared the end of the alley, a man stepped suddenly in front of them. Grant reacted immediately, shoving Jane aside, but before he could swing the rifle around there was a pistol in his face, and several more men stepped into the alley, all of them armed, all of them with their weapons pointed at Grant. Jane stopped breathing, her eyes wide with horror. Then she recognized the man in the middle, and her heart stopped. Was Grant going to die now, because of her?

She couldn't bear it. She had to do something, anything.

"Manuel!" she cried, filling her voice with joy. She ran to him and flung her arms around him. "I'm so glad you found me!"

_____ *Chapter Ten*

It was a nightmare. Grant hadn't taken his narrowed gaze off her, and the hatred that glittered in his eyes made her stomach knot, but there was no way she could reassure him. She was acting for all she was worth, clinging to Turego and babbling her head off, telling him how frightened she'd been and how this madman had knocked her out and stolen her away from the plantation, all the while clinging to Turego's shirt as if she couldn't bear to release him. She had no clear idea of what she was going to do, only that somehow she had to stay unfettered so she could help Grant, and to do that she had to win Turego's trust and soothe his wounded vanity.

The entire situation was balanced on a knife edge; things could go in either direction. Wariness was in Turego's dark eyes, as well as a certain amount of cruel satisfaction in having cornered his prey. He wanted to make her suffer for having eluded him, she knew, yet for the moment she was safe from any real harm, because he still wanted the microfilm. It was Grant whose life was threatened, and it would take only a word from Turego for those men to kill him where he stood. Grant had to know it, yet there wasn't even a flicker of fear in his expression, only the cold, consuming hatred of his glare as he stared at Jane. Perhaps it was that, in the end, that eased Turego's suspicions somewhat. He would never relax his guard around her again, but Jane could only worry about one thing at a time. Right now, she had to protect Grant in any way she could.

Turego's arm stole around her waist, pulling her tightly against him. He bent his head and kissed her, a deeply intimate kiss that Jane had to steel herself not to resist in any way, even though she shuddered at having to endure the touch and taste of him. She knew what he was doing; he was illustrating his power, his control, and using her as a weapon against Grant. When he lifted his head, a cruel little smile was on his handsome mouth.

"I have you now, *chiquita*," he reassured her in a smooth tone. "You are quite safe. This...madman, as you called him, will not bother you again, I promise. I am impressed," he continued mockingly, inclining his head toward Grant. "I have heard of you, *señor*. Surely there can be only one with the yellow eyes and scarred face, who melts through jungles like a silent cat. You are a legend, but it was thought that you were dead. It has been a long time since anything was heard of you."

Grant was silent, his attention now on Turego, ignoring Jane as if she no longer existed. Not a muscle moved; it was as if he'd turned to stone. He wasn't even breathing. His utter stillness was unnerving, yet there was also the impression of great strength under control, a wild animal waiting for the perfect moment to pounce. Even though he was only one against many, the others were like jackals surrounding a mighty tiger; the men who held their weapons trained on him were visibly nervous.

"Perhaps it would be interesting to know who now pays you for your services. And there are others who would like very much to have an opportunity to question you, yes? Tie him, and put him in the truck," Turego ordered, still keeping his arm around Jane. She forced herself not to watch as Grant was roughly bound and dragged over to a two ton military-type truck, with a canvas top stretched over the back. Instead she gave Turego her most dazzling smile and leaned her head on his shoulder.

"I've been so frightened," she whispered.

"Of course you have, *chiquita*. Is that why you resisted my men when they found you in the forest yesterday?"

She might have known he was too sharp to simply believe her! She let her eyes widen incredulously. "Those were *your* men? Well, why didn't they say so? They were shoving me around, and I was afraid they wanted to... to attack me. I had managed to slip away from that crazy man; I'd have made it, too, if it hadn't been for all the noise your men made! They led him right to me!" Her voice quivered with indignation.

"It is over; I will take care of you now." He led her to the truck and assisted her into the cab, then climbed in beside her and gave terse instructions to the driver.

That was exactly what she was afraid of, being taken care of by Turego, but for the moment she had to play up to him and somehow convince him that she was totally innocent of her escape from under the noses of his guards. He hadn't gotten where he was by being a gullible idiot; though she'd successfully fooled him the first time, the second time would be much more difficult.

"Where are we going?" she asked innocently, leaning against him. "Back to the plantation? Did you bring any of my clothes with you? *He* brought me this blouse this morning," she said, plucking at the soft white fabric, "but I'd really like to have my own clothes."

"I have been so worried about you that I did not think of your clothes, I confess," Turego lied smoothly. His hard arm was around her shoulders, and Jane smiled up at him. He was unnaturally handsome, with perfect features that would have done better on a statue than a man, though perhaps Turego wasn't quite human. He didn't show his age; he looked to be in his twenties, though Jane knew that he was in his early forties. Emotion hadn't changed his face; he had no wrinkles, no attractive crinkles at the corners of his eyes, no signs that time or life had touched him. His only weakness was his vanity; he knew he could force himself on Jane at any time, but he wanted to seduce her into giving herself willingly to him. She would be another feather in his cap; then, once he had the microfilm, he could dispose of her without regret.

She had only the microfilm to protect her, and only herself to protect Grant. Her mind raced, trying to think of some way she could free him from his bonds, get some sort of weapon to him. All he needed was a small advantage.

"Who *is* he? You seem to know him."

"He hasn't introduced himself? But you have spent several days alone with him, my heart. Surely you know his name."

Again she had to make a split second decision. Was Grant's real name commonly known? Was Grant his real name, anyway? She couldn't take the chance. "He told me that his name is Joe Tyson. Isn't that his real name?" she asked in an incredulous voice, sitting up to turn the full force of her brown eyes on him, blinking as if in astonishment.

Oddly, Turego hesitated. "That may be what he calls himself now. If he is who I think he is, he was once known as the Tiger."

He was uneasy! Grant was tied, and there were ten guns on him, but still Turego was made uneasy by his presence! Did that slight hesitation mean that Turego wasn't certain of Grant's real name and didn't want to reveal his lack of knowledge—or was the uncertainty of a greater scope?

Was he not entirely certain that Grant was the Tiger? Turego wouldn't want to make himself look foolish by claiming to have captured the Tiger, only to have his prisoner turn out to be someone much less interesting.

Tiger. She could see how he had gained the name, and the reputation. With his amber eyes and deadly grace, the comparison had been inevitable. But he was a man, too, and she'd slept in his arms. He'd held her during the long hours of darkness, keeping the night demons away from her, and he'd shown her a part of herself that she hadn't known existed. Because of Grant, she felt like a whole person, capable of love and passion, a warm, giving woman. Though she could see what he had been, the way she saw him now was colored by love. He was a man, not a supernatural creature who melted through the dark, tangled jungles of the world. He could bleed, and hurt. He could laugh, that deep, rusty laugh that caught at her heart. After Grant, she felt contaminated just by sitting next to Turego.

She gave a tinkling laugh. "That sounds so cloak-and-daggerish! Do you mean he's a spy?"

"No, of course not. Nothing so romantic. He is really just a mercenary, hiring himself out to anyone for any sort of dirty job."

"Like kidnapping me? Why would he do that? I mean, no one is going to pay any ransom for me! My father doesn't even speak to me, and I certainly don't have any money of my own!"

"Perhaps something else was wanted from you," he suggested.

"But I don't have anything!" She managed to fill her face and voice with bewilderment, and Turego smiled down at her.

"Perhaps you have it and are not aware of it."

"What? Do you know?"

"In time, love, we shall find out."

"No one tells me anything!" she wailed, and lapsed into a pout. She allowed herself to hold the pout for about thirty seconds, then roused to demand of him again, like an impatient child, "Where are we going?"

"Just down this street, love."

They were on the very fringes of the town, and a dilapidated tin warehouse sat at the end of the street. It was in sad shape, its walls sagging, the tin roof curled up in several places, sections of it missing altogether in others. A scarred blue door hung crookedly on its hinges. The warehouse was their destination, and when the truck stopped beside the blue door and Turego helped Jane from the cab, she saw why. There were few people about, and those who were in the vicinity quickly turned their eyes away and scurried off.

Grant was hauled out of the back of the truck and shoved toward the door; he stumbled and barely caught his balance before he would have crashed headlong against the building. Someone chuckled, and when Grant straightened to turn his unnerving stare on his captors, Jane saw that a thin trickle of blood had dried at the corner of his mouth. His lip was split and puffy. Her heart lurched, and her breath caught. Someone had hit him while he had his hands tied behind his back! Right behind her first sick reaction came fury, raw and powerful, surging through her like a tidal wave. She shook with the effort it took to disguise it before she turned to Turego again.

"What are we going to do here?"

"I just want to ask a few questions of our friend. Nothing important."

She was firmly escorted into the building, and she gasped as the heat hit her in the face like a blow. The tin building was a furnace, heating the air until it was almost impossible to breathe. Perspiration immediately beaded on her skin, and she felt dizzy, unable to drag in enough oxygen to satisfy her need.

Evidently Turego had been using the warehouse as a sort of base, because there was equipment scattered around. Leaving Grant under guard, Turego led Jane to the back of the building, where several small rooms connected with each other, probably the former offices. It was just as hot there, but a small window was opened and let in a measure of fresh air. The room he took her to was filthy, piled with musty smelling papers and netted with cobwebs. An old wooden desk, missing a leg, listed drunkenly to one side, and there was the unmistakable stench of rodents. Jane wrinkled her nose fastidiously. "Ugh!" she said in completely honest disgust.

"I apologize for the room," Turego said smoothly, bestowing one of his toothpaste-ad smiles on her. "Hopefully, we won't be here long. Alfonso will stay with you while I question our friend about his activities, and who hired him to abduct you."

What he meant was that she was also under guard. Jane didn't protest, not wanting to arouse his suspicions even more, but her skin crawled. She was very much afraid of the form his "questioning" would take. She had to think of something fast! But nothing came to mind, and Turego tilted her chin up to kiss her again. "I won't be long," he murmured. "Alfonso, watch her carefully. I would be very upset if someone stole her from me again."

Jane thought she recognized Alfonso as one of the guards who had been at the plantation. When Turego had gone, closing the door behind him, Jane gave Alfonso a slow glance from under lowered lashes and essayed a tentative smile. He was fairly young and good-looking. He had probably been warned against her, but still he couldn't help responding to her smile.

"You were a guard at the plantation?" she asked in Spanish.

He gave a reluctant nod.

"I thought I recognized you. I never forget a good-looking man," she said with more enthusiasm than precision, her pronunciation mangled just enough to bring a hint of amusement to Alfonso's face. She wondered if he knew what Turego was up to, or if he had been told some fabrication about protecting her.

Whatever he had been told, he wasn't inclined toward conversation. Jane poked around the room, looking for anything to use as a weapon, but trying not to be obvious about it. She kept straining her ears for any sound from the warehouse, her nerves jumping. What was Turego doing? If he harmed Grant...

How long had it been? Five minutes? Ten? Or less than that? She had no idea, but suddenly she couldn't stand it any longer, and she went to the door. Alfonso stretched his arm in front of her, barring her way.

"I want to see Turego," she said impatiently. "It's too hot to wait in here."

"You must stay here."

"Well, I won't! Don't be such a stuffed shirt, Alfonso; he won't mind. You can come with me, if you can't let me out of your sight."

She ducked under his arm and had the door open before he could stop her. With a muffled oath he came after her, but Jane darted through the door and the connecting offices. Just as she entered the main warehouse she heard the sickening thud of a fist against flesh, and the blood drained from her face.

Two men held Grant between them, holding him up by his bound arms, while another stood before him, rubbing his fist. Turego stood to the side, a small, inhuman smile on his lips. Grant's head sagged forward on his chest, and drops of blood spotted the floor at his feet.

"This silence will gain you nothing but more pain, my friend," Turego said softly. "Tell me who hired you. That is all I want to know, for now."

Grant said nothing, and one of the men holding him grabbed a fistful of hair, jerking his head up. Just before Alfonso took her arm, Jane saw Grant's face, and she jerked free, driven by a wild strength.

"Turego!" she cried shrilly, drawing everyone's attention to her. Turego's brows snapped together over his nose.

"What are you doing here? Alfonso, take her back!"

"No!" she yelled, pushing Alfonso away. "It's too hot back there, and I won't stay! Really, this is too much! I've had a miserable time in that jungle, and I thought when you rescued me that I'd be comfortable again, but no, you drag me to this miserable dump and leave me in that grungy little room. I insist that you take me to a hotel!"

"Jane, Jane, you don't understand these things," Turego said, coming up to her and taking her arm. "Just a few moments more and he will tell me what I want to know. Aren't you interested in knowing who hired him?" He turned her away, leading her back to the offices again. "Please be patient, love."

Jane subsided, letting herself be led docilely away. She risked a quick glance back at Grant and his captors, and saw that they were waiting for Turego's return before resuming the beating. He was sagging limply in their grasp, unable even to stand erect.

"You are to stay here," Turego said sternly when they reached the office again. "Promise me, yes?"

"I promise," Jane said, turning toward him with a smile on her face; he never saw the blow coming. She caught him under the nose with the bridge of her hand, snapping his head back and making blood spurt. Before he could yell with pain or surprise, she slammed her elbow into his solar plexus and he doubled over with an agonized grunt. As if in a well-choreographed ballet, she brought her knee up under his unprotected chin, and Turego collapsed like a stuffed doll. Jane cast a quick thought of thanks to her father for insisting that she take all of those self-defense classes, then bent down and quickly jerked the pistol from Turego's holster.

Just as she started through the doorway again, a shot reverberated through the tin building, and she froze in horror. "No," she moaned, then launched herself toward the sound.

When Jane had hurled herself into Turego's arms, Grant had been seized by a fury so consuming that a mist of red had fallen over his vision, but he'd been trained to control himself, and that control had held, even though he had been on the edge of madness. Then the mist had cleared, and cold contempt had taken its place. Hell, what had he expected? Jane was a survivor, adept at keeping her feet. First she had charmed Turego, then Grant had stolen her from Turego and she'd charmed him as effortlessly as she had put Turego under her spell. Now Turego was back, and since he had the upper hand, it was a case of So long, Sullivan. He even felt a sort of bitter admiration for the way she had so quickly and accurately summed up the situation, then known exactly the tone to set to begin bringing Turego back to heel.

Still, the sense of betrayal was staggering, and nothing would have pleased him at that moment as much as to get his hands on her. Damn her for being a lying, treacherous little bitch! He should have known, should have suspected that her patented look of wide-eyed innocence was nothing but a well-rehearsed act.

The old instincts, only partially shelved, suddenly returned in full force. Forget about the bitch. He had to look out for himself first, then see to her. She was curling in Turego's arms like a cat, while Grant knew that his own future was nonexistent unless he did some fast thinking.

Part of the thinking was done for him when Turego put two and two together and came up with an accurate guess about Grant's identity. A year had been far too short a time for people in the business to even begin forgetting him. After he'd disappeared, his absence had probably made his reputation grow to legendary proportions. Well, let Turego think that he was after the missing microfilm, too; Grant felt no compunction about using Jane in any way he could. She'd not only used him, she'd had him dancing to her tune like a puppet on a fancy little string. If he hadn't agreed to bring her out of Costa Rica, he would have wished the joy of her on Turego, and gotten himself out any way he could. But he'd taken the job, so he had to finish it—if he came out of this alive. When he got his hands on her again she'd find that there would be no more kid glove treatment.

Turego was curious. With his hands tied behind his back, supported between two of the hired goons, Grant found out just how curious.

"Who hired you? Or are you an independent now?"

"Naw, I'm still a Protestant," Grant said, smiling smoothly. At a nod from Turego, a fist crashed into his face, splitting his lip and filling his mouth with blood. The next blow was into his midsection, and he'd have jacknifed if it hadn't been for the cruel support of his twisted arms.

"Really, I don't have the time for this," Turego murmured. "You are the one known as the Tiger; you aren't a man who works for nothing."

"Sure I am; I'm a walking charity."

The fist landed on his cheekbone, snapping his head back. This guy was a real boxer; he placed his blows with precision. The face a couple of times, then the ribs and kidneys. Pain sliced through Grant until his stomach heaved. He gasped, his vision blurred even though his mind was still clear, and he deliberately let all his weight fall on his two supporters, his knees buckling.

Then he heard Jane's voice, petulant and demanding, as he'd never heard it before, followed by Turego's smooth reassurances. The men's attention wasn't on him; he sensed its absence, like a wild animal acutely sensitive to every nuance. He sagged even more, deliberately putting stress on the bonds around his wrists, and fierce satisfaction welled in him as he felt them slip on his right hand.

He had powerful hands, hands that could destroy. He used that power against the cord that bound him, extending his hand to the fullest and stretching the cord, then relaxing and letting the cord slip even lower. Twice he did that, and the cord dropped around his fingers in loose coils.

Looking about through slitted eyes, he saw that no one was paying much attention to him, not even the boxer, who was absently rubbing his knuckles and waiting for Turego to return from wherever he'd gone. Jane was nowhere in sight, either. Now was the time.

The two men holding him were off guard; he threw them away from him like discarded toys. For a split second everyone was disconcerted, and that split second was all he needed. He grabbed a rifle and kicked its butt up under the chin of the soldier he'd taken it from, sending him staggering backward. He whirled, lashing out with his feet and the stock of the rifle. The soldiers really didn't have much of a chance; they didn't have a fraction of the training he'd had, or the years of experience. They didn't know how to react to an attacker who struck and whirled away before anyone could move. Only one managed to get his rifle up, and he fired wildly, the bullet zinging far over Grant's head. That soldier was the last one standing; Grant took him out with almost contemptuous ease. Then he hesitated only the barest moment as he waited for movement from any of them, but there was none. His gaze moved to the door at the far end of the warehouse, and a cold, twisted smile touched his bruised and bloody lips. He went after Jane.

She'd never known such terror; even her fear of the dark was nothing compared to the way she felt now. She couldn't move fast enough; her feet felt as if they were slogging through syrup. Oh, God, what if they'd killed him? The thought was too horrible to be borne, yet it swelled in her chest until she couldn't breathe. No, she thought, no, no, *no*!

She burst through the door, the pistol in her hand, half-crazed with fear and ready to fight for her man, for her very life. She saw a confused scene of sprawled men and her mind reeled, unable to comprehend why so many were lying there. Hadn't there been only one shot?

Then an arm snaked around her neck, jerking her back and locking under her chin. Another arm reached out, and long fingers clamped around the hand that held the pistol, removing it from her grip.

"Funny thing, sweetheart, but I feel safer when you're unarmed," a low voice hissed in her ear.

At the sound of that voice, Jane's eyes closed, and two tears squeezed out from under the lids. "Grant," she whispered.

"Afraid so. You can tell me how glad you are to see me later; right now we're moving."

He released his arm lock about her neck, but when she tried to turn to face him, he caught her right arm and pulled it up behind her back, not so high that she was in pain, but high enough that she would be if he moved it even a fraction of an inch higher. "Move!" he barked, thrusting her forward, and Jane stumbled under the force of the motion, wrenching her arm and emitting an involuntary cry.

"You're hurting me," she whimpered, still dazed and trying to understand. "Grant, wait!"

"Cut the crap," he advised, kicking open the door and shoving her out into the searing white sunlight. The transport truck was sitting there, and he didn't hesitate. "Get in. We're going for a ride."

He opened the door and half-lifted, half-threw Jane into the truck, sending her sprawling on the seat. She cried out, her soft cry knifing through him, but he told himself not to be a fool; she didn't need anyone to look after her. Like a cat, she always landed on her feet.

Jane scrambled to a sitting position, her dark eyes full of tears as she stared at his battered, bloody face in both pain and horror. She wanted to reassure him, tell him that it had all been an act, a desperate gamble to save both their lives, but he didn't seem inclined to listen. Surely he wouldn't so easily forget everything they'd shared, everything they'd been to each other! Still, she couldn't give up. She'd lifted her hand to reach out for him when a movement in the door beyond them caught her eye, and she screamed a warning.

"Grant!"

He whirled, and as he did Turego lifted the rifle he held and fired. The explosive crack of sound split the air, but still Jane heard, felt, sensed the grunt of pain that Grant gave as he dropped to one knee and lifted the pistol. Turego lunged to one side, looking for cover, but the pistol spat fire, and a small red flower bloomed high on Turego's right shoulder, sending him tumbling back through the door.

Jane heard someone screaming, but the sound was high and far away. She lunged through the open door of the truck, falling to her hands and knees on the hot, rocky ground. Grant was on his knees, leaning against the running board of the truck, his right hand clamped over his upper left arm, and bright red blood was dripping through his fingers. He looked up at her, his golden eyes bright and burning with the fire of battle, fierce even in his swollen and discolored face.

She went a little mad then. She grabbed him by his undershirt and hauled him to his feet, using a strength she'd had no idea she possessed. "Get in the truck!" she screamed, pushing him in the door. "Damn it, get in the truck! Are you trying to get yourself killed?"

He winced as the side of the seat smashed into his bruised ribs; Jane was shoving at him and screaming like a banshee, tears streaming down her face. "Would you shut up!" he yelled, painfully pulling himself inside.

"Don't you tell me to shut up!" she screamed, pushing him until he moved over. She slapped the tears from her cheeks and climbed into the truck herself. "Get out of the way so I can get this thing started! Are there any keys? Where are the keys? Oh, damn!" She dove headfirst under the steering wheel, feeling under the dash and pulling wires out frantically.

"What're you doing?" Grant groaned, his mind reeling with pain.

"I'm hot-wiring the truck!" she sobbed.

"You're tearing the damned wiring out!" If she was trying to disable their only transportation, she was doing a good job of it. He started to yank her out from under the steering wheel when suddenly she bounced out on her own, jamming the clutch in and touching two wires together. The motor roared into life, and Jane slammed the door on her side, shoved the truck into gear and let out on the clutch. The truck lurched forward violently, throwing Grant against the door.

"Put it in low gear!" he yelled, pulling himself into a sitting position and getting a tighter grip on the seat.

"I don't know where the low gear is! I just took what I could find!"

Swearing, he reached for the gear shift, the pain in his wounded arm like a hot knife as he closed his hand over the knob. There was nothing he could do about the pain, so he ignored it. "Put the clutch in," he ordered. "I'll change gears. Jane, put the damned clutch in!"

"Stop yelling at me!" she screamed, jamming in the clutch. Grant put the truck in the proper gear and she let out on the clutch; this time the truck moved more smoothly. She put her foot on the gas pedal, shoving it to the floor, and slung the heavy truck around a corner, sending its rear wheels sliding on the gravel.

"Turn right," Grant directed, and she took the next right.

The truck was lunging under her heavy urging, its transmission groaning as she kept her foot down on the gas pedal.

"Change gears!"

"Change them yourself!"

"Put in the clutch!"

She put in the clutch, and he geared up. "When I tell you, put in the clutch, and I'll change the gears, understand?"

She was still crying, swiping at her face at irregular intervals. Grant said, "Turn left," and she swung the truck in a turn that sent a pickup dodging to the side of the road to avoid them.

The road took them out of town, but they were only a couple of miles out when Grant said tersely, "Pull over." Jane didn't question him; she pulled over to the side of the road and stopped the truck.

"Okay, get out." Again she obeyed without question, jumping out and standing there awkwardly as he eased himself to the ground. His left arm was streaked with blood, but from the look on his face Jane knew that he wasn't about to stop. He shoved the pistol into his belt and slung the rifle over his shoulder. "Let's go."

"Where are we going?"

"Back into town. Your boyfriend won't expect us to double back on him. You can stop crying," he added cruelly. "I didn't kill him."

"He's not my boyfriend!" Jane spat, whirling on him.

"Sure looked like it from where I was."

"I was trying to catch him off guard! One of us had to stay free!"

"Save it," he advised, his tone bored. "I bought your act once, but it won't sell again. Now, are you going to walk?"

She decided that there was no use trying to reason with him now. When he'd calmed down enough to listen, when she'd calmed down enough to make a coherent explanation, then they'd get this settled. As she turned away from him, she looked in the open door of the truck and caught a glimpse of something shoved in the far corner of the floor. Her backpack! She crawled up in the truck and leaned far over to drag the pack out from under the seat; in the excitement, it had been totally overlooked and forgotten.

"Leave the damned thing!" Grant snapped.

"I need it," she snapped in return. She buckled it to her belt-loop again.

He drew the pistol out of his belt and Jane swallowed, her eyes growing enormous. Calmly he shot out one of the front tires of the truck, then stuck the pistol back into his belt.

"Why did you do that?" she whispered, swallowing again.

"So it'll look as if we were forced to abandon the truck."

He caught her upper arm in a tight grip and pulled her off the road. Whenever he heard an engine he forced her to the ground and they lay still until the sound had faded. Her blouse, so white and pretty only an hour or so before, became streaked with mud and torn in places where the thorns caught it. She gave it a brief glance, then forgot about it.

"When will Turego be after us again?" she panted.

"Soon. Impatient already?"

Grinding her teeth together, she ignored him. In twenty more minutes they approached the edge of the town again, and he circled it widely. She wanted to ask him what he was looking for, but after the way he'd just bitten her head off, she kept silent. She wanted to sit down to wash his bruised face, and bandage the wound in his arm, but she could do none of those things. He didn't want anything from her now.

Still, what else could she have done? There was no way she could have known he was going to be able to escape. She'd had to use the best plan she had at the time.

Finally they slipped into a ramshackle shed behind an equally ramshackle house and collapsed on the ground in the relatively cool interior. Grant winced as he inadvertently strained his left arm, but when Jane started toward him, he gave her a cold glare that stopped her in her tracks. She sank back to the ground and rested her forehead on her drawn up knees. "What are we going to do now?"

"We're getting out of the country, any way we can," he said flatly. "Your daddy hired me to bring you home, and that's what I'm going to do. The sooner I turn you over to him, the better."

_____ *Chapter Eleven*

After that Jane sat quietly, keeping her forehead down on her knees and closing her eyes. A cold desolation was growing inside her, filling her, thrusting aside anxiety and fear. What if she could never convince him that she hadn't betrayed him? With the life he'd led, it was probably something that he'd had to guard against constantly, so he wasn't even surprised by betrayal. She would try again to reason with him, of course; until he actually left her, she wouldn't stop trying. But... what if he wouldn't listen? What would she do then? Somehow she just couldn't imagine her future without Grant. The emotional distance between them now was agonizing, but she could still lift her head and see him, take comfort in his physical proximity. What would she do if he weren't there at all?

The heat and humidity began building, negating the coolness of the shade offered by the old, open-sided shed, and in the distance thunder rumbled as it announced the approach of the daily rain. A door creaked loudly, and soon a stooped old woman, moving slowly, came around the side of the house to a small pen where pigs had been grunting occasionally as they lay in the mud and tried to escape the heat. Grant watched her, his eyes alert, not a muscle moving. There wasn't any real danger that she would see them; weeds and bushes grew out of control, over waist-high, between the house and the shed, with only a faint little-used path leading to the shed. The pigs squealed in loud enthusiasm when the old woman fed them, and after chatting fondly to them for a moment she laboriously made her way back into the shack.

Jane hadn't moved a muscle, not opening her eyes even when the pigs had begun celebrating the arrival of food. Grant looked at her, a faint puzzlement creeping into the coldness of his eyes. It was unlike her to sit so quietly and not investigate the noise. She knew it was the pigs, of course, but she hadn't looked up to see what was making them squeal so loudly, or even when the old woman had begun talking to them. She was normally as curious as a cat, poking her nose into everything whether it concerned her or not. It was difficult to tell, the way she had her head down, but he thought that she was pale; the few freckles he could see stood out plainly.

An image flashed into his mind of Turego bending his head to press his mouth to Jane's, and the way Jane had stood so quiescently to accept that kiss. Rage curled inside him again, and his fists knotted. Damn her! How could she have let that slime touch her?

The thunder moved closer, cracking loudly, and the air carried the scent of rain. Wind began to swirl, darting through the shed and bringing with it welcome coolness. The air was alive, almost shining with the electrical energy it carried. The small creatures began to take shelter, birds winging back and forth in an effort to find the most secure perch to wait out the storm.

During the rain would be a good time to leave, as everyone else would take shelter until it was over, but his body ached from the beating he'd received, and his left arm was still sullenly oozing blood. They were in no immediate danger here, so he was content to rest. Night would be an even better time to move.

The rain started, going from a sprinkle to a deluge in less than a minute. The ground wasn't able to soak up that enormous amount of water, and a small stream began to trickle through the shed. Grant got up, stifling a groan as his stiff body protested, and found a seat on top of a half-rotten vegetable crate. It gave a little, but held his weight.

Jane still hadn't moved. She didn't look up until the moisture began to dampen the seat of her pants; then her head lifted and she realized that a river was beginning to flow around her. She didn't look at Grant, though she moved away from the water, shifting to the side. She sat with her back to him and resumed her earlier posture, with her knees drawn up, her arms locked around her legs, and her head bent down to rest on her knees.

Grant knew how to wait; patience was second nature to him. He could hold a position all day long, if necessary, ignoring physical discomfort as if it didn't exist. But the silence and lack of motion in the shed began to grate on his nerves, because it wasn't what he'd learned to expect from Jane. Was she planning something?

Eventually the rain stopped, and the steamy heat began to build again. "Are we going to sit here all day?" Jane finally asked fretfully, breaking her long silence.

"Might as well. I don't have anything better to do. Do you?"

She didn't answer that, or ask any more questions, realizing that he wasn't in the mood to tell her anything. She was so hungry that she was sick, but there wasn't any food in her pack, and she wasn't about to complain to him. She dropped her head back to her knees and tried to seek refuge in a nap; at least then she could forget how miserable she was.

She actually managed to sleep, and he woke her at twilight, shaking her shoulder. "Let's go," he said, pulling her ιo her feet. Jane's heart stopped because just for that moment his touch was strong but gentle, and she had the crazy hope that he'd cooled down and come to his senses while she was napping. But then he dropped her arm and stepped away from her, his face hard, and the hope died.

She followed him like a toy on a string, right in his footsteps, stopping when he stopped, always the same distance behind him. He went boldly into the center of town, walking down the streets as if no one at all was looking for him, let alone a small army. Several people looked at them oddly, but no one stopped them. Jane supposed they did look strange: a tall blond man with a bruised, swollen face and a rifle carried easily in one hand, followed by a woman with wild tangled hair, dirty clothes and a backpack buckled to her belt and swinging against her legs as she walked. Well, everything seemed strange to her, too. She felt as if they'd gotten lost in a video game, with crazy neon images flashing at her. After a moment she realized that the images were real; a street sign advertising a cantina flashed its message in neon pink and blue.

What was he doing? They were attracting so much notice that Turego would have to hear of it if he asked any questions at all. For all Grant knew, Turego could have the local law enforcement looking for them under trumped-up charges; Turego certainly had enough authority to mobilize any number of people in the search. It was as if Grant *wanted* Turego to find them.

He turned down a side street and paused outside a small, dimly lit cantina. "Stay close to me, and keep your mouth shut," he ordered tersely, and entered.

It was hot and smoky in the small bar, and the strong odor of alcohol mixed with sweat permeated the air. Except for the waitress, a harried looking girl, and two sultry prostitutes, there were no other women there. Several men eyed Jane, speculation in their dark eyes, but then they looked at Grant and turned back to their drinks, evidently deciding that she wasn't worth the trouble.

Grant found them space at a small table at the back, deep in the shadows. After a while the waitress made it over to them, and without asking Jane her preference, Grant ordered two tequilas.

Jane stopped the waitress. "Wait—do you have lime juice?" At the young woman's nod, she heaved a sigh of relief. "A glass of lime juice, instead of the tequila, please."

Grant lit a cigarette, cupping his hands around the flame. "Are you on the wagon or something?"

"I don't drink on an empty stomach."

"We'll get something to eat later. This place doesn't run to food."

She waited until their drinks were in front of them before saying anything else to him. "Isn't it dangerous for us to be here? Any of Turego's men could have seen us walking down the street."

His eyes were narrow slits as he stared at her through the blue smoke of his cigarette. "Why should that worry you? Don't you think he'd welcome you back with open arms?"

Jane leaned forward, her own eyes narrowed. "Listen to me. I had to buy time, and I did it the only way I could think of. I'm sorry I didn't have time to explain it to you beforehand, but I don't think Turego would have let me call 'time out' and huddle with you! If he'd tied me up, too, there would have been no way I could help you!"

"Thanks, honey, but I can do without your sort of help," he drawled, touching his left eye, which was puffy and red.

Anger seared her; she was innocent, and she was tired of being treated like Benedict Arnold. She thought of pouring the lime juice in his lap, but her stomach growled and revenge took a distant second place to putting something in her empty stomach, even if it was just fruit juice. She sat back in her chair and sipped, wanting to make the juice last as long as possible.

The minutes crawled by, and Jane began to feel a twitch between her shoulder blades. Every second they sat there increased the danger, gave Turego a better chance of finding them. The abandoned truck wouldn't fool him for long.

A man slipped into the chair beside her and Jane jumped, her heart flying into her throat. He gave her only a cursory glance before turning his attention to Grant. He was a nondescript character, his clothing worn, his face covered by a couple of days' growth of beard, and his smell of stale alcohol made Jane wrinkle her nose. But then he said a few words to Grant, so quietly that she couldn't understand them, and it all clicked into place.

Grant had advertised their presence not because he wanted Turego to find them, but because he wanted someone else to find them. It had been a gamble, but it had paid off. He was no longer in the business, but he was known, and he'd trusted his reputation to pull in a contact. This man was probably just a peripheral character, but he would have his uses.

"I need transport," Grant said. "Within the hour. Can you manage it?"

"*Sì*," the man said, slowly nodding his head for emphasis.

"Good. Have it sitting behind the Blue Pelican exactly one hour from now. Put the keys under the right seat, get out, and walk away."

The man nodded again. "Good luck, amigo."

That hard, lopsided smile curved Grant's lips. "Thanks. I could use some about now."

The man blended in with the crowd, then was gone. Jane slowly twirled the glass of juice between her palms, keeping her eyes on the table. "Now that you've made your contact, shouldn't we get out of here?"

Grant lifted the tequila to his mouth, his strong throat working as he swallowed the sharp tasting liquid. "We'll wait a while longer."

No, it wouldn't do to follow the other man too closely. George had always told her how important it was to make contact without seeming to. The man had taken a chance by walking up to them so openly, but then, Grant had taken a chance by making himself so available. It had probably been clear that the situation was desperate, though Grant looked as if he was thinking about nothing more important than going to sleep. He was sprawled in his chair, his eyes half-closed, and if Jane hadn't noticed that he kept his left hand on the rifle she would have thought that he was totally relaxed.

"Do you suppose we could find a bathroom?" she asked, keeping her tone light.

"In here? I doubt it."

"Anywhere."

"Okay. Are you finished with that?" He downed the rest of his tequila, and Jane did the same with her lime juice. Her skin was crawling again; she felt that tingling on the back of her neck, and it intensified as she stood up.

They threaded their way through the tangle of feet and tables and chairs to the door, and as soon as they stepped outside Jane said, "I think we were being watched."

"I know we were. That's why we're going in the opposite direction of the Blue Pelican."

"What on earth is the Blue Pelican? How do you know so much about this town? Have you been here before?"

"No, but I keep my eyes open. The Blue Pelican is the first cantina we passed."

Now she remembered. It was the cantina with the flashing neon sign, the one that had given her such an intense feeling of unreality.

They were walking down the small side street into a yawning cave of darkness. The street wasn't paved, and there were no sidewalks, no street lights, not even one of the incongruous neon signs to lend its garish light. The ground was uneven beneath her boots, and the sour smell of old garbage surrounded her. Jane didn't think; her hand shot out, and she grabbed Grant's belt.

He hesitated, then resumed walking without saying anything. Jane swallowed, belatedly realizing that she could have found herself sailing over his shoulder again, as she had the first time she'd grabbed him from behind. What would she do if she no longer had him to cling to in the dark? Stand around wringing her hands? She'd already come a long way from the child who had sat in a terrified stupor for days, and perhaps it was time for one step more. Slowly, deliberately, Jane released her grip on his belt and let her arm drop to her side.

He stopped and looked around at her, darkness shrouding his features. "I don't mind you holding on to my belt."

She remained silent, feeling his reluctant curiosity, but unable to give him any explanation. All her milestones had been inner ones, attained only by wrenching effort, and this wasn't something she could easily talk about. Not even the frighteningly expensive child psychologist to whom her parents had taken her had been able to draw her out about the kidnapping. Everyone knew about the nightmares she'd had, and her abrupt, unreasonable fear of the dark, but she'd never told anyone the details of her experience. Not her parents, not even Chris, and he'd been her best friend long before he'd been her husband. In all the years since the kidnapping, she'd told only one person, trusted only one person enough. Now there was a distance between them that she'd tried to bridge, but he kept pushing her away. No matter how she wanted to throw herself into his arms, she had to stand alone, because soon she might have no choice in the matter.

The fear of being alone in the dark was nothing compared to the fear that she might be alone for the rest of her life.

He wove a crazy path through the town, crisscrossing, backtracking, changing their route so many times that Jane completely lost her sense of direction. She chugged along doggedly, staying right on his heels. He stopped once, and stood guard while Jane sneaked in the back of the local version of a greasy spoon. The plumbing was pre-World War II, the lighting was a single dim bulb hanging from the ceiling, and the carcass of an enormous cockroach lay on its back in the corner, but she wasn't in the mood to quibble. At least the plumbing worked, and when she turned on the water in the cracked basin a thin, lukewarm stream came out. She washed her hands and, bending over, splashed water on her face. There was no towel, so she wiped her hands on her pants and left her face to dry naturally.

When she tiptoed out of the building, Grant stepped from the shadows where he had concealed himself and took her arm. They weren't far from the Blue Pelican, as it turned out; when they turned the corner, she could see the blue and pink sign flashing. But Grant didn't walk straight to it; he circled the entire area, sometimes standing motionless for long minutes while he waited, and watched.

At last they approached the old Ford station wagon that was parked behind the cantina, but even then he was cautious. He raised the hood and used his cigarette lighter to examine the motor. Jane didn't ask what he was looking for, because she had the chilling idea that she knew. He closed the hood as quietly as possible, evidently reassured.

"Get in, and get the keys out from under the seat."

She opened the door. The dome light didn't come on, but that was to be expected. Doing a little checking on her own, she peered over the back of the seat, holding her breath in case there was actually someone there. But the floorboard was empty, and her breath hissed out of her lungs in relief.

Leaning over, she swept her hand under the seat, searching for the keys. The other door opened, and the car swayed under Grant's weight. "Hurry," he snapped.

"I can't find the keys!" Her scrabbling fingers found a lot of dirt, a few screws, a scrap of paper, but no keys. "Maybe this isn't the right car!"

"It'll have to do. Check again."

She got down on the floor and reached as far under the seat as she could, sweeping her hands back and forth. "Nothing. Try under yours."

He leaned down, extending his arm to search under his seat. Swearing softly, he pulled out a single key wired to a small length of wood. Muttering under his breath about damned people not being able to follow simple instructions, he put the key in the ignition and started the car.

Despite its age, the engine was quiet and smooth. Grant shifted into gear and backed out of the alley. He didn't turn on the headlights until they were well away from the Blue Pelican and the well-lit main street.

Jane leaned back in the musty smelling seat, unable to believe that at last they seemed to be well on their way. So much had happened since that morning that she'd lost her sense of time. It couldn't be late; it was probably about ten o'clock, if that. She watched the road for a while, hypnotized by the way it unwound just ahead of the reach of their headlights, tired but unable to sleep. "Are we still going to Limon?"

"Why? Is that what you told your lover?"

Jane sat very still, clenching her teeth against the anger that shook her. All right, she'd try one more time. "He isn't my lover, and I didn't tell him anything. All I was trying to do was to stay untied until I could catch one of them off guard and get his gun." She spat the words out evenly, but her chest was heaving as she tried to control her anger. "Just how do you think I got the pistol that you took away from me?"

She felt that was a point that he couldn't ignore, but he did, shrugging it away. "Look, you don't have to keep making explanations," he said in a bored tone. "I'm not interested—"

"Stop the car!" she shouted, enraged.

"Don't start pitching one of your fits," he warned, slanting her a hard look.

Jane dived for the steering wheel, too angry to care if she caused them to crash. He pushed her off with one hand, cursing, but Jane ducked under his arm and caught the wheel, wrenching it violently toward her. Grant hit the brake, fighting to keep the car under control with one hand while he held Jane off with the other. She caught the wheel again and pulled it, and the car jolted violently as it hit the shoulder of the road.

Grant let go of her and wrestled with the car as it slewed back and forth on the narrow road. He braked sharply, finally bringing the car to a complete halt so he could give his full attention to Jane, but even before the car had completely stopped she threw the door open and jumped out. "I'll get myself out of Costa Rica!" she yelled, slamming the door.

He got out of the car. "Jane, come back here," he warned as she started walking off.

"I'm not going another mile with you, not another *inch*!"

"You're going if I have to hog-tie you," he said, coming after her, his stride measured.

She didn't stop. "That's your remedy for everything, isn't it?" she sneered.

Without warning, he sprinted. He moved so fast that Jane didn't have time to run. She gave a startled cry, twisting away as he reached her; his outstretched hand caught her blouse and Jane jerked as he stopped her. It was doubly infuriating to find herself so easily caught, and with a fresh burst of rage she threw herself away from him, twisting and doubling her lithe body, trying to break his grip.

He caught her wildly flailing arm and pinned it to her side. "Damn, woman, why do you have to do everything the hard way?" he panted.

"Let . . . *go*!" she shouted, but he wrapped his arms around her, holding her arms pinned down. She kicked and shrieked, but he was too strong; there was nothing she could do as he carried her back to the car.

But he had to release her with one arm so he could open the car door, and when he did she twisted violently, at the same time lifting her feet. The combination of the twist and the sudden addition of weight broke his grip, and she slid under his arm. He grabbed for her again, his fingers hooking in the low neckline of the blouse. The fabric parted under the strain, tearing away from her shoulders.

Tears spurted from Jane's eyes as she scrambled to cover her breasts, holding the ruined cloth over them. "Now look what you've done!" Turning away from him, she burst into sobs, her shoulders shaking.

The raw, hard sobs that tore from her throat were so violent that he dropped his outstretched arms. Wearily he rubbed his face. Why couldn't she cry with sedate little sniffles, instead of these sobs that sounded as if she had been beaten? Despite everything that had happened, he wanted to take her in his arms and hold her head to his chest, stroke her dark hair and whisper that everything was going to be all right.

She whirled on him, wiping her face with one hand and clutching the ruined blouse to her breasts with the other. "Think about a few things!" she said hoarsely. "Think about how I got that pistol. And think about Turego. Remember when he came up behind you with the rifle, and I warned you? Did you notice, before you shot him, that his face was bloody? Do you remember the way his nose was bleeding? Do you think it was the altitude that made his nose bleed? You big, stupid, boneheaded *jackass*!" she bellowed, so beside herself with fury that she was shaking her fist under his nose. "Damn it, can't you tell that I love you?"

Grant was as still as stone, not a muscle moving in his face, but he felt winded, as if he'd just taken a huge blow in the chest. Everything hit him at once, and he staggered under the weight of it. She was right. Turego's face had been bloody, but he hadn't thought anything about it at the time. He'd been so damned angry and jealous that he hadn't been thinking at all, only reacting to what had

looked like betrayal. Not only had she done some quick
thinking to avoid being tied up, she'd charged to his rescue as soon as she could, and when he remembered the way
she'd looked when she came through that door, so white
and wild—Turego's goons were probably lucky that he'd
gotten free first. *She loved him!* He stared down at her, at
the small fist that was waving dangerously close to his
nose. She was utterly magnificent, her hair a wild tangle
around her shoulders, her face filled with a temper that
burned out of control, yelling at him like some banshee.
She clutched that ridiculous scrap of cloth to her breasts
with the hand that wasn't threatening his profile. Indom-
itable. Courageous. Maddening. And so damned desirable that he was suddenly shaking with need.

He caught her fist and jerked her to him, holding her to
him so tightly that she gasped, his face buried against her
hair.

She was still struggling against him, beating at his back
with her fists and crying again. "Let me go! Please, just let
me go."

"I can't," he whispered, and caught her chin, turning
her face up to him. Fiercely he ground his mouth down on
hers and, like a cornered cat, she tried to bite him. He
jerked his head back, laughing, a wild joy running through
him. The torn blouse had fallen away, and her naked
breasts were flattened against him, their soft fullness reminding him of how good it felt when she wasn't fighting
him. He kissed her again, roughly, and cupped her breast
in his palm, rubbing his thumb over the velvet nipple and
making it tighten.

Jane whimpered under the onslaught of his mouth, but
her temper had worn itself out, and she softened against
him, suddenly aware that she'd gotten through to him. She
wanted to hold on to her anger, but she couldn't hold a

grudge. All she could do was kiss him back, her arms sliding up to lock around his neck. His hand burned her breast, his thumb exciting her acutely sensitive skin and beginning to tighten the coil of desire deep in her loins. He had no need to hold her still for his kisses now, so he put his other hand on her bottom and urged her against him, demonstrating graphically that she wasn't the only one affected.

He lifted his mouth from hers, pressing his lips to her forehead. "I swear, that temper of yours is something," he whispered. "Do you forgive me?"

That was a silly question; what was she supposed to say, considering that she was hanging around his neck like a Christmas ornament? "No," she said, rubbing her face into the hollow of his throat, seeking his warm, heady male scent. "I'm going to save this to throw up at you the next time we have a fight." She wanted to say "for the rest of our lives," but though his arms were hard around her, he hadn't yet said that he loved her. She wasn't going to dig for the words, knowing that he might not be able to say them and mean it.

"You will, too," he said, and laughed. Reluctantly his arms loosened, and he reached up, removing her arms from his neck. "I'd like to stay like this, but we need to get to Limon." He looked down at her breasts, and a taut look came over his battered face. "When this is over with, I'm going to take you to a hotel and keep you in bed until neither of us can walk."

They got back in the car, and Jane removed the remnants of the blouse, stuffing it in the backpack and pulling on Grant's camouflage shirt that she'd put in the pack that morning. It would have wrapped around her twice, and the shoulder seams hung almost to her elbows. She rolled the sleeves up as far as they would go, then gathered the long tails and tied them at her waist. Definitely not high fashion, she thought, but she was covered.

The Ford rolled into Limon in the early hours of the morning, and though the streets were nearly deserted, it was obvious that the port was a well-populated city of medium size. Jane's hands clenched on the car seat. Were they safe, then? Had Turego been fooled by the abandoned truck?

"What now?"

"Now I try to get in touch with someone who can get us out tonight. I don't want to wait until morning."

So he thought Turego's men were too close for safety. Was it never going to end? She wished they had remained in the jungle, hidden so deeply in the rain forest that no one would ever have found them.

Evidently Grant had been in Limon before; he negotiated the streets with ease. He drove to the train station, and Jane gave him a puzzled look. "Are we going to take the train?"

"No, but there's a telephone here. Come on."

Limon wasn't an isolated jungle village, or even a tiny town at the edge of the forest; it was a city, with all of the rules of a city. He had to leave the rifle in the back of the station wagon, but he stuck the pistol into his boot. Even without his being obviously armed, Jane thought there was no chance at all of them going anywhere without being noticed. They both looked as if they'd come fresh from a battle, which, in effect, they had. The ticket agent eyed them with sharp curiosity, but Grant ignored him, heading straight for a telephone. He called someone named Angel, and his voice was sharp as he demanded a number. Hanging up, he fed more coins into the slot, then dialed another number.

"Who are you calling?" Jane whispered.

"An old friend."

The old friend's name was Vincente, and intense satisfaction was on Grant's face when he hung up. "They're pulling us out of here. In another hour we'll be home free."

"Who's 'they'?" Jane asked.

"Don't ask too many questions."

She scowled at him, then something else took her attention. "While we're here, could we clean up a little? You look awful."

There was a public bathroom—empty, she was thankful to see—and Grant washed his face while Jane brushed her hair out and quickly pulled it back into a loose braid. Then she wet a towel and painstakingly cleaned the wound on Grant's arm; the bullet hadn't penetrated, but the graze was deep and ugly. After washing it with a strong smelling soap, she produced a small first-aid kit from her backpack.

"One of these days I'm going to see what all's in that thing," Grant growled.

Jane uncapped a small bottle of alcohol and poured it on the graze. He caught a sharp breath, and said something extremely explicit. "Don't be such a baby," Jane scolded. "You didn't make this much fuss when you were shot."

She smeared an antibiotic cream on the wound, then wrapped gauze snugly around his arm and tied the ends together. After replacing the kit, she made certain the pack was still securely buckled to her belt-loop.

Grant opened the door, then abruptly stepped back and closed it again. Jane had been right behind him, and the impact of their bodies made her stagger. He caught her arm, keeping her from falling. "Turego and a few of his men just came into the station." He looked around, his eyes narrowed and alert. "We'll go out a window."

Her heart pounding, Jane stared in dismay at the row of small, high windows that lined the restroom. They were well over her head. "I can't get up there."

"Sure you can." Grant bent down and grasped her around the knees, lifting her until she could reach the windows. "Open one, and go through it. Quick! We only have a minute."

"But how will you get up—"

"I'll make it! Jane, get through that window!"

She twisted the handle and shoved the window open. Without giving herself time to think about how high above the ground on the other side it might be, she grasped the bottom edge of the frame and hauled herself through, jumping into the darkness and hoping she didn't kill herself on a railroad tie or something. She landed on her hands and knees in loose gravel, and she had to bite back a cry of pain as the gravel cut her palms. Quickly she scrambled out of the way, and a moment later Grant landed beside her.

"Are you all right?" he asked, hauling her to her feet.

"I think so. No broken bones," she reported breathlessly.

He started running along the side of the building, dragging her behind him. They heard a shot behind them, but didn't slow down or look back. Jane stumbled and was saved from falling only by his grip on her hand. "Can't we go back for the Ford?" she wailed.

"No. We'll have to get there on foot."

"Get where?"

"To the pick up point."

"How far is that?"

"Not too far."

"Give it to me in yards and miles!" she demanded

He dodged down a street and pulled her into the deep shadows of an alley. He was laughing. "Maybe a mile," he said, and kissed her, his mouth hard and hungry, his tongue finding hers. He hugged her fiercely.

"Whatever you did to Turego, honey, he looks like hell."

"I think I broke his nose," she admitted.

He laughed again. "I think you did, too. It's swollen all over his face. He won't forget you for a long time!"

"Never, if I have anything to do with it. We're going to tell the government about that man," she vowed.

"Later, honey. Right now, we're getting out of here."

Chapter Twelve

A helicopter came in low and fast, and settled lightly on its runners, looking like a giant mosquito. Grant and Jane ran across the small field, bent low against the wind whipped up by the rotors, which the pilot hadn't cut. Behind them people were pouring out of their houses to see what the uproar was about. Jane began to giggle, lightheaded with the triumph of the moment; by the time Grant boosted her into the helicopter, she was laughing so hard she was crying. They'd done it! Turego couldn't catch them now. They would be out of the country before he could mobilize his own helicopters to search for them, and he wouldn't dare pursue them across the border.

Grant flashed her a grin, telling her that he understood her idiotic laughter. He shouted, "Buckle up!" at her, then levered himself into the seat beside the pilot and gave him the thumbs-up sign. The pilot nodded, grinned, and the helicopter rose into the night. Grant put on the headset that would allow him to talk to the pilot, but there wasn't one in the back. Jane gave up trying to hear what they were saying and gripped the sides of her seat, staring out through the open sides of the helicopter. The night air swirled around her, and the world stretched out beyond the small craft. It was the first time she'd ever been in a helicopter, and it was a totally different sensation from being in a jet. She felt adrift in the velvet darkness, and she wished that it wasn't night, so she could see the land below.

The flight didn't take long, but when they set down, Jane recognized the airport and reached up to grab Grant's shoulder. "We're in San Jose!" she yelled, anxiety filling her voice. This was where it had all begun. Turego had plenty of men in the capitol!

Grant took off the headset. The pilot cut the rotors, and the noise began to decrease. They shook hands, and the pilot said, "Nice to see you again! Word filtered down that you were in the area, and that we should give you any assistance you asked for. Good luck. You'd better run. You have just enough time to get on that flight."

They jumped to the asphalt and began running toward the terminal. "What flight is that?" Jane panted.

"The flight to Mexico City that's leaving in about five minutes."

Mexico City! That sounded more like it! The thought lent her strength.

The terminal was almost deserted at that time of night, because the flight for Mexico City had already boarded. The ticket clerk stared at them as they approached, reminding Jane once again of how they looked. "Grant Sullivan and Jane Greer," Grant said tersely. "You're holding our tickets."

The clerk had regained his composure. "Yes, sir, and the plane," he returned in perfect English, handing over two ticket folders. "Ernesto will take you directly aboard."

Ernesto was an airport guard, and he led the way, running. Grant held Jane's hand to make certain she kept up with them. She had a fleeting thought about the pistol stuck in his boot, but they bypassed all checkpoints. Grant certainly had connections, she thought admiringly.

The jet was indeed waiting, and the smiling stewardess welcomed them aboard as calmly as if there was nothing unusual about them. Jane wanted to giggle again; maybe they didn't look as outlandish as she felt they did. After all, camouflage clothing was all the rage in the States. So what if Grant was sporting an almost black eye, a puffy lip and a bandage on his arm? Maybe they looked like journalists who had had a rough time in the field.

As soon as they were seated, the plane began rolling. As they buckled their seat belts, Grant and Jane exchanged glances. It was well and truly over now, but they still had some time together. The next stop was Mexico City, an enormous international city with shops, restaurants... and hotels. Her body longed for a bed, but even deeper than her weariness ran the tingling awareness that Grant would be in that bed with her. He lifted the armrest between their seats and pulled her over so her head nestled into the hollow of his shoulder. "Soon," he murmured against her temple. "In a couple of hours we'll be in Mexico. Home free."

"I'm going to call Dad as soon as we get there, so he and Mom will stop worrying." Jane sighed. "Do you have anyone to call? Does your family know where you were?"

His eyes took on that remote look. "No, they don't know anything about what I do. I'm not close to my family, not anymore."

That was sad, but Jane supposed that when someone was in the business Grant had been in, it was safer for his family not to be close to him. She turned her face into his neck and closed her eyes, holding tightly to him in an effort to let him know that he wasn't alone anymore. Had his nights been spent like hers, lying awake in bed, so achingly alone that every nerve in her body cried out against it?

She slept, and Grant did, too, exhaustion finally sweeping over him as he allowed his bruised body to relax. With her in his arms, it was easy to find the necessary relaxation. She nestled against him as trustingly as a child, but he could never forget that she was a woman, as fierce and elemental as wind or fire. She could have been the spoiled debutante he'd expected. It was what she *should* have been, and no one would have thought the less of her for being the product of her environment—no one expected her to be any more than that. But she'd risen above that, and above the crippling trauma of her childhood, to become a woman of strength and humor and passion.

She was a woman in whose arms a wary, battered, burnt-out warrior could sleep.

The sky was turning pearl pink with dawn when they landed in Mexico City. The terminal was teeming with people scurrying to catch early flights, a multitude of languages and accents assailing the air. Grant hailed a cab, which took them on a hair-raising ride through traffic that made every moment an exercise in survival—or it would have been hair-raising if Jane had had the energy to care. After what she'd been through, the Mexico City traffic looked mundane.

The city was beautiful at dawn, with its wide avenues and fragrant trees; and the white of the buildings glowed rosily in the early morning sun. The sky was already a deep blue bowl overhead, and the air carried that velvet feel that only the warmer climes achieved. Despite the odor of exhaust fumes she could smell the sweetness of orange blossoms, and Grant was warm beside her, his strong leg pressed against hers.

The desk clerk in the pristine white, high-rise hotel was reluctant to give them a room without a reservation. His black eyes kept wandering to Grant's bruised face as he rattled off excuses in rapid-fire Spanish. Grant shrugged, reached into his pocket and peeled off a couple of bills from a roll. The clerk suddenly smiled; that changed everything. Grant signed them in, and the clerk slid a key across the desk. After taking a few steps, Grant turned back. "By the way," he said easily, "I don't want any interruptions. If anyone calls or asks, we aren't here. *¿Comprende?* I'm dead tired, and I get irritable if I'm jerked out of a sound sleep."

His voice was full of silky, lazy menace, and the clerk nodded rapidly.

With Grant's arm draped across her shoulders, they walked over to the bank of elevators. He punched the button for the nineteenth floor, and the doors slid silently shut. Jane said dazedly, "We're safe."

"Having trouble believing it?"

"I'm going to get that man. He's not going to get off scot-free!"

"He won't," Grant drawled. "He'll be taken care of, through channels."

"I don't want 'channels' to take care of him! I want to do it myself!"

He smiled down at her. "You're a bloodthirsty little wench, aren't you? I almost think you enjoyed this."

"Only parts of it," she replied, giving him a slow smile.

Their room was spacious, with a terrace for sunning, a separate sitting area with a dining table and a stunningly modern bath. Jane poked her head into it and withdrew with a beatific smile on her face. "All the modern conveniences," she crowed.

Grant was studying the in-house registry for room service. Picking up the phone, he ordered two enormous breakfasts, and Jane's mouth watered at the thought. It had been almost twenty-four hours since they'd eaten.

While they were waiting for their food, she began the process of making a phone call to Connecticut. It took about five minutes for the call to go through, and Jane sat with the receiver gripped tightly in her hand, taut with the need to hear her parents' voices.

"Mom? Mom, it's Jane! I'm all right—don't cry, I can't talk to you if you're crying," Jane said, and wiped away a few tears herself. "Put Dad on the line so I can tell him what's going on. We'll blubber together just as soon as I get home, I promise." She waited a few moments, smiling mistily at Grant, her dark eyes liquid.

"Jane? Is it really you?" Her father's voice boomed across the line.

"Yes, it really is. I'm in Mexico City. Grant got me out; we just flew in a few minutes ago."

Her father made a choked sound, and Jane realized that he was crying, too, but he controlled himself. "Well, what now?" he demanded. "When are you going to be here? Where are you going from there?"

"I don't know," she said, lifting her brows at Grant and taking the receiver from her ear. "Where are we going next?"

He took the phone from her. "This is Sullivan. We'll probably be here for a couple of days, getting some paperwork straightened out. We came in here without being checked for passports, but I'll have to make some calls before we can get into the States. Yes, we're okay. I'll let you know as soon as I find out something."

When he hung up, he turned to find Jane surveying him with pursed lips. "How *did* we get here without being checked for passports?"

"A few people turned their heads, that's all. They knew we were coming through. I'll report our passports as being lost, and get duplicates from the American Embassy. No big deal.''

"How did you manage to set all that up so quickly? I know this wasn't the original plan."

"No, but we had some inside help." Sabin had been as good as his word, Grant reflected. All the old contacts had been there, and they had all been notified to give him whatever he needed.

"Your... former business associates?" Jane hazarded a guess.

"The less you know, the better. You pick up on this too damned quickly. Like hot-wiring that truck. Had you ever done it before?"

"No, but I watched you do it the first time," she explained, her eyes full of innocence.

He grunted. "Don't waste your time giving me that wide-eyed look."

A tap on the door and a singsong voice announced that room service had arrived in record time. Grant checked through the fish-eye viewer, then unbolted the door and let the young boy in. The aroma of hot coffee filled the room, and Jane's mouth started watering. She hovered over the boy as he set the food out on the table.

"Look at this," she crooned. "Fresh oranges and melon. Toast. Apricot Danish. Eggs. Butter. Real coffee!"

"You're drooling," Grant teased, giving the boy a generous tip, but he was just as ravenous, and between them they destroyed the array of food. Every crumb was gone and the pot of coffee was empty before they looked at each other and smiled.

"I feel almost human again," Jane sighed. "Now for a hot shower!"

She began unlacing her boots, pulling them off and sighing in relief as she wiggled her toes. Glancing at him, she saw that he was watching her with that lopsided smile that she loved so much. Her heart kicked into time and a half rhythm. "Aren't you going to shower with me?" she asked innocently, sauntering into the bathroom.

She was already under the deliciously warm spray of water, her head tilted up so it hit her directly in the face, when the shower door slid open and he joined her. She turned, wiping the moisture from her eyes, a smile ready on her lips, but the smile faded when she saw the mottled bruises on his ribcage and abdomen. "Oh, Grant," she whispered, reaching out to run her fingers lightly over the dark, ugly splotches. "I'm so sorry."

He gave her a quizzical look. He was sore and stiff, but nothing was broken and the bruises would fade. He'd suffered much worse than this, many times. Of course, if Turego had been able to carry the beating as far as he'd wanted, Grant knew that he probably would have died of internal injuries. But it hadn't happened, so he didn't worry about it. He caught her chin, turning her face up to him. "We're both covered with bruises, honey, in case you haven't noticed. I'm okay." He covered her mouth with his, tasting her sweetness with his tongue, easing her against him.

Their wet, naked bodies created a marvelous friction against each other, heating them, tightening the coil of desire. The rather boring process of soaping and rinsing became a lingering series of strokes, her hands slipping over the muscles and intriguing hardness of his body, his finding the soft curves and slopes of hers, the enticing depths. He lifted her off her feet and bent her back over his arm, kissing her breasts and sucking at her nipples until they were hard and reddened, tasting the freshness of newly soaped skin and the sweetness of her flesh that no soap could ever disguise. Jane writhed against him, her legs twining with his, and heat fogged his mind as he thrust himself against the juncture of her thighs.

She wanted him, wanted him, wanted him. Her body ached and burned. The bed was suddenly too far away. Her legs parted, lifting to wrap around his waist, and with a hoarse cry he pinned her to the wall. She shuddered as he drove into her, going as deep as he could with a single, powerful thrust, as if any distance at all between them was far too much. Digging his fingers into her hair, he pulled her head back and kissed her, his mouth wild and rough, the kiss deep, his tongue twining with hers, the water beating down on them. The power of his thrusts made her consciousness dim, but she clung to him, whimpering, begging him not to stop. He couldn't have stopped, couldn't even have slowed, his body demanding release inside her. The red mists that clouded his mind blocked out everything but the hot ecstasy of the way her body sheathed him, so softly, so tightly.

She cried out again and again as the almost unbearable waves of pleasure crashed over her. She clung tightly to his shoulders, trembling and shivering, the velvet clasp of her body driving him to the edge. He poured himself into her, heaving against her, feeling that he was dying a little, and yet so intensely alive that he almost screamed from the conflict.

They barely made it to the bed. Drying off had taken all their energy, and Jane was so weak she could barely walk. Grant was shaking in every muscle of his big body. They tumbled onto the bed, not caring that their wet hair soaked the pillows.

Grant reached out for her. "Crawl up here," he rumbled, hauling her on top of him. Blissfully, her eyes closing, she made herself comfortable on the hard expanse of his chest. He adjusted her legs, parting them, and her lashes fluttered open as he eased into her. A purr of pleasure escaped her lips, but she was so sleepy, so tired . . . "Now we can sleep," he said, his lips moving on her hair.

The room was hot when they awoke, the Mexican sun broiling through the closed curtains. Their skin was stuck together with perspiration and made a wet, sucking noise as Grant lifted her off him. He got up and turned the air-conditioning on full blast, and stood for a moment with the cold air hitting his naked body. Then he came back to the bed and turned her onto her back.

They scarcely left the bed that day. They made love, napped and woke to make love again. She couldn't get enough of him, nor he, it seemed, of her. There was no sense of urgency now to their lovemaking, only a deep reluctance to be parted from each other. He taught her the unlimited reaches of her own sensuality, tasting her all over, making love to her with his mouth until she was shivering and shuddering with pleasure, mindless, helpless. She told him that she loved him. She couldn't keep the words unsaid, not now, when she'd already told him anyway and soon the world would intrude on them again.

Night came, and finally they left the room. Walking hand in hand in the warm Mexican night, they sought out some shops that were open late. Jane bought a pink sundress that made her tanned skin look like honey, a pair of sandals and new underwear. Grant wasn't much on shopping, so she blithely picked out jeans, loafers and a white polo shirt for him. "You might as well change," she instructed, pushing him toward the dressing room. "We're going out to eat tonight."

There wasn't any talking her out of it, either. It wasn't until he was seated across from her in a dimly lit restaurant with a bottle of wine between them that he realized this was the first time in years that he'd been with a woman in a strictly social setting. They had nothing to do but eat and talk, sip the wine, and think about what they were going to do when they got back to the hotel. Even after he'd retired, he'd kept to himself on the farm, sometimes going for weeks without seeing another human being. When the need for supplies had forced him to go into town, he'd gone straight there and back, a lot of times without speaking to anyone. He hadn't been able to stand anyone else around him. But now he was relaxed, not even thinking about the strangers surrounding him, accepting their presence but not noticing them, because his mind and his senses were on Jane.

She was radiant, incandescent with energy. Her dark eyes shone; her tanned skin glowed; her laughter sparkled. Her breasts thrust against the bodice of the sundress, her nipples puckered by the coolness of the restaurant, and desire began to stir inside him again. They didn't have much more time together; soon they would be back in the States, and his job would be finished. It was too soon, far too soon. He hadn't had his fill yet of the taste of her, the wild sweetness of her body beneath him, or the way her laughter somehow eased all the knots of tension inside him.

They went back to the hotel, and back to bed. He made love to her furiously, trying to sate himself, trying to hoard enough memories to hold him during the long, empty years ahead. Being alone was a habit deeply ingrained in him; he wanted her, but couldn't see taking her back to the farm with him, and there was no way he could fit into her world. She liked having people around her, while he was more comfortable with a wall at his back. She was outgoing, while he was controlled, secretive.

She knew, too, that it was almost over. Lying on his chest, with the darkness wrapped around them like a blanket, she talked. It was a gift that she gave him, the tales of her childhood, where she'd gone to school, her food and music preferences, what she liked to read. Because she talked, he found it easier to return the favor, his voice low and rusty as he told her about the white-haired young boy he'd been, his skin burned dark by the hot, south Georgia summers, running wild in the swamp. He'd learned to hunt and fish almost as soon as he'd learned how to walk. He told her about playing football during high school, chasing after the cheerleaders, getting drunk and raising hell, then trying to sneak into the house so his mother wouldn't catch him.

Her fingers played in the hair on his chest, aware that silence had fallen because he'd reached the point in his story where his life had changed. There were no more easy tales of growing up.

"Then what happened?" she whispered.

His chest rose and fell. "Vietnam happened. I was drafted when I was eighteen. I was too damned good at sneaking through jungles, so that's where they put me. I went home, once, for R & R, but the folks were just the same as always, while I was nothing like what I had been. We couldn't even talk to each other. So I went back."

"And stayed?"

"Yeah. I stayed." His voice was flat.

"How did you get into the secret agent business, or whatever you call it?"

"Covert activities. High risk missions. The war ended, and I came home, but there was nothing for me to do. What was I going to do, work in a grocery store, when I'd been trained to such an edge that people would be taking their lives in their hands to walk up to me and ask the price of eggs? I guess I'd have settled down eventually, but I didn't want to hang around to find out. I was embarrassing the folks, and I was a stranger to them anyway. When an old colleague contacted me, I took him up on his offer."

"But you're retired now. Did you go back to Georgia?"

"Just for a few days, to let them know where I'd be. I couldn't settle there; too many people knew me, and I wanted to be left alone. So I bought a farm close to the mountains in Tennessee, and I've been hibernating there ever since. Until your dad hired me to fetch you home."

"Have you ever married? Been engaged?"

"No," he said, and kissed her. "That's enough questions. Go to sleep."

"Grant?"

"Hmmm?"

"Do you think he's really given up?"

"Who?"

"Turego."

Amusement laced his voice. "Honey, I promise you, he'll be taken care of. Don't worry about it. Now that you're safe and sound, steps can be taken to neutralize him."

"You're using some ominous sounding phrases. What do 'taken care of' and 'neutralize' mean?"

"That he's going to be spending some time in those gracious Central American jails that everyone hears so much about. Go to sleep."

She obeyed, her lips curved in a contented smile, his arms securely around her.

* * *

Someone had pulled strings again. It could have been her father, or the mysterious "friend" of Grant's who kept arranging things, or possibly Grant had intimidated someone at the embassy. However it happened, the next afternoon they had passports. They could have taken the next flight to Dallas, but instead they spent another night together, making love in that king-size bed, the door securely bolted. She didn't want to leave. As long as they were still in Mexico City, she could pretend that it wasn't over, that the job wasn't finished. But her parents were waiting for her, and Grant had his own life to go back to. She had to find another job, as well as take care of the little chore that had gotten her into so much trouble to begin with. There was no way they could stay in Mexico.

Still, tears burned the back of her eyes when they boarded the jet that would take them to Dallas. She knew that Grant had booked separate flights for them from Dallas; she was going on to New York, and he was flying to Knoxville. Their goodbyes would be said in the vast, busy Dallas-Ft. Worth airport, and she couldn't stand it. If she didn't get a tight hold on herself she'd be squalling like a baby, and he wouldn't want that. If he wanted more of her than what he'd already had, he'd have asked her, because she'd made it more than obvious that she was willing to give him whatever he wanted. But he hadn't asked, so he didn't want her. She'd known that this time would come, and she'd accepted it, taken the risk, grabbed for what happiness she could get. Pay up time had come.

She controlled her tears. She read the airline magazine; and was even able to comprehend what she was reading. For a while she held his hand, but she released it when the in-flight meal was served. She ordered a gin and tonic, gulped it down, then ordered another.

Grant eyed her narrowly, but she gave him a bright, glittering smile, determined not to let him see that she was shattering on the inside.

Too soon, far too soon, they landed at Dallas and filed out of the plane through the portable tunnel. Jane clutched the dirty, battered backpack, for the first time realizing that his boots and fatigues were in it along with her clothing. "I need your address," she chattered brightly, nervously. "To mail your clothes to you. Unless you want to buy a bag in the airport shop, that is. We have plenty of time before our flights."

He checked his watch. "You have twenty-eight minutes, so we'd better find your gate. Do you have your ticket?"

"Yes, it's right here. What about your clothes?"

"I'll be in touch with your father. Don't worry about it."

Yes, of course; there was the matter of payment for dragging her out of Costa Rica. His face was hard and expressionless, his amber eyes cool. She held out her hand, not noticing how it was shaking. "Well, goodbye, then. It's—" She broke off. What could she say? *It's been nice meeting you?* She swallowed. "It's been fun."

He looked down at her extended hand, then back up at her, disbelief edging into the coolness of his eyes. He said slowly, "The hell you say," caught her hand, and jerked her into his arms. His mouth was hot, covering hers, his tongue curling slowly into her mouth as if they weren't surrounded by curiously gawking people. She clung to him, shaking.

He set her away from him. His jaw was clenched. "Go on. Your folks are waiting for you. I'll be in touch in a few days." The last slipped out; he'd intended this to be the final break, but her dark eyes were so lost and full of pain, and she'd kissed him so hungrily, that he couldn't stop the words. One more time, then. He'd give himself one more time with her.

She nodded, drawing herself up. She wasn't going to break down and cry all over him. He almost wished she would cry, because then he'd have an excuse to hold her again. But she was stronger than that. "Goodbye," she said, then turned and walked away from him.

She barely saw where she was going; people blurred in her vision, and she stubbornly blinked her eyes to keep the tears back. Well, she was alone again. He'd said he'd be in touch, but she knew he wouldn't. It was over. She had to accept that and be grateful for the time she'd had. It had been obvious from the first that Grant Sullivan wasn't a man to be tied down.

Someone touched her arm, the touch warm and strong, a man's touch. She stopped, wild hope springing into her breast, but when she turned she found that it wasn't Grant who had stopped her. The man had dark hair and eyes, and his skin was dark, his features strongly Latin. "Jane Greer?" he asked politely.

She nodded, wondering how he'd known her name and recognized her. His grip tightened on her arm. "Would you please come with me," he said, and though his voice remained polite, it was an order, not a question.

Alarm skittered through her, jerking her out of her misery. She smiled at the man and swung the backpack by its straps, catching him on the side of the head with it and sending him staggering. From the solid 'thunk' it made, she knew Grant's boots had hit him.

"Grant!" she screamed, her voice slicing through the bustle of thousands of people. *"Grant!"*

The man caught himself and lunged for her. Jane began running back in the direction she'd come from, dodg-

ing around people. Up ahead she saw Grant coming
through the crowd like a running back, shoving people out
of his path. The man caught up with her, catching her arm;
then Grant was there. People were screaming and scattering, and the airport guards were running toward them.
Grant sent the man sprawling, then grabbed Jane's arm
and ran for the nearest exit, ducking past the milling
crowds and ignoring the shouts to stop.

"What the hell's going on?" he roared, jerking her out
into the bright Texas sunlight. The humid heat settled over
them.

"I don't know! That man just came up to me and asked
if my name was Jane Greer; then he caught my arm and
told me to come with him, so I hit him in the head with the
backpack and started screaming."

"Makes perfect sense to me," he muttered, flagging a
cab and putting her in it, then crawling in beside her.

"Where to, folks?" the cab driver asked.

"Downtown."

"Any particular place downtown?"

"I'll tell you where to stop."

The driver shrugged. As they pulled away from the curb
there seemed to be a lot of people spilling out of the terminal, but Jane didn't look back. She was still shaking. "It
can't be Turego again, can it?"

Grant shrugged. "It's possible, if he has enough money.
I'm going to make a phone call."

She'd thought she was safe, that they were both safe.
After the two peaceful days spent in Mexico, the sudden
fear seemed that much sharper and more acrid. She
couldn't stop trembling.

They didn't go all the way into Dallas. Grant instructed
the driver to drop them at a shopping mall. "Why a shopping mall?" Jane asked, looking around.

"There are telephones here, and it's safer than standing in a phone booth on the side of a street." He put his arm around her and hugged her briefly to him. "Don't look so worried, honey."

They went inside and found a bank of pay telephones, but it was a busy day and all the lines were in use. They waited while a teenager argued extensively with her mother about how late she could stay out that night, but at last she hung up and stormed away, evidently having lost the argument. Grant stepped in and commandeered the telephone before anyone else could reach it. Standing close by him, Jane watched as he dropped in the coins, punched in a number, then dropped in more coins. He leaned casually against the fieldstone nook that housed the telephone, listening to the rings on the other end.

"Sullivan," he finally drawled when the phone was answered. "She was nearly grabbed in DFW." He listened a moment; then his eyes flicked to Jane. "Okay, I got it. We'll be there. By the way, that was a dumb move. She could've killed the guy." He hung up, and his lips twitched.

"Well?" Jane demanded.

"You just belted an agent."

"An agent? You mean, one of your friend's men?"

"Yeah. We're taking a little detour. You're going to be debriefed. It was left up to some other people to pick you up, and they decided to pick you up after we'd parted company, since I'm no longer in the business and this doesn't officially concern me. Sabin will pin their ears back."

"Sabin? Is he your friend?"

He was smiling down at her. "He's the one." He stroked her cheekbone very gently with the backs of his fingers. "And that's a name you're going to forget, honey. Why don't you call your parents and let them know that you won't be in tonight? It'll be tomorrow; you can call them again when we know something definite."

"Are you going, too?"

"I wouldn't miss it." He grinned a little wolfishly, already anticipating Kell's reaction to Jane.

"But where are we going?"

"Virginia, but don't tell your parents that. Just tell them that you missed your flight."

She reached for the phone, then stopped. "Your friend must be pretty important."

"He's got some power," Grant understated.

So, they must know about the microfilm. Jane punched in her credit card number. She'd be glad to get the whole thing over with, and at least Grant was going to be with her one more day. Just one more day! It was a reprieve, but she didn't know if she'd have the strength for another goodbye.

_____ *Chapter Thirteen*

The Virginia countryside around the place was quiet and serene, the trees green, the flowering shrubs well-tended. It looked rather like her father's Connecticut estate. Everyone was polite, and several people greeted Grant, but Jane noticed that even the ones who spoke to him did so hesitantly, as if they were a little wary of him.

Kell's office was right where it had always been, and the door still had no name on it. The agent who had escorted them knocked quietly. "Sullivan is here, sir."

"Send them in."

The first thing Jane noticed was the old-fashioned charm of the room. The ceilings were high; the mantel was surely the original one that had been built with the house over a hundred years before. Tall glass doors behind the big desk let in the late afternoon sun. They also placed the man behind the desk in silhouette, while anyone who came in the door was spotlighted by the blazing sun, something George had told her about. He rose to his feet as they entered, a tall man, maybe not quite as tall as Grant, but lean and hard with a whipcord toughness that wasn't maintained by sitting behind a desk.

He stepped forward to greet them. "You look like hell, Sullivan," he said, and the two men shook hands; then he turned his eyes on her, and for the first time Jane felt his power. His eyes were so black that there was no light in

them at all; they absorbed light, drawing it into the depths
of the irises. His hair was thick and black, his complexion
dark, and there was an intense energy about him that
seared her.

"Ms. Greer," he said, holding out his hand.

"Mr. Sabin," she returned, calmly shaking his hand.

"I have a very embarrassed agent in Dallas."

"He shouldn't be," Grant drawled behind her. "She let
him off easy."

"Grant's boots were in the pack," Jane explained.
"That's what stunned him so badly when I hit him in the
head."

There was the first hint in Sabin's eyes that Jane wasn't
quite what he'd expected. Grant stood behind her, his arms
calmly folded, and waited.

Sabin examined her open expression, the catlike slant of
her dark eyes, the light dusting of freckles across her
cheekbones. Then he quickly glanced at Grant, who was
planted like the Rock of Gibraltar behind her. He could
question her, but he had the feeling that Grant wouldn't let
her be harrassed in any way. It wasn't like Sullivan to get
involved, but he was out of the business now, so the old
rules didn't apply. She wasn't a great beauty, but there was
a lively charm about her that almost made Sabin want to
smile. Maybe she'd gotten close to Sullivan. Sabin didn't
trust that openness, however, because he knew more about
her now than he had in the beginning.

"Ms. Greer," he began slowly, "did you know that
George Persall was—"

"Yes, I did," Jane interrupted cheerfully. "I helped him
sometimes, but not often, because he liked to use different methods every time. I believe this is what you want."
She opened the backpack and began digging in it. "I know

it's in here. There!'' She produced the small roll of film, placing it on his desk.

Both men looked thunderstruck. "You've just been carrying it around?'' Sabin asked in disbelief.

"Well, I didn't have a chance to hide it. Sometimes I put it in my pocket. That way Turego could search my room all he wanted and he'd never find anything. All of you spy types try to make everything too complicated. George always told me to keep it simple.''

Grant began to chuckle. He couldn't help it; it was funny. "Jane, why didn't you tell me you had the microfilm?''

"I thought it would be safer for you if you didn't know about it.''

Again Sabin looked thunderstruck, as if he couldn't believe anyone would actually feel the need to protect Grant Sullivan. As Kell was normally the most impassive of men, Grant knew that Jane had tilted him off balance, just as she did everyone she met. Sabin coughed to cover his reaction.

"Ms. Greer,'' he asked cautiously, "do you know what's on the film?''

"No. Neither did George.''

Grant was laughing again. "Go ahead,'' he told Sabin. "Tell her about the film. Or, better yet, show her. She'll enjoy it.''

Sabin shook his head, then picked up the film and pulled it out, unwinding it. Grant produced his cigarette lighter, leaned forward, and set the end of the film on fire. The three watched as the flames slowly ate up the length of celluloid until it burned close to Sabin's fingers and he dropped it into a large ashtray. "The film,'' Sabin explained, "was a copy of something we don't want anyone else to know. All we wanted was for it to be destroyed before anyone saw it.''

With the stench of burning plastic in her nostrils, Jane silently watched the last of the film curl and crumble. All they'd wanted was for it to be destroyed, and she'd hauled it through a jungle and across half a continent—just to hand it over and watch it burn. Her lips twitched; she was afraid of making a scene, so she tried to control the urge. But it was irresistible; it rolled upward, and a giggle escaped. She turned, looking at Grant, and between them flashed the memory of everything they'd been through. She giggled again, then they were both laughing, Jane hanging on to his shirt because she was laughing so hard her knees had gone limp.

''I fell down a cliff,'' she gasped. ''We stole a truck... shot another truck...I broke Turego's nose...all to watch it *burn!*''

Grant went into another spasm of laughter, holding his sore ribs and bending double. Sabin watched them clinging to each other and laughing uproariously. Curiosity seized him. ''Why did you shoot a truck?'' he asked; then suddenly he was laughing, too.

An agent paused outside the door, his head tilted, listening. No, it was impossible. Sabin never laughed.

They lay in bed in a hotel in the middle of Washington, D.C., pleasantly tired. They had made love as soon as the door was locked behind them, falling on the bed and removing only the necessary clothing. But that had been hours before, and now they were completely nude, slipping gradually into sleep.

Grant's hand moved up and down her back in a lazy pattern. ''Just how involved were you in Persall's activities?''

"Not very," she murmured. "Oh, I knew about them. I had to know, so I could cover for him if I had to. And he sometimes used me as a courier, but not very often. Still, he talked to me a lot, telling me things. He was a strange, lonely man."

"Was he your lover?"

She lifted her head from his chest, surprised. "George? Of course not!"

"Why 'of course not'? He was a man, wasn't he? And he was in your bedroom when he died."

She paused. "George had a problem, a medical one. He wasn't capable of being anyone's lover."

"So that part of the report was wrong, too."

"Deliberately. He used me as a sort of shield."

He put his hand in her hair and held her for his kiss. "I'm glad. He was too old for you."

Jane watched him with wise, dark eyes. "Even if he hadn't been, I wasn't interested. You might as well know, you're the only lover I've ever had. Until I met you, I'd never . . . wanted anyone."

"And when you met me . . . ?" he murmured.

"I wanted." She lowered her head and kissed him, wrapping her arms around him, slithering her body over his until she felt his hardening response.

"I wanted, too," he said, his words a mere breath over her skin.

"I love you." The words were a cry of pain, launched by desperation, because she knew this was definitely the last time unless she took the chance. "Will you marry me?"

"Jane, don't."

"Don't what? Tell you that I love you? Or ask you to marry me?" She sat up, moving her legs astride him, and shook her dark hair back behind her shoulders.

"We can't live together," he explained, his eyes turning dark gold. "I can't give you what you need, and you'd be miserable."

"I'll be miserable anyway," she said reasonably, striving for a light tone. "I'd rather be miserable with you than miserable without you."

"I'm a loner. Marriage is a partnership, and I'd rather go it alone. Face it, honey. We're good together in bed, but that's all there is."

"Maybe for you. I love you." Despite herself, she couldn't keep the echo of pain out of her voice.

"Do you? We were under a lot of stress. It's human nature to turn to each other. I'd have been surprised if we hadn't made love."

"Please, spare me your combat psychology! I'm not a child, or stupid! I know when I love someone, and damn it, I love you! You don't have to like it, but don't try to talk me out of it!"

"All right." He lay on his back, looking up into her angry eyes. "Do you want me to get another room?"

"No. This is our last night together, and we're going to spend it *together*."

"Even if we're fighting?"

"Why not?" she dared.

"I don't want to fight," he said, lunging up and twisting. Jane found herself on her back, blinking up at him in astonishment. Slowly he entered her, pushing her legs high. She closed her eyes, excitement spiraling through her. He was right; the time was far better spent making love.

She didn't try again to convince him that they had a future together. She knew from experience just how hardheaded he was; he'd have to figure it out for himself. So she spent her time loving him, trying to make certain that he never forgot her, that no other woman could begin to give him the pleasure that she did. This would be her goodbye.

Late in the night she leaned over him. "You're afraid," she accused softly. "You've seen so much that you're afraid to let yourself love anyone, because you know how easily a world can be wrecked."

His voice was tired. "Jane, let it be."

"All right. That's my last word, except for this: if you decide to take a chance, come get me."

She crept out of bed early the next morning and left him sleeping. She knew that he was too light a sleeper not to have awakened some time during the shower she took, or while she was dressing, but he didn't roll over or in any way indicate that he was awake, so she preserved the pretence between them. Without even kissing him, she slipped out the door. After all, they'd already said their goodbyes.

At the sound of the door closing Grant rolled over in the bed, his eyes bleak as he stared at the empty room.

Jane and her parents fell into each other's arms, laughing and crying and hugging each other exuberantly. Her return called for a family celebration that lasted hours, so it was late that night before she and her father had any time alone. Jane had few secrets from her father; he was too shrewd, too realistic. By silent, instinctive agreement, they kept from her mother the things that would upset her, but Jane was like her father in that she had an inner toughness.

She told him how the entire situation in Costa Rica had come about, and even told him about the trek through the rain forest. Because he was shrewd, he picked up on the nuances in her voice when she mentioned Grant.

"You're in love with Sullivan, aren't you?"

She nodded, sipping her glass of wine. "You met him. What did you think about him?" The answer was important to her, because she trusted her father's judgment of character.

"I thought him unusual. There's something in his eyes that's almost scary. But I trusted him with my daughter's life, if that tells you what you want to know, and I'd do so again."

"Would you mind having him in the family?"

"I'd welcome him with open arms. I think he could keep you in one place," James said grumpily.

"Well, I asked him to marry me, but he turned me down. I'm going to give him a while to stew over it; then I'm going to fight dirty."

Her father grinned, the quick, cheerful grin that his daughter had inherited. "What are you planning?"

"I'm going to chase that man like he's never been chased before. I think I'll stay here for a week or two; then I'm going to Europe."

"But he's not in Europe!"

"I know. I'll chase him from a distance. The idea is for him to know how much he misses me, and he'll miss me a lot more when he finds out how far away I am."

"But how is he going to find out?"

"I'll arrange that somehow. And even if it doesn't work, a trip to Europe is never a waste!"

It was odd how much he missed her. She'd never been to the farm, but sometimes it seemed haunted by her. He'd think he heard her say something and turn to find no one there. At night...God, the nights were awful! He couldn't sleep, missing her soft weight sprawled on top of him.

He tried to lose himself in hard physical work. Chores piled up fast on a farm, and he'd been gone for two weeks.

With the money he'd been paid for finding Jane, he was able to free the farm from debt and still have plenty left over, so he could have hired someone to do the work for him. But the work had been therapy for him when he'd first come here, still weak from his wounds, and so tightly drawn that a pine cone dropping from a tree in the night had been enough to send him diving from the bed, reaching for his knife.

So he labored in the sun, doing the backbreaking work of digging new holes for the fence posts, putting up new sections of fencing, patching and painting the barn. He reroofed the house, worked on the old tractor that had come with the farm; and thought about doing more planting the next spring. All he'd planted so far was a few vegetables for himself, but if he was going to own a farm, he might as well farm it. A man wouldn't get rich at it, not on this scale, but he knew how to do it. Working the earth gave him a measure of peace, as if it put him in contact with the boy he'd once been, before war had changed his life.

In the distance loomed the mountains, the great, misty mountains where the ghosts of the Cherokee still walked. The vast slopes were uninhabited now, but then, only a few hardy souls other than the Cherokee had ever called the mountains home. Jane would like the mountains. They were older, wreathed in silvery veils, once the mightiest mountain range on earth, but worn down by more years than people could imagine. There were places in those mountains where time stood still.

The mountains, and the earth, had healed him, and the process had been so gradual that he hadn't realized he was healed until now. Perhaps the final healing had come when Jane had shown him how to laugh again.

He had told her to let it be, and she had. She had left in the quiet morning, without a word, because he'd told her to go. She loved him; he knew that. He'd pretended that it was something else, the pressure of stress that had brought them together, but even then he'd known better, and so had she.

Well, hell! He missed her so badly that he hurt, and if this wasn't love, then he hoped he never loved anyone, because he didn't think he could stand it. He couldn't get her out of his mind, and her absence was an empty ache that he couldn't fill, couldn't ease.

She'd been right; he was afraid to take the chance, afraid to leave himself open to more hurt. But he was hurting anyway. He'd be a fool if he let her get away.

But first there were old rifts to try to heal.

He loved his parents, and he knew they loved him, but they were simple people, living close to the earth, and he'd turned into someone they didn't recognize. His sister was a pretty, blond woman, content with her job at the local library, her quiet husband, and her three children. It had been a couple of years since he'd even seen his nephew and two nieces. When he'd stopped by the year before to tell his parents that he'd retired and had bought a farm in Tennessee, they'd all been so uncomfortable that he'd stayed for only a few hours, and had left without seeing Rae, or the kids.

So he drove down to Georgia, and stood on the weathered old porch, knocking on the door of the house where he'd grown up. His mother came to the door, wiping her hands on her apron. It was close to noon; as always, as it had been from the time he could remember, she was cooking lunch for his father. But they didn't call it lunch in this part of the country; the noon meal was dinner, and the evening meal was supper.

Surprise lit her honey-brown eyes, the eyes that were so like his, only darker. "Why, son, this is a surprise. What on earth are you knocking for? Why didn't you just come in?"

"I didn't want to get shot," he said honestly.

"Now, you know I don't let your daddy keep a gun in the house. The only gun is that old shotgun, out in the barn. What makes you say a thing like that?" Turning, she went back to the kitchen, and he followed. Everything in the old frame house was familiar, as familiar to him as his own face.

He settled his weight in one of the straight chairs that were grouped around the kitchen table. This was the table he'd eaten at as a boy. "Mama," he said slowly, "I've been shot at so much that I guess I think that's the normal way of things."

She was still for a moment, her head bent; then she resumed making her biscuits. "I know, son. We've always known. But we didn't know how to reach you, how to bring you back to us again. You was still a boy when you left, but you came back a man, and we didn't know how to talk to you."

"There wasn't any talking to me. I was still too raw, too wild. But the farm that I bought, up in Tennessee . . . it's helped."

He didn't have to elaborate, and he knew it. Grace Sullivan had the simple wisdom of people who lived close to the land. She was a farm girl, had never pretended to be anything else, and he loved her because of it.

"Will you stay for dinner?"

"I'd like to stay for a couple of days, if I won't be messing up any plans."

"Grant Sullivan, you know your daddy and I don't have any *plans* to go off gallivanting anywhere."

She sounded just like she had when he had been five years old and had managed to get his clothes dirty as fast as she could put them on him. He remembered how she'd looked then, her hair dark, her face smooth and young, her honey-gold eyes sparkling at him.

He laughed, because everything was getting better, and his mother glanced at him in surprise. It had been twenty years since she'd heard her son laugh. "That's good," he said cheerfully. "Because it'll take me at least that long to tell you about the woman I'm going to marry."

"What!" She whirled on him, laughing, too. "You're pulling my leg! Are you really going to get married? Tell me about her!"

"Mama, you'll love her," he said. "She's nuts."

He'd never thought that finding her would be so hard. Somehow he'd thought that it would be as simple as calling her father and getting her address from him, but he should have known. With Jane, nothing was ever as it should be.

To begin with, it took him three days to get in touch with her father. Evidently her parents had been out of town, and the housekeeper either hadn't known where Jane was, or she'd been instructed not to give out any information. Considering Jane's circumstances, he thought it was probably the latter. So he cooled his heels for three days until he was finally able to speak to her father, but that wasn't much better.

"She's in Europe," James explained easily enough. "She stayed here for about a week, then took off again."

Grant felt like cursing. "Where in Europe?"

"I don't really know. She was vague about it. You know Jane."

He was afraid that he did. "Has she called?"

"Yes, a couple of times."

"Mr. Hamilton, I need to talk to her. When she calls again, would you find out where she is and tell her to stay put until I get in touch?"

"That could be a couple of weeks. Jane doesn't call regularly. But if it's urgent, you may know someone who knows exactly where she is. She did mention that she's talked to a friend of yours...let's see, what was his name?"

"Sabin," Grant supplied, grinding his teeth in rage.

"Yes, that's it. Sabin. Why don't you give him a call? It may save you a lot of time."

Grant didn't want to call Kell; he wanted to see him face to face and strangle him. Damn him! If he'd recruited Jane into that gray network ...!

He was wasting time and money chasing over the country after her, and his temper was short when he reached Virginia. He didn't have the clearance to go in, so he called Kell directly. "Sullivan. Clear me through. I'll be there in five minutes."

"Grant—"

Grant hung up, not wanting to hear it over the phone.

Ten minutes later he was leaning over Kell's desk. "Where is she?"

"Monte Carlo."

"Damn it!" he yelled, pounding his fist on the desk. "How could you drag her into this?"

"I didn't drag her," Kell said coolly, his dark eyes watchful. "*She* called *me*. She said she'd noticed something funny and thought I might like to know. She was right; I was highly interested."

"How could she call you? Your number isn't exactly listed."

"I asked her the same thing. It seems she was standing beside you when you called me from Dallas."

Grant swore, rubbing his eyes. "I should have known. I should have been expecting it after she hot-wired that truck. She watched me do it, just once, then did it herself the next time."

"If it's any consolation, she didn't get it exactly right. She remembered the numbers, but not the right order. She told me I was the fifth call she'd placed."

"Oh, hell. What kind of situation is she in?"

"A pretty explosive one. She's stumbled across a high rolling counterfeiter. He has some high quality plates of the pound, the franc and several denominations of our currency. He's setting up the deal now. Some of our comrades are very interested."

"I can imagine. Just what does she think she can do?"

"She's going to try to steal the plates."

Grant went white. "And you were going to let her?"

"Damn it, Grant!" Kell exploded. "It's not a matter of letting her and you know it! The problem is stopping her without tipping the guy off and sending him so deep underground we can't find him. I've got agents tiptoeing all around her, but the guy thinks he's in love with her, and his buyer has watchdogs sniffing around, and we simply can't snatch her without blowing the whole thing sky high!"

"All right, all right. I'll get her out of it."

"How?" Kell demanded.

"I'll get the plates myself, then jerk her out of there and make damned certain she never calls you again!"

"I would deeply appreciate it," Kell said. "What are you going to do with her?"

"Marry her."

Something lightened in Kell's dark face, and he leaned back in his chair, looping his hands behind his head. "Well, I'll be damned. Do you know what you're getting into? That woman doesn't think like most people."

That was a polite way of saying it, but Kell wasn't telling him anything he didn't already know. Within moments of meeting her, Grant had realized that Jane was just a little unorthodox. But he loved her, and she couldn't get into too much trouble on the farm.

"Yeah, I know. By the way, you're invited to the wedding."

Jane smiled at Felix, her eyes twinkling at him. He was such a funny little guy; she really liked him, despite the fact that he was a counterfeiter and was planning to do something that could really damage her country. He was slightly built, with shy eyes and a faint stutter. He loved to gamble, but had atrocious luck; that is, he'd had atrocious luck until Jane had started sitting beside him. Since then he'd been winning regularly, and he was now devoted to her.

Despite everything she was having fun in Monte Carlo. Grant was being slow coming around, but she hadn't been bored. If she had trouble sleeping, if she sometimes woke to find her cheeks wet, that was something she had to accept. She missed him. It was as if part of herself were gone. Without him there was no one she could trust, no one in whose arms she could rest.

It was a dangerous tightrope she was walking, and the excitement of it helped keep her from settling into depression. The only thing was, how much longer was it going to last? If she saw that Felix was finally going to make up his mind who to sell to, she would be forced to do something—fast—before the plates got into the wrong hands.

Felix was winning again, as he had every night since he'd met Jane. The elegant casino was buzzing, and the chandeliers rivaled in brilliance the diamonds that were roped about necks and dripping from ears. The men in their formal evening wear, the women in their gowns and jewels, casually wagering fortunes on the roll of the dice or the turn of a card, all created an atmosphere that was unequaled anywhere in the world. Jane fit into it easily, slim and graceful in her black silk gown, her shoulders and back bare. Jet earrings dangled to her shoulders, and her hair was piled on top of her head in a careless, becoming twist. She wore no necklace, no bracelets, only the earrings that touched the glowing gold of her skin.

Across the table Bruno was watching them closely. He was becoming impatient with Felix's dithering, and his impatience was likely to force her hand.

Well, why not? She'd really waited as long as she could. If Grant had been interested, he'd have shown up before now.

She stood and bent down to kiss Felix on the forehead. "I'm going back to the hotel," she said, smiling at him. "I have a headache."

He looked up, dismayed. "Are you really ill?"

"It's just a headache. I was on the beach too long today. You don't have to leave; stay and enjoy your game."

He began to look panicky, and she winked at him. "Why don't you see if you can win now without me? Who knows, it may not be me at all."

He brightened, the poor little man, and turned back to his game with renewed fervor. Jane left the casino and hurried back to the hotel, going straight to her room. She always allowed for being followed, because she sensed that she always was. Bruno was a very suspicious man. Swiftly she stripped off her gown, and she was reaching into the closet for a dark pair of pants and a shirt when a hand closed over her mouth and a a muscular arm clamped around her waist.

"Don't scream," a low, faintly raspy voice said in her ear, and her heart jumped. The hand left her mouth, and

Jane turned in his arms, burying her face against his neck, breathing in the delicious, familiar male scent of him.

"What are you doing here?" she breathed.

"What do you think I'm doing here?" he asked irritably, but his hands were sliding over her nearly-naked body, reacquainting himself with her flesh. "When I get you home, I just may give you that spanking I've threatened you with a couple of times. I get you away from Turego, and as soon as my back is turned you plunge right back into trouble."

"I'm not in trouble," she snapped.

"You couldn't prove it by me. Get dressed. We're getting out of here."

"I can't! There are some counterfeit plates that I've got to get. My room is being watched, so I was going to climb out the window and work my way around to Felix's room. I have a pretty good idea where he's hidden them."

"And you say you're not in trouble."

"I'm not! But really, Grant, we've got to get those plates."

"I've already got them."

She blinked, her brown eyes owlish. "You do? But... how? I mean, how did you know—never mind. Kell told you, didn't he? Well, where did Felix have them hidden?"

She was enjoying this. He sighed. "Where do you think he had them?"

"In the ceiling. I think he pushed up a square of the ceiling and hid the plates in there. It's really the only good hiding place in the room, and he isn't the type to put them in a safety deposit box in a bank, which is where I'd have put them."

"No, you wouldn't," he said, annoyed. "You'd have put them in the ceiling, just like he did."

She grinned. "I was right!"

"Yes, you were right." And he probably never should have told her. Turning her around, he gave her a pat on the bottom. "Start packing. Your little friend is probably the nervous sort who checks his hidey-hole every night before he goes to bed, and we want to be long gone before he does."

She dragged down her suitcases and started throwing clothes into them. He watched her, sweat popping out on his brow. She looked even better than he remembered, her breasts ripe and round, her legs long and shapely. He hadn't even kissed her. He caught her arm, swinging her around and catching her close to him. "I've missed you," he said, and lowered his mouth to hers.

Her response was instantaneous. She rose on tiptoe, moving against him, her arms coiled around his neck and her fingers deep in his hair. He'd had a haircut, and the dark blond strands slipped through her fingers to fall back in place, shaped perfectly to his head. "I've missed you, too," she whispered when he released her mouth.

His breathing was ragged as he reluctantly let her go. "We'll finish this when we have more time. Jane, would you please put on some clothes?"

She obeyed without question, pulling on green silk trousers and a matching green tunic. "Where are we going?"

"Right now? We're driving to the beach and turning the plates over to an agent. Then we're going to catch a flight to Paris, London and New York."

"Unless, of course, Bruno is waiting just outside the door, and instead we end up sailing across the Mediterranean."

"Bruno isn't waiting outside the door. Would you hurry?"

"I'm finished."

He picked up the suitcases and they went downstairs, where he checked her out. It all went like clockwork. There was no sign of Bruno, or any of the men she had dubbed "Bruno's goons." They turned the plates over to the promised agent and drove to the airport. Jane's heart was thudding with a slow, strong, powerful beat as Grant slipped into the seat beside her and buckled himself in. "You know, you never did actually tell me what you're doing here. You're retired, remember? You're not supposed to be doing things like this."

"Don't play innocent," he advised, giving her a look from molten gold eyes. "I saw your fine hand in this from the beginning. It worked. I came after you. I love you; I'm taking you to Tennessee; and we're going to be married. But you'd better remember that I'm on to your tricks now, and I know you're too slick for your own good. Did I leave anything out?"

"No," Jane said, settling back in her seat. "I think you have everything covered."

_____ *Epilogue*

He lay on his back in the bed, his arms around Jane. Her dark hair was spread across his shoulder, and he stroked her head, her back, the rounded curve of her buttocks. "I couldn't sleep without you," he murmured. "I got used to you using me as a bed."

She was silent, but he knew that she wasn't asleep. They were tired, but too wound up to sleep. Once they'd arrived in Paris, going on to London and New York hadn't seemed that important. Instead they'd checked into a hotel, and the loving had been even better than before, the sensations sharpened by the time they'd spent apart.

"What would I have done if you hadn't come after me?" she whispered, and the desolation of the lonely days without him was in her voice.

"You knew I'd come."

"I hoped. I wasn't certain."

"You can be certain from now on," he said, rolling over and pinning her beneath him. "I love you. I hope you can be happy in Tennessee, because I really don't think I can live in a city, not now. That's been worrying me."

A slow smile touched her lips. "Haven't you learned by now that I'm not addicted to cities, either? I can be happy anywhere; if you're there with me. Besides, I think the country will be a good place for the kids to grow up."

"We haven't talked about that, have we? I'd like to have kids, but if you want to wait a while, I'm willing."

She traced the outline of his mouth with her fingertip. "It's a little too late now to think about waiting. If you wanted to wait, you should have stayed away from me in the jungle. And in Mexico City. And in D.C."

He swallowed, staring at her. "Are you telling me what I think you're telling me?"

"I think I am. I'm not certain yet, but all the signs are there. Do you mind?"

"Mind? God, no!"

The thick emotion in his voice warmed her all over, and she put her arms around him, closing her eyes and hugging him closely. She no longer minded the dark, because Grant was there.